"WE haven't had much chance to speak for the past few days, Jeremiah," Letty said as they strolled through the garden. "Mr. Bassett has been occupying so much of your time."

"I like Worth very much," Jeremiah replied. "He is my friend. My skin is black, but Worth treats me as a white man. And he wants to take me to Russia to study ballet with the masters there. Oh, Miss Letty . . . I do want to go. But I will miss being with you." He paused and a look of pain came into his eyes.

"You're not going because I'm white and a girl and you're black—it's not . . . I mean—"

"You are my best friend in the whole world, Letty, and I love you, but . . ." He could not continue.

Letty ran to him and threw her arms around him, hugging him as tightly as she could. "Why is it wrong? *Why is it wrong?*"

Jeremiah was unable to reply. And Letty did not see the tears streaming down his cheeks as he slowly allowed his hands to touch her back . . . .

...imbrough:

THE SAGA OF THE PHENWICK WOMEN

- [ ] JANE, THE COURAGEOUS   00278 $1.75
- [ ] PATRICIA, THE BEAUTIFUL   00294 $1.25
- [ ] RACHEL, THE POSSESSED   00304 $1.50
- [ ] SUSANNAH, THE RIGHTEOUS   00312 $1.25
- [ ] REBECCA, THE MYSTERIOUS   00320 $1.75
- [ ] JOANNE, THE UNPREDICTABLE   00347 $1.25
- [ ] HARRIET, THE HAUNTED   00382 $1.75
- [ ] NANCY, THE DARING   00399 $1.50
- [ ] MARCIA, THE INNOCENT   00413 $1.75
- [ ] KATE, THE CURIOUS   00430 $1.50
- [ ] BARBARA, THE VALIANT   03228 $1.75
- [ ] RUTH, THE UNSUSPECTING   04037 $1.75
- [ ] DOROTHY, THE TERRIFIED   04133 $1.50
- [ ] ANN, THE GENTLE   04168 $1.75
- [ ] NELLIE, THE OBVIOUS   04202 $1.75
- [ ] ISABELLE, THE FRANTIC   04238 $1.75
- [ ] EVELYN, THE AMBITIOUS   04265 $1.75
- [ ] LOUISE, THE RESTLESS   04298 $1.75
- [ ] POLLY, THE WORRIED   04343 $1.75
- [ ] YVONNE, THE CONFIDENT   04383 $1.75
- [ ] JOYCE, THE BELOVED   04438 $1.75
- [ ] AUGUSTA, THE SECOND   04472 $1.75
- [ ] CAROL, THE PURSUED   04505 $1.75
- [ ] PEGGY, THE CONCERNED   04563 $1.95
- [ ] OLGA, THE DISILLUSIONED   04594 $1.95
- [ ] PHYLLIS, THE CAUTIOUS   04613 $1.95
- [ ] URSALA, THE PROUD   04627 $1.95
- [ ] LETITIA, THE DREAMER   04638 $2.25

Buy them at your local bookstore or use this handy coupon for ordering.

COLUMBIA BOOK SERVICE (a CBS Publications Co.)
32275 Mally Road, P.O. Box FB, Madison Heights, MI 48071

Please send me the books I have checked above. Orders for less than 5 books must include 75¢ for the first book and 25¢ for each additional book to cover postage and handling. Orders for 5 books or more postage is FREE. Send check or money order only.

Cost $_____   Name _____

Sales tax*_____   Address _____

Postage_____   City _____

Total $_____   State _____ Zip _____

*The government requires us to collect sales tax in all states except AK, DE, MT, NH and OR.

This offer expires 1 November 81   8999

DEDICATED TO

WILLIAM COMSTOCK

Book 35—LETITIA, THE DREAMER
CAST OF CHARACTERS

JIM PHENWICK	The eldest of the Savannah, Georgia Phenwicks.
MATTIE PHENWICK	His deranged sister.
LETITIA PHENWICK	His attractive and talented granddaughter.
JASPAR CALHOUN	Jim's great-nephew. A man of self-importance, yet unscrupulous in his dealings.
Todd Potter	Jaspar's assistant.
Horace James	A Negro tenant at Moss Grove who has been Jim Phenwick's longtime friend.
Cissy James	Horace's wife.
JEREMIAH JAMES	His eldest son, a boy with remarkable talent and charm.
Lucas and Pansy	The James' other two children.
MADAME ROSELLE IVANOVICH	A former ballerina who has turned to teaching. She is the ex-wife of a famed dancer.
VLADIMIR POPKIN	Roselle's long time associate, a talented pianist in his own right.
LAURA DONNALLY	The wife of wealthy Pruman Donnally, she is a lady who seeks her own interests and desires to become involved with the arts.
GEORGES LEVEQUE	A producer of ballets.
TIZIANO SPOLINI	An impresario with a glib tongue and a persuading charm.
WORTH BASSETT	An eccentric pianist and artist, who is also very much interested in ballet.
Madison Davis	The playwright.

ALEXANDRIA MUZAKOVA	A young ballerina and close friend of Letty. Exotically beautiful, she has an air of mystery about her.
Fazio	Tiziano Spolini's servant.
DANIEL CHARLES PHENWICK	Head of the Phenwick family in London.
LOUISE PHENWICK	His wife. A respected Phenwick woman who is very much a patron of the arts.
CHARLES	His eldest son.
AUGUSTUS	His second son.
TIMOTHY	His youngest son, a student of the classics.
ALEXANDER (XAN) PHENWICK	Daniel Charles's younger half-brother.
URSALA PHENWICK	Xan's bride.
BARON CONRAD VON KLOOTZ	A nobleman in the Hapsburg lineage.

GENEALOGY
THE PHENWICK FAMILY

*AUGUSTA — Founder of the family. 1st mar. to Arthur Barrywell, mother of Rodney, Selwynn and Agatha; then mar. to JOSHUA PHENWICK, mother of DANIEL CHARLES. Later mar. to Charles Signoret. No children. Augusta adopted EDWARD and JANE MUNSK, whom she raised as PHENWICKS.

DANIEL — Father of ELIAS (by Kate Mumford); mar. to *MARGARET O'PLAGGERTY: father of ALEXANDER, PETER AND *RACHEL.

ELIAS — Mar. to *PATRICIA KELBURN: father of *REBECCA.

*REBECCA — 1st mar. to JOHNNY ORNBY; 2nd mar. to Robert Cathcart; mother of *KATE PHENWICK CATHCART.

*KATE — Mar. to JOHN COLLIER: mother of *NELLIE, Elizabeth, George and Rupert.

*NELLIE — Mar. to THADIUS PHENWICK: mother of PHILIP, MORGAN, JEROME and MARY MAUDE.

PHILIP — Mar. to *KATHERINE PHENWICK: father of Yolanda and Matthew.

MORGAN

ALEXANDER — Mar. to *SUSANNAH PHENWICK: they adopt *MARCIA and GREGORY WING.

*MARCIA — Mar. to STUART PHENWICK: mother of DANIEL CHARLES II and ANN MARIE.

DANIEL CHARLES II — Mar. to *LOUISE ORNBY: father of Charles, Augustus and Timothy.

CHARLES — Mar. to Alexandria

AUGUSTUS

TIMOTHY

GREGORY — Mar. to *ILENE DUMPHY: father of *ISABELLE, ELENA (twins), Alexandria and ALBERT.

*ISABELLE — Mar. to JOHN PHENWICK: mother of SIMON and LAURA.

ALBERT — Mar. to *POLLY PHENWICK: father of Annabelle, Eugenia, *PAULA, *URSALA and William David.

*PAULA

*URSALA

AUGUSTA

DANIEL (CONTINUED)

PETER — 1st mar. to Helen Barnfather: father of AUGUSTUS, *JOANNE, PRENTISE and JOSHUA. 2nd mar. to *NANCY COX: father of THADIUS, JOHN, PAUL and DANIEL LOUIS.

AUGUSTUS — Mar. to Lillian Webb: father of STUART and GORDON.

STUART — 1st mar. to *MARCIA PHENWICK: father of DANIEL CHARLES II and ANN MARIE. ALEXANDER (born to *BARBARA PHENWICK); 2nd mar. to *RUTH ELDRIDGE: father of Richard, *POLLY and DONALD.

DANIEL CHARLES II — Mar. to *LOUISE ORNBY: father of Charles, Augustus and Timothy.

ALEXANDER — Mar. to *YVONNE SINCLAIR: father of *KATHERINE. 2nd mar. to *URSALA KRUGGER.

*KATHERINE — Mar. to PHILIP PHENWICK. (See under PHILIP.)

RICHARD

*POLLY — Mar. to ALBERT PHENWICK (See under ALBERT.)

DONALD — Mar. to *PEGGY PHENWICK.

GORDON — Mar. to *MILLIJOY GRAY: father of THOMAS.

THOMAS — Mar. to *EVELYN JACKSON: father of Gordon Thomas.

GORDON THOMAS — Mar. to Melany (LANY). No children.

*JOANNE — Only daughter of Peter. Unmarried actress.

PRENTISE — Mar. to *HARRIET PETTIJOHN: father of JAMES, Frances, Louis, Martha, Patrick, Sam and Tom.

JAMES — Mar. to *DOROTHY WILKES: father of Henry, Lela and Frances.

HENRY — Mar. to Thomasina Clark: father of *LETITIA and John Charles.

*LETITIA

FRANCES — Mar. to Schuyler Callahan. 2nd mar. Enoch Calhoun; mother of Virginia, Clayborn and George.

CLAYBORN — Mar. to Sybil Wilcox. father of Jaspar, Caleb and Fanny.

JOSHUA — Mar. to *OLIVIA PRITCHARD: father of *OPHELIA, ARNOLD LEON (LEO), Ruth Carrie, Elizabeth and David.

*OPHELIA — Mar. to Henry Ashton: mother of Michael, Joanna and Marcia.

AUGUSTA	
DANIEL	
PETER (CONTINUED)	
ARNOLD LEON (LEO)	Married to *ANN ORNBY: father of Edwin, *AUGUSTA II, Joshua Leon, Eva Rose and Matthew.
*AUGUSTA II	Unmarried.
THADIUS	Mar. to *NELLIE COLLIER: father of PHILIP, MORGAN, JEROME and Mary Maude.
PHILIP	Mar. to *KATHERINE PHENWICK.
MORGAN	
JEROME	
JOHN	Mar. to *ISABELLE PHENWICK: father of SIMON and LAURA.
SIMON	Mar. to *Phyllis Burdick; father of David, Terence and Rita Marie.
LAURA	Mar. to R. Pruman Donnally. No children.
PAUL	Mar. to Lottie Wells; father of JOHN ADAM, LUKE, HAYDEN, *PEGGY and LOLA.
JOHN ADAM	Mar. to *CAROL INGRAHAM: father of George, Raymond and Malcolm.
LUKE	Mar. to *JOYCE CALDER MUMFORD: father of OLIVER.
OLIVER	
HAYDEN	Mar. to *OLGA DUVANE: father of Cornellius and Belinda.
*PEGGY	Mar. to DONALD PHENWICK. No children.
LOLA	Mar. to William Stocker.
DANIEL LOUIS	Unmarried.
*RACHEL	Daniel's only daughter, died in teens.
EDWARD (MUNSK) PHENWICK	Adopted son of AUGUSTA: mar. to *PATRICIA KELBURN: father of David and *SUSANNAH.(He is the actual son of John and Lydia Munsk.)
DAVID	Killed during the war of 1812.
*SUSANNAH	Mar. to ALEXANDER PHENWICK: foster mother of *MARCIA and GREGORY WING. (See under children of Peter Phenwick.)
*JANE (MUNSK)	Adopted daughter of AUGUSTA: married to Jeffrey Ornby; mother of FREDERICK, JOHNNY and ANDREW. (Actual daughter of John and Lydia Munsk.)
THE ORNBYS	
FREDERICK	Married to Henrietta Ellsworth; father of John and Edward.

AUGUSTA
JANE
FREDERICK (CONTINUED)

JOHN	Married Dorothy Wren; children: Millicent, Crandall and Virginia.
EDWARD	Married to Sarah Hadley; father of Thomas, Mary and John Frederick.
THOMAS	Married to Zelda Casey. No children.
MARY	Died in teens.
JOHN FREDERICK	Married Sally Battel; father of *ANN ROSE and FREDERICK.
*ANN ROSE	Married to ARNOLD LEON PHENWICK: mother of EDWIN, *AUGUSTA II, JOSHUA LEON, EVA ROSE and MATTHEW.
*AUGUSTA II	Not married.
JOHNNY	Married to Olivia Barnfather; children: ADRIANNE and LYDIA; second marriage to *REBECCA PHENWICK. No children.
ADRIANNE	Murdered in England.
LYDIA	Unmarried.
ANDREW	Married to Livinia Hendricks; father of JANE AUGUSTA, DANIEL, THEODORE, ANGELA, BERTHA and JEFFREY.
JANE AUGUSTA	Married to Eustace Clark. No children.
DANIEL	An attorney. Wife: Mellissa Kesler; children: JAMES, HENRY, THOMAS and SARAH.
THEODORE	(Dr. Ted) Wife: Louise Lacy; children: JOSEPH, AUGUSTUS, COLLIN, MARY ROSE and RUTH.
JOSEPH	A physician. Wife: Sheila Dumphy. No children.
AUGUSTUS	A physician. Wife: Nell Willet; children: CHARLES and *LOUISE.
CHARLES	
*LOUISE	Married to DANIEL CHARLES PHENWICK. (See under DANIEL CHARLES.)

PROLOGUE

Reconstruction in the South was a slow process. At times there seemed to be little headway being made, only fragmentary progress. The grandeur of antebellum aristocracy was gone, wisped away with the winds of defeat and the flames of destruction. It would be a hard, long and tedious road back. Bitterness, remorse, heartbreak and poverty conditions intimidated both whites and blacks. The North had won and the defeated had to claw their own ways out of the destitution that followed.

Medallion Enterprises had never greatly flourished in Savannah, due to the lack of business sense and the weakness of Prentise Phenwick's character. He was easily manipulated and overpowered by Milton Callahan. When Jim Phenwick was put in charge of the Southern branch of the power that Medallion empire based in Boston, he managed to make the family business survive for a short period of time as long as he had assistance from his relatives at a distance. Yet, in time, he fell under the negative aspects of despair that prevailed.

Jim's mother, Harriet, had been known as a Phenwick woman; but she had become deranged with a madness from which she never escaped. Both of his sisters, Franny and Mattie; had seemed to inherit their mother's insanity. Franny passed over while still young, but Mattie endured and became a burden to her brother. Other of the Phenwick children had scattered into anonymity and disappeared, never to attempt to reestablish communication with Jim or others of the family.

Jim's wife, Dorothy, died shortly after the birth of her fourth child, and he never married again. The fact is, Jim gave up. With ambition gone, he sat back to observe the rest of his life pass by. Still, it went on and he managed to exist. As he crept into old age, one light brightened his eye, one hope that something of his lineage would amount to something, perhaps even become important—the beloved granddaughter whom he had raised.

Chapter One

1913

MAGNOLIAS. THE SCENT WAS SUBTLE mingled with the fading aroma of honeysuckle. Chickens clucked as they picked around the front of the old mansion called Moss Grove, just outside of lethargic Savannah, Georgia. Moss dripped lazily from the wide oaks. Weeds grown high a month before had turned to straw. Morning glories vined over the dilapidated fenceposts and climbed across the wild berry branches with their prickly stems.

Shortly after the roosters had crowed the announcement of dawn and the first hint of pink colored the daylight, the spry young supple figure moved from the house. Her long cotton dress was faded, patched and serviceable. Bare feet padded over the wooden boards of the porch past the decaying Corinthian columns. Pretty face turned upward, she inhaled of the fresh morning air, already warm and humid, before she went out to gather eggs and place them in the worn basket she carried. She stopped by the old maple that had been struck by lightning and appeared to be only half alive. Stretching her graceful body and undulating to

15

an unheard rhythm, toes were pointed as the skirt was lifted and the leg was thrust forward, then to the side and finally back as far as it would go.

Letty used the tree trunk to brace herself as she did her other limbering up exercises. Periodically she would stop and listen. Chattering birds, squabbling hens, buzzing flies, hogs snorting in the distance, the soft gurgle of the stream that meandered through the pasture; these were the accompanying sounds to which she danced. The early morning was her favorite time of day especially in summer. With a leap she went to collect eggs only to be pecked at by a red setting hen.

Letty gently stroked the chicken and cooed softly to her. "I won't take your eggs, lady, but you just let me get th' others."

Letty used her apron to dry the eggs after she had washed them by the well. When they were returned to the basket, neatly arranged and packed with cotton rags, she went back to the porch, where she set the basket while she pulled into the pair of scuffed, high-top shoes. She retied the faded blue gingham poke bonnet with the long beak before she picked up the basket and hurried toward the dusty road.

Well over an hour later Letty arrived in the downtown area of Savannah. By then the fragrance of magnolias was almost overpowering. She stopped in the town square where the black man who had raped her great-grandmother had been hanged and stepped to the watering trough to splash cool water on her face.

There was movement in the streets, whites and blacks slowly going about their chores. Most people kept to their houses in extremely hot weather or sat in the shade of the great sprawling trees.

Suddenly perceiving that she was being watched, Letty picked up the basket of eggs before she cautiously glanced around. Usually she appeared to be oblivious of other people, especially when she was in town. Even if something or someone caught her attention, she made a point of never staring.

The man was resting on a rickety bench. He rose as she briefly focused on him and quickly looked away. A handsome man, she thought, with a most attractive smile. She started to move away before she recognized a familiar fragrance that was neither the essence of magnolias nor honeysuckle. Roses? Where were they? She turned her attention in several directions before she became aware that the man was moving toward her. The closer he came, the stronger the scent of roses grew. Why couldn't she move away?

"Good morning."

Letty stared at the man who appeared to be far too overdressed for that time of day, for the street and for the weather. Yet he seemed to be cool and comfortable.

"Mornin'," Letty replied. She wanted to leave, but she felt mysteriously compelled to remain. "Excuse me, I've these eggs t' take t' market and—" Words seemed dry in her throat. Again aware of the rose fragrance, she darted her eyes to the sides to find the source of the aroma. There were no roses to be seen.

"I'll only detain you a moment, Letitia."

"Letitia? How do y'all know my name?" she asked, peering into that handsome face that insisted on her attention.

"My people have lived in Savannah for generations. Perhaps you've heard of the Truffs."

"Are you a Truff? Lawsy, you don't much look like any of th' Truffs I know. Belinda Truff used t' be my best friend before she off an' got married. They moved out yonder somewhere."

"Belinda lives near Atlanta now."

"Oh, yes. Seems as how I recall her sayin' that's where they were fixin' t' move to." She smiled before she cocked her head to get a closer look at the stranger. "Which Truff are you?"

"Adam."

"Hmm. Don't quite recollect havin' heard that name before. Belinda was th' only Truff I was real acquainted with." She wiped the back of her hand over her brow. "Do you smell roses?"

She received only a smile.

"I sure do, but I don't see any."

"There's one there in your egg basket, Letitia."

"How *do* you know my name?"

"You are *Letitia Phenwick, aren't you?"*

"Yes. But how do you know that? Fact is, no one's called me Letitia much except Madame Ivanovich. I'm just plain Letty t' everyone around here."

"I like the name of Letitia. It has an elegant sound to it that suits you."

"Elegant?" Letty laughed. "Go on with you, Mr. Truff."

"You may call me Adam."

She looked down demurely. "How did that rose get in my egg basket? It wasn't there when I left home."

"Sometimes mysterious things happen, Letitia. You will receive many other roses someday. This will not be your last. We will meet from time to time."

A clock bonged the hour in the distance.

"Lord have mercy! It's eight o'clock. I'm way behind my time," Letty exclaimed. "Madame Ivanovich will be furious. An' I still have these eggs t' leave off at th' store so I can pay Madame Ivanovich."

"Then you'd better go, hadn't you?"

"Yes, sir. Excuse me." Letty turned and began to run in the direction of the watering trough. She wanted to douse her face again.

"Does yo' always talks t' yo'se'f like dat, girl?" a small black boy asked as the cold water touched her face.

"Talk t' myself? I was speakin' t' that man over yonder."

"What man?" Large black eyes glanced over toward the rickety bench and back to Letty's attractive features. "Ain't no man over dere, girl." He scratched his head and laughed.

"There ain't?" Letty scanned the area around the

18

bench, then over the rest of the square. "But he—"

"Ain't no one dere, an' ain't no one bin dere." He laughed again and sauntered off.

Letty followed the boy with her eyes before she looked back at the bench, shrugged, picked up the egg basket and headed in the direction of the store.

Tall, gaunt, long-fingered Vladimir Popkin poured corn whiskey from a jug into a metal cup and swilled it down with a coughing reaction. A fierce expression distorted his coarse Slavic features in reaction to the invasion of liquid fire before he shoved the jug back under the bed. Veins stood out in his angular arms as he pulled suspenders up over sleeveless underwear. The rumpled trousers bagged and appeared to be several sizes too large for him. Unshaven, with weeks of grime beneath his fingernails, he briefly examined his face in the broken mirror above the washbasin and chipped pitcher. What difference did appearance make at his time of life? Graying brown hair, almost pure white stubble of beard, pale eyes, red-lined and watery; he recognized the reflection, but he didn't want much to do with it.

"Popkin!" came the rasping call of the unmistakable voice of Madame Roselle Ivanovich from the next room. "Popkin! I need you *now!*"

Vladimir made a halfhearted attempt at a salute and went toward the sound of her voice. He stopped momentarily as he entered the large room and let his somewhat dazed eyes survey the near perfect form of Letty as she stood at the ballet *barre* in front of the long mirror.

"Mam'selle has warmed up without you," the aging, diminutive woman with the face of a crow stated, wrinkling her facial features into an even more unattractive expression. Silver-streaked hair wrapped in a bun atop her head, cane firmly held in hand, she sniffed deeply but chose not to comment on the man's early morning imbibing.

Vladimir made a noncommittal movement of his head and stepped to the piano stool. The instrument was old and out of tune. Several hammers missing left blank spaces in the melodies his long fingers picked out. He sat with his legs crossed. The fingers were agile and played with virtuosity. He immediately appeared to be absorbed in the playing.

Under Madame Roselle Ivanovich's sharp eye, Letty danced for an hour. The room had become sweltering and the young girl was melting with perspiration. Still, with the conscientiousness of a devout artist, she persisted, only periodically stopping to mop her brow with a damp towel.

"You must stop now, mam'selle," Roselle commanded, fanning herself with an almost ineffectual paper fan. "The summer is too hot for anyone to dance."

"I can come an hour earlier next week, Madame Ivanovich," Letty replied, gasping slightly as she caught her breath.

Vladimir rose from the stool, took another glance at Letty and shuffled out of the room.

"No more whiskey!" Roselle called. "It raises your temperature."

Vladimir muttered something in Russian and closed the door behind him.

Letty stretched back on the *barre*.

"There will be no ballet lesson here next week, mam'selle," Madame Ivanovich said as she watched the beautiful and talented girl. "Nor will there be any more until after the end of summer. I am too old to teach in all this heat. Besides, I am going away in two weeks."

"Goin' away?" Letty stood up and gracefully stepped nearer to the older woman. "No more ballet lessons?"

"I have been sent for to go to London, and later on to Paris," Roselle stated. "Georges LeVeque has sent me traveling money. He wants me to act in an advisory capacity for a new ballet company he is forming. I knew Georges when he was only in the corps de ballet.

He never gained much prominence as a dancer, but he has achieved some fame as a choreographer and an impresario."

"But what will become of my dancin'?"

"You will continue to practice as I have taught you, and when I return—ah, autumn when it is not so hot—you will study with me again," Roselle commented, "unless—"

"Unless?" Letty scowled. "You're th' only person in all of Savannah who teaches ballet."

"And you, mam'selle, are the only dancer of any quality I have encountered since being here. It was foolish of me to think I could teach in a place like Savannah. But I didn't come here to teach, I came to retire. Sometimes I think I am not old enough to retire, and at other times I feel as if I am ancient."

"You said 'unless.' What did you start t' say?" Letty asked.

"Letitia, I will tell you something." Roselle reached to take the girl's hand. She spoke in perfect English with only a trace of a European accent. "In my time I have seen many dancers, exceptional ballerinas. I myself received my share of acclaim and accolades of praise. I say that in all modesty, of course."

"Of course."

"I have seen other dancers who were mediocre at best," the woman continued. "I believe from the depth of my heart that you, Letitia Phenwick, are among the most talented dancers I've ever had the honor to work with. I do not say you are perfect, or that you have achieved mastery of your ability, but you show far greater promise than I've ever before seen. But look at you! An impoverished waif who must sell eggs to pay for her dancing lessons. What chance have you for a future among the greats of my art? Yet—"

"What are y'all gettin' at, Madame Ivanovich?" Letty's soft voice had a lilting melody to it.

"I once dined with kings and princes for a brief interlude of grandeur," Roselle went on. "I have tasted

21

champagne and the sparkling glitter of fame. Ah, but only tasted of it! Then I fell in love with Monsieur Ivanovich, a fine dancer himself, and I abandoned it all for an even briefer interlude of romance. We came to Savannah fifteen years ago, but my love was not strong enough to hold Monsieur Ivanovich. I was stranded and had to teach—for what else did I know? What was I getting at? Oh, yes. I might have had wealth. I haven't. What do I have? Vladimir, who passes out from intoxication by mid-afternoon. But if I could afford it, I would invite you to come along to London with me."

"Me? Go t' London, France?"

"London, *England*," Roselle corrected. She laughed. "What a dream fulfilled it would be if I could take you to Europe and mold you into a great ballerina. You *do* have the talent. Of that I am certain."

Letty's cheeks were flushed. She had always become embarrassed whenever Madame Ivanovich spoke of her talent.

"I have met your grandfather a time or two," Roselle said. "Basically he is a very good man. If it were possible for him to finance your trip?"

"Grandpa don't have no money. He don't even try t' farm th' land no more." Letty looked away. "I reckon I better take th' shoes off an' get my things together." She turned toward where she had left her high-top shoes.

"Mam'selle! You're a Phenwick!" Roselle called.

"I'm one of th' poor Phenwicks," Letty said as she sat to untie the worn pair of ballet shoes Madame Ivanovich allowed her to practice in. "We're nothin' but poor whites, that's all we are."

"Vladimir knows about your family," Roselle persisted, grunting to rise from the rocking chair in which she had been seated. "The Phenwicks of Boston are among the richest people in the United States, maybe in the world."

"I don't know anythin' about that." Letty appeared

22

sullen. "I'll miss not takin' my ballet lessons, Madame Ivanovich."

Roselle stood before the girl with her arms held open to her. A moment later she hugged Letty's lithe body to hers. "Letitia, Letitia! Dearest child, if only I had the money, I would see that you became one of the greatest dancers of all time. Maybe if I were to speak with your grandfather."

"Y'all can't get blood from a turnip, you know. Grandpa ain't got no money."

"But he *is a* Phenwick."

"I think Grandpa's been forgotten by th' other Phenwicks long ago," Letty replied and held tightly to the woman.

"Tell him what I've told you, especially tell him about London and Paris, and how much talent I truly believe you possess, mam'selle. It would be a sin—no, an absolute crime for such talent to remain buried in obscurity."

"There's no money. There never has been. If I didn't sell th' eggs, I wouldn't have been able t' take lessons with you."

Roselle held Letty at arm's length. Tired eyes grew moist as if tears were about to flow. "I will write to LeVeque and tell him about you. Maybe—just maybe, —he will send enough money."

Letty moved away from the woman to pick up the egg basket.

"If you only had the enthusiasm I have, mam'selle."

"I'm tryin' t' be realistic. Even if I were filled with dreams an' enthusiasm, what is *is*."

"Yet you have a compulsion to dance. I believe there is a reason for that." Roselle went to where the girl was standing. "I do believe there is a reason. I will pray. And I will not give up hope. It's a feeling I have about you, mam'selle, a strange and wonderful and somewhat mystifying feeling." Her attention fell to the basket. "Ah, a rose!" She put her hand into the basket and raised the flower to get a closer look. "What perfection! And you've not had it in water. Still it is perfect, not the least bit wilted and here the room is as hot as an oven. It's an omen!"

Letty laughed uneasily. "You may keep it, Madame Ivanovich. It's sure to wilt before I get home. I had forgotten about it."

"But where did you get it?"

"I believe a man by th' name of Truff gave it t' me," Letty said and quickly explained about what had happened earlier that day. "Now I must go before I'm trudgin' home in th' heat of th' day."

"Truff?" Roselle questioned. "Why is that name—? Ah, Belinda Truff. She married a man with money, didn't she?"

"He didn't have much money. Besides, Belinda is in Atlanta."

Roselle thought a moment. "No, *you* must keep the rose. But I beg of you to speak to your grandfather about what we have discussed. And, if necessary, I'll go out to see him. I believe if he were really to set his mind to it that he would be able to raise money for you."

Letty embraced Roselle and kissed her affectionately on the cheek.

"We will visit again before I leave for London," Roselle stated.

"Yes, Madame Ivanovich, we will speak."

"Vladimir!" Roselle called a few minutes after Letty had departed. "Vladimir! Do you hear me?"

A scuffing sound of footsteps preceded Vladimir's entrance. He moved unsteadily and appeared to have difficulty focusing on the former ballerina. "What is it?"

"The Phenwicks? Where did you get your information about them?"

"I don't remember," Vladimir mumbled. "What difference does it make?"

"You silly drunken sot, you bore me! Think, Vladimir, think!"

24

Vladimir scratched his head, nearly bald and dry with flakiness. "It was one of them Calhouns, that's who. I forget which one."

"Dolt! Never mind. I will find what I must by myself." Roselle didn' watch as Vladimir lurched from the room. The man, she thought, had once been a brilliant pianist. Now look at him. Life is most unkind to the artist!

"But the rose?" Roselle question aloud. "The *rose?*"

Letty walked slowly. Her clothing was soaked with perspiration. No breeze. Hot furnace rays of sun. No clouds. She had stopped several times along the road to sit in the shade of a tree. No one had passed, not even in a wagon. Hunger pains came and she gathered a few berries to eat. Realizing she had nearly a mile farther to go, she stretched out in the shade of a large hickory tree after removing her shoes. Flies buzzed around her and shooing them away was the only thing that kept her from falling asleep.

Then she fell into her favorite form of preoccupation: dreaming of becoming a great ballerina. She had never in her life seen a ballet performed. How did she know about it? Why should she have such a compulsive desire to want to become a successful dancer? It didn't matter, she thought, she had her dreams into which she could escape.

Dreams. Those wonderful illusions of fantasy, the creations of her imaginative mind were her escape from the mundane reality of everyday boredom. Day-to-day life was humdrum in Savannah, miserable, lonely, and just plain dull. It often amazed her, however, to receive thoughts about situations and things she had no conscious awareness of knowing about. Still she did know of them and, even if they were projected fantasies, they had an eerie reality to them that was inexplicable. There was music, melodious orchestrations of symphonic grandeur—yet she had never attended a concert of any kind. Could it be possible that she had only imagined such things? Often when Vladimir Popkin played with gusto on the archaic, out-of-tune piano, Letty perceived the sounds of many musical instruments playing in majestic accompanying harmony.

Were these only dreams, chance imaginings? Or was she somehow in tune with mystical forces that crescendoed through the ether, sounds that perhaps circled the earth—sounds to which sensitive creative souls could be attuned?

And why did she so obsessively dream about dancing? From where had such notions come?

Chapter Two

MOSS GROVE PLANTATION HAD SURVIVED the years with a continual decaying process. Little or no improvement had been made. A monument to days that once had been, to gaiety once known, to beauty, lovely ladies and handsome gentlemen who celebrated life in elegant splendor. Did their ghosts still linger to waltz in the magic of a forgotten past time?

The old man—old before his years—mopped his leathered hand over a deeply furrowed brow where the residue of dust clung to the perspiration. Tired eyes looked toward the woods as he recalled the stream-fed pond beyond the trees where he had splashed many happy boyhood hours. He was too old to skinny dip, his joints too stiff to climb the trees and perch for long hours among the branches as he had done when his youthful dreams were wide-eyed fantasies of the unknown.

Jim Phenwick scratched at a freshly smarting mosquito bite and sighed. He believed he had seen and done all that life had in store for him—except to die. Death was no stranger to him, and because it had become so common in his experience. he accepted the inevitability of it with a kind of quiet anticipation. Life would go on and he would endure, but, if he had any enthusiasm concerning anything it was for his contemplation of the great unknown beyond the pains and desperations of mortal existence. Not a religious man as such, he had had brushes with certain philosophical thoughts that gave him a sense of continuity: ideas which he had received for the most part years ago when he had gone to spend a length of time with his late Uncle Joshua Phenwick in London. If there had been any truly happy days in his life, they had occurred during his sojourn away from Savannah when he had tasted of the opulent lifestyle of the affluent Phenwicks. Quite frankly, since he believed his earthly existence had reached an irreversible stalemate, he was becoming anxious to see what he called "the other side of the rainbow."

Painfully thin, emaciated-looking, hair straggly and unkempt, Martha Phenwick, whom they called Mattie, ambled from the grotesquely deteriorating old house. Vacant, watery eyes stared at nothing. The soiled and patched gray dress hung on her frail body like an ill-fitting shroud. One of the dogs loped toward her before he recognized who she was and detoured his course, circled about and sauntered over to the well where Jim was still standing.

The hard hand with stiff fingers stroked the dog's head as the whiplike tail swished back and forth in appreciation. "What's th' matter, ol' Blue?"

Blue barked.

Jim squinted as he observed his sister. "Mattie, don't ya go a-wand'rin' off now, ya hear? I ain't a-comin' after ya if you-all get lost in the woods. You-all'll just have to spend the night out there with th' wild animals. Ya hear, sistah?"

Mattie seemingly heard nothing except the constant din of voices that chattered incoherently in her head. She picked at her fingers and stuck one into her mouth to gnaw on a fingernail. "I reckon th' Yankees is a-comin'. I reckon that was th' commotion I heard. Ya-all go away, ya hear?" She screamed.

Jim trotted toward her, Blue close at his heels. "Mattie, ya know ya ain't s'pose t' come outside. Now you-all git on back in that house."

Mattie stared witlessly at her brother. "Ya damn Yankee, go on with ya!" She screamed again. "Ya-ll'll not take me like ya done before!"

Jim panted as he came up to where she was standing. "Mattie, now I ain't a-tellin' ya ag'in. Ya-all go back in that house."

"Damn Yankee! Damn Yankee!"

"I ain't no Yankee. I'm ya brothah Jim."

Beyond reason and reasoning with, Mattie clutched her fists and began assailing her brother. Jim caught her by the wrists. Screaming like a banshee, Mattie struggled with remarkable strength and soon was on the verge of overpowering him.

Sauntering up the road, the basket dangling in her hand, Letty at first did not hear the hysterical cries of her great-aunt Mattie; nor, when she did perceive them, did she realize they were not coming from the old house. The accompaniment of Blue's barking made her identify that the sound was outside. Because of Mattie's abnormal fear of men, Jim had depended on Letty to handle his sister, especially at times like these when she didn't seem to remember that he was her own brother. Dropping the basket, Letty ran as fast as she could toward the well.

"Aunt Mattie!" Letty called. "Aunt Mattie, do ya hear me?"

Mattie continued to struggle with Jim as Letty reached the place they were located. Immediately the girl got a hold from behind around the distraught woman and jerked her backwards, knocking the two of them off balance and freeing Mattie's hold from Jim's arms. The two women fell to the ground on their backsides. Rolling her over and sitting atop her, Letty straddled Mattie as she pinned her arms down.

"Now ya jus' hold still, Aunt Mattie," Letty warned, "or I'll tie up ya hands with rope." Mattie struggled. "Gran'daddy, ya best go fetch some rope. She ain't cooperatin' none."

"Mattie, ya-all behave ya' se'f, ya hear?" Jim called before he turned toward the house.

"No!" Mattie screamed. "No! Don't tie me up like th' Yankees done! Don't rip off my pantaloons! Don't hurt me!"

"Nobody's gonna hurt ya, Aunt Mattie, if'n ya-all behave yaself. What ya doin' outside, anyway?"

Mattie had become somewhat calmer. "Th' room was stiflin', that's what it was, an' I thought I was gonna die from suffocatin'."

"Did ya open th' winders for cross-ventilation?" Letty asked, a tone of serenity in her voice.

"I never did. I couldn't git 'em open," Mattie whined.

"If'n ya'll behave ya'self, I'll go with ya an' open 'em for ya," Letty coaxed softly, gently.

"I'll be good, Letitia, I'll be good. Don't tie me up! Please don't tie me up!"

Before Jim had reached the house, Letty helped Mattie to her feet and hugged her affectionately, reassuringly. The beautiful girl had a way of handling Mattie far better than anyone else had ever been able to. Her honest compassionate attitude had a way of calming. Arm about Mattie, and leaning against her, Letty guided the older woman to the house.

"We're gonna have t' put a lock on her door," Jim said a short while later when Letty arrived at his large room on the second floor. The furnishings were plain, simple, functional, but well worn and in need of repair. The walls were stained and grimy, the floors scratched and dusty, the windows so incrusted that they couldn't be seen through. The pieces of curtains that remained were in tatters. The smell of chewing tobacco, urine and coal oil mingled to create an offensive aroma. The smell was worse in Mattie's room since the demented woman had little control over her bladder or her bowels.

"Ya may be right, Gran'daddy, ya may be right," Letty sighed.

"I swear, Letty, ya-all better let me take Mattie on up t' the crazy farm an' jus' leave her," Jim said as he sat in the creaky rocking chair and pushed it back and forth.

"We cain't do that, Gran'daddy, we jus' cain't," Letty returned. "She's our flesh an' blood, ya only livin' sistah."

Jim held his hand out to the girl. "Letty, it ain't fair t' you. Ya're a-blossomin' forth into womanhood an' it ain't right for ya t' have t' take care a' a crazy ol' woman like Mattie. Three times she was attacked an' raped by a whole platoon a' Yankee soldiers, an' they jus' drove th' sanity outa' her. She ain't never bin right since then. An' she's a-gittin' worse."

Letty squeezed her grandfather's hand and walked to the window. It was as wide open as it would go. She stared out and thought of Madame Ivanovich's words. Then she thought of Mattie and the terrible looks of horror she had seen in her face. "Gran'daddy? Why don't ya sell Moss Grove? Y'all could buy a little shack in closer t' town. There's good rich soil on this ol' plantation, but it's jus' gone t' weed."

"Who'd wanta buy a place like this?" Jim moaned and reached for his chewing tobacco. "No one's got much money—an' even if they done had, who'd want it, anyway? I was born here, an' I reckon I'll die here."

"But there's acres an' acres of land as far as th' eye kin see," Letty protested. "It's jus' a-goin' t' waste. I reckon if'n I was t' talk t' Jaspar Calhoun about it, he'd figure some way a' buyin' it."

"An' rob me in th' end!" Jim belched. "None a' them Calhouns or Callahans are any good. They gits that from ol' Milton Callahan."

"But ya sistah, Great-aunt Franny, she was married t' Mistah Callahan's son."

"I'll tell ya somethin', Letty," Jim said as he stared at Letty as she gazed out the window. "Schuyler

Callahan never sired no children by Franny—they was done by ol' Milton Callahan hisself. That's what. Schuyler Callahan never could a' done it, because he jus' plain couldn't. It weren't physically possible for him t' do. Adam Truff told me that, jus' th' same as my stepmama done."

Letty turned slowly, a silhouette against the afternoon light. "What did you say?"

"Ya know my own mama died crazy like Mattie an'—well, Franny in her last days," Jim said. "Milton Callahan forced my daddy to marry his daughter Barbara. Alexander, who I always thought was my half-brothah, was really sired by my cousin Stuart Phenwick. Adam Truff tol' me that, too."

Letty stepped toward the old man, an incredulous expression straining her features. "Adam Truff?"

"Ya've heard me tell about th' time I was captured near Charleston an' held in th' stockade. It was Adam Truff what was responsible for gittin' me out, he an' an Injun."

"Adam Truff?"

"He was th' second son a' Milton Callahan's overseer before th' War," Jim went on. "Lordy, he was a handsome devil with dark hair an' eyes that'ud stare right through ya. Anyway, Callahan maneuvered t' git Adam t' be a spy for th' Confederacy an' sent him up t' Boston, where he met my cousin Stuart. They become friends an' Adam became a spy for th' North because he hated ol' man Callahan so much. He got away with it most a' th' War. Adam was a good friend a' my stepmama an' ol' Millijoy Phenwick. Then after th' War, he came down an' got Alexander an' took up t' live with Stuart, who was his real daddy. Him an' Alexander was real close over th' years. Alexander was called 'Xan' by Adam. I envied Alexander. I woulda given anythin' if'n I coulda traveled with Adam."

"Adam—?"

"There was only one Adam Truff." Jim chuckled to himself. "I reckon th' Truffs hated Adam as much as th' Callahans done. He was never considered much by his family, so I allow as how they wouldn'ta named any a' their kin after him."

It was all Letty could do to contain the queer feeling that was tingling inside of her. After staring incredulously at her grandfather for several moments, she lifted her skirts and dashed from the room.

"Where ya goin', Letty?" Jim called.

"I'll be right back," Letty replied as she ran down the hallway with the creaky floorboards and took the steps two at a time. Moments later she was outside, Blue trotting behind her as she went to where she had dropped the egg basket. Flying feet returned her to the house as quickly as they had taken her.

Gasping for breath as she leaned against the doorsill, Letty gazed as if she thought Jim could read her mind.

"What is it, Letty-girl?" Jim asked and made a direct hit into the spittoon beside the old table.

Letty reached into the basket to remove the still perfectly formed red rose that showed no sign of wilting. She held it toward her grandfather. "Ya see this rose? It ain't been in water all day, an' it's still as fresh as if it had jus' been picked, ain't it?"

"Ye-us, I kin see that. Where'd ya-all git it?"

"I don't rightly know, Gran'daddy. It jus' appeared in my egg basket, a-layin' there right on top a' th' eggs." Letty's innocent face was alive with amazement. "I seen a man who said he was Adam Truff a-sittin' on th' park bench, he was."

Jim's lower lip sagged and he blinked several times before he was able to speak. "Last I heared Adam Truff was dead."

"Well, this Adam Truff wasn't dead—least ways he never appeared to be," Letty said. "However—"

"However?" Jim questioned when his granddaughter fell silent.

"A nigra boy said he seen me a-talkin' t' myself."

Jim stood and hobbled to the water pitcher to pour

himself a drink. "You tell me 'xactly what happened this mornin'."

Letty explained the early morning events as best she could and went on to tell Jim about Madame Ivanovich's proposal.

"One thin' at a time, now, girl," Jim interrupted. "Ya-all was a-speakin' 'bout Adam Truff, then ya went right into carryin' on 'bout dancin' an' traipsin' off t' England an' th' like. Don't confuse me with too many confusin' thin's at once. My mind ain't what it used t' be." He went back to the table where he had left the rose. Hesitatingly he touched it. "It's real, all right. Ya-all kin tell by th' feel a' it."

"Of course it's real, Gran'daddy. It even smells real. No one could make an artificial rose like that."

"I'll have t' puzzle that out," Jim said as he repositioned himself in the rocking chair. His mind went to other thoughts of Adam Truff and distant memories of the past.

Letty watched him for a good five minutes before she broke the silence. "Reckon there ain't no way there's any money for me t' go with Madame Ivanovich, is there?"

Jim shook his head without looking up. "Ain't got none. Travelin's for rich people, an' we're th' poor Phenwicks. If'n I hadn'ta bin so dang stubborn an' proud years ago, I woulda kept in touch with my kin in Boston. But I jus' never, not after I lost Medallion. Reckon it was partly my fault, an' partly th' fault a' th' times. I'm sorry, Letty. I wish there was some way."

"I understand, Gran'daddy, I never counted much on there a-bein' any money." Letty sagged onto the bed and looked forlorn. "Reckon I'll go wash up an' git on with my chores."

"Come here, Letty," Jim ordered as he stretched his hand toward her. His pouty lips tried to smile as she moved toward him. "I ain't got much in th' world. My daddy lost a lotta money. An' then there was th' War. But money ain't ever' thin'. Ya know, I onc't loved your

34

gran'ma more'n anythin' in th' world. An' I reckon as how I loved my kids in a way, but th' real love a' my life is you, Letty. Ya know, years ago my stepmama tol' me a funny thin'. 'Tweren't funny, actual, it was kinda mysterious an' spooky. She said that before she married my daddy she had a vision a' what she called a lavender-gray lady who smelled all like vi'lets. Well, I never thought much a' that at th' time, until my own Dorothy tol' me 'bout smellin' vi'lets an' a-seein' that same lavender-gray lady. I asked Millijoy 'bout it, an' she'd had a similar experience an' she done said it was because she'd bin chosen t' be a Phenwick woman. Well, th' other two who'd seen th' lavender-gray lady, they become knowed as Phenwick women."

"Who was the lavender-gray lady, Gran'daddy?" Letty was perched on the edge of the bed staring with fascinated interest.

"My Aunt Olivia over in London, who'd also seen th' lady, tol' me that she was th' spirit a' Augusta Phenwick what chooses th' Phenwick women." Jim wiped his hand over his head and scratched. "It all sounded kind a' crazylike t' me. Th' thin' that drew that t' mind was the scent a' flowers. Maybe—well, I ain't gonna say what I'm a-thinkin'. It'll sound crazy, too. But jus' maybe there was a connection between you gettin' this rose, th' man who called hisself Adam Truff, an' Madame Ivanovich a-askin' ya t' London with her."

Letty wanted to retaliate with a statement, but she needed to gather her thoughts and consider the entire matter. She kissed her grandfather on the forehead and patted him gently. "I'm gonna go wash up now. An' I got chores t' do."

"Ya-all know what I'm a-gonna do? I'm a-gonna git right down here on my knees an' pray, that's what. An' if'n th' Lord wants ya t' go t' London, He'll find th' way."

"Oh, Gran'daddy!" Letty laughed and hugged him. "I love ya, Gran'daddy. You-all're about all I got in th' world, too." Another kiss and Letty darted toward the door.

Jim could hear her running down the hallway. He fingered the rose. "Adam Truff . . . hmm. Well, maybe it was ol' Adam." He, too, laughed, but it was a different kind of laughter.

The offices of Jaspar Calhoun were in the center of town, near the courthouse. Stocky, bald on top, ruddy complexion, beady eyes that squinted through thick-lensed eyeglasses, Jaspar Calhoun was known for his fiery temper, belligerent attitude and a downright arrogant personality. A cigar was perpetually held in his mouth, although not always lit, and he wore two large diamond rings on short pudgy fingers that glistened when he twisted the cigar around between his lips. An artificial smile was mechanically projected when he greeted a client, and his raucous laughter had a superficial ring that only the most naïve individuals could possibly believe. Pompous, wily, crafty, underhanded, blatantly dishonest, he was known for defending notorious legal cases and pulling shady deals. On the other hand, he religiously attended church, made magnificent financial contributions, held the position of deacon and played a significant role in the local Democratic party. In short, he was considered to be one of the foremost citizens of Savannah.

A widower at the age of twenty-eight—(his wife had met accidental death under suspicious circumstances which were neatly covered over)—Jaspar kept two mistresses and flirted with the notion of remarrying for the sake of appearance. Neither Betsy Bueler nor Maura Weston, the ladies with whom he had had long-time liaisons, were considerations to be the second Mrs. Calhoun. In his opinion, those ladies were hardly more than common doxies. Besides, he was the grandson of the former Frances Phenwick and the notorious Milton Callahan, although he thought that the latter was actually his *great*-grandfather. Quite frankly, he toyed with the thought of marrying his third cousin, Letitia Phenwick. Not only did he consider Letty a remarkable beauty—as did everyone else who ever saw her—,he had long had his eyes on the Moss Grove property which he had several times attempted to purchase from his great-uncle Jim for an absurdly small price, claiming that the land was virtually worthless. When Jaspar learned that Jim intended eventually to leave the property to Letty, unbeknownst to her, his lovely cousin appeared all the more attractive to him.

Blessed with the patience of Job, Jaspar had made no overt motions toward attempting to court Letty. When he had shown interest in her, she had openly rejected his overtures and had certainly not taken him seriously—nor was it likely that she ever would. His one hope, he concluded, would be to eventually get Letty or her grandfather into a compromising position and move in to work his will.

"I don't know no Madam Ivanovich," Jaspar snorted late that same afternoon when his clerk, Todd Potter, announced the lady and advised that she was waiting to see him. "Madam? Does she run a house or somethin'?" He laughed licentiously.

"She says it's important that ya see her, Mistah Calhoun," the intimidated, middle-aged clerk replied.

"Look like she's got any money?"

Todd Potter shook his head and shrugged.

"Cain't be bothered none! I give charity t' my church—where it's deserved, not t' tiresome poor whites who come in off th' street. She is white, ain't she?"

"Ye-us, suh. But she does speak with a little accent."

"Tell her I ain't in."

"I've done tol' her ya was in."

"Idiot!"

"She said she come somethin' 'bout th' Phenwicks."

"Th' Phenwicks? Dear Uncle Jim. I trust nothin's happen t' him."

"I b'lieve she done mentioned a Miss Phenwick," Todd

said almost as if he were purposefully baiting Jaspar to observe his reaction.

Jaspar made a noncommittal wave of his hand and looked down at a paper on his desk. Not hearing the clerk leave, he glanced up. "Tell her I cain't see her for five or ten minutes. I'll thinka somethin' t' kill th' time."

Todd Potter restrained a smirk and turned to leave the office.

Jasper leaned back in the chair and bounced his fingertips together. After whittling a point on a lead pencil, he stood at the open window and contemplated the situation. Finally he went to the door, opened it a crack to observe the small woman with the austere face and the stoic posture. Their eyes met before he opened the door wider.

"You the madam who wants t' see Jaspar Calhoun?"

Roselle's eyelids lowered halfway before she used a cane to lift herself. "You, I take it, are the same Mr. Jaspar Calhoun."

"I am. C'mon in." Jaspar motioned with his hand and preceded her into the room. He was behind the desk and seated before she entered. "C'mon in—an' take a chair." Watching as she sat, he drummed his fingers in a show of restless impatience. "Who, may I ask, is Madam Ivan-whatever?"

"Ivanovich. I am Madame Roselle Ivanovich. I am a former ballerina who presently teaches dancing lessons here in Savannah," she announced with precise articulation as she adjusted herself comfortably in the wooden chair. "I doubt you would have had the occasion to know of me, Mr. Calhoun. Not surprising. I will, however, come to the point of my business with you. I have several pupils who make a feeble attempt at dancing. They mean well, they simply lack appreciable talent. Be that as it may. Of all those who study with me, one, and only one, shows virtuoso skill and promise. I refer to Miss Letitia Phenwick."

Jaspar squinted as the side of his face involuntarily

twitched. "Letitia Phenwick?" he questioned. "I presume you mean Letty Phenwick. If so, she's my third cousin."

"Ah! I was not certain how you were related."

"At a respectable distance." Jaspar laughed. "What 'bout Letty?"

"I would like you to give her five hundred dollars." Roselle didn't as much as blink.

"Ya-all want me—" More laughter. "Ya-all want me t' give Letty five hundred dollars? I said we was *distantly* related. And for that matter, we're practically strangers."

"I take that to mean that you *won't* give her the money." Roselle started to rise. "Forgive me for usurping your precious time, Mr. Calhoun."

"Jus' a moment. Perhaps if'n ya was t' explain why ya want me t' give money t' Letty, I might—*'might'* I said—reconsider." Jaspar suddenly beamed an expression of Christian charity.

Once Roselle had repositioned herself, she explained the situation in full.

Jaspar sat in silent contemplation after she completed her narration. As their eyes met, he slowly shook his head. "I ain't a wealthy man, madam, an' I ain't a benefactor a' such thin's as dancin'. As t' Letty herself, I reckon it'ud be jus' plumb crazy for her t'go traipsin' off t' England or France—or wherever."

"Again I apologize for taking up your time, Mr. Calhoun," Roselle said as she pushed herself up. "My last hope is going directly to Mr. James Phenwick and beseeching him for assistance."

"Uncle Jim ain't got no money!" Jaspar replied, trying not to sound contemptuous. "Th' ol' fool's stubbornly set in his ways. He's got a little money stashed away, but he'd be even more foolish t' give it t' Letty t' go off with ya-all an' ya foolishness."

"Art may be foolish to you, Mr. Calhoun," Roselle stated as she reached the door and turned back, "it is not so with me. The United States is so barbaric when it comes to comprehension of the artist—especially the former Confederate states. Nothing progresses without the arts. And civilizations decay when the arts are abused and neglected. Good day, Mr. Calhoun."

Jaspar remained seated until Roselle left the room, then he rose and went to the window to watch her emerge into the street. Before he returned to the desk, a scheme began formulating in his mind. The more he considered it, the more excited he became about its possibilities. Maybe the little lady with the faint accent had opened a new door to him.

Chapter Three

FIRMLY STRUCTURED with the artistic proportions of a young god, golden-bronze in the late afternoon sun, the sixteen-year-old Negro youth stretched his shirtless body before he stood on one foot, lifted his arms and spun himself around, leapt and took a pose. His features were sensuously handsome, his body a masterpiece of perfection. Hard work had developed his musculature, long hours of hoeing, plowing, chopping wood.

The old slave quarters at Moss Grove, which were comprised of four buildings, had been fixed over to house several liberated Negro slaves after the Civil War. While their lot was little better than it had been prior to Emancipation, they lived as free people and worked for the Phenwicks for lodging and food. By the end of the nineteenth century, only one black family remained. They had taken the surnames of James, for Jim Phenwick. Horace and Cissy tended the garden and prepared meals in the plantation house, while their three children, Jeremiah, Lucas and Pansy assisted as best they could. Other than for the period they were involved with domestic work, the Jameses kept pretty much to themselves, living a simple life.

Young Jeremiah James was two years younger than Letty, but they had grown up as childhood friends. Both Horace and Cissy had mulatto blood and were exceptionally handsome, as were their children. As Letty had learned to dance, she had taught Jeremiah what she had been taught and the agile youth was quick to pick it up. Letty often stated that she would not have become as accomplished as she was if she had not had Jeremiah with whom to practice.

"Lawsy, Miss Letty," Jeremiah exclaimed when she told him of Madame Ivanovich's proposed trip, "y'all wouldn't go clean across th' ocean, would ya?"

"I will, if I get the chance."

"What yo' gran'daddy say 'bout dat?"

"Ya know there ain't much money—but he'll think 'bout it."

"How long will yo' be gone?" Jeremiah asked.

Letty shrugged. "Maybe I'll never return t' Savannah."

I would miss yo' if'n yo' never come back. I believes I'd miss yo' some' un terrible. Yo' taught me t' dance an' t' read an' t' write an' do numbers. Why, I'd be clean lost was yo' neber t' return."

There was still another two hours of daylight. The young friends had strolled through the woods to the pond. Theirs was a special relationship that reached beyond color or gender. They were simply two people, somehow kindred souls in a world that so often judged by outer appearances. The warmth of their friendship was unsurpassed. Still, Letty was being made more and more aware of the fact that Jeremiah was of the black race and that he was a man. Certainly she had never entertained romantic feelings for him, nor had she ever had lustful thoughts concerning him, which was also the situation as far as Jeremiah was concerned in his attitude toward her. Still, people being as they are had begun to make little insinuating remarks

42

about the two, and none the least of these was Cissy James, the boy's mother. She had even mentioned the closeness of the young people's relationship to Jim Phenwick. The old man lightly passed the matter off, but the subject had been planted in his mind.

The buggy rumbled up the deeply furrowed lane to Moss Grove. Dust clouded, and the road was bumpy. The ride proved to be uncomfortable and harrowing as Jaspar Calhoun held tightly to either side of the carriage to maintain his position as best he could.

The gray-haired black driver slowed the horse when the old plantation loomed into view as they rounded the bend. Jaspar sighed with relief and instructed the man to pull up to the carriage entrance.

Jaspar dusted himself before he entered the rambling old house. Aware that there were no servants and himself a part of the family, he made himself at home as he circled about the large room before he stopped to cock his head and listen. There was no sound. He struck a match and puffed on the short cigar. The clicking of his heels broke the silence as he went to climb the stairs to the second floor. He knew where Mattie stayed, so he avoided that part of the house.

The door to Jim's room was open. He was napping in the chair.

"Uncle Jim?" Jaspar called softly. Fear of disturbing Mattie restrained him from his customary volume. "Uncle Jim? Are ya awake?"

"I ain't, but ya done solved that." Jim squinted and yawned. "Who is it?"

"Your nephew, Jaspar Calhoun."

"Jaspar Calhoun?" Jim straightened in the chair. "What brings ya t' Moss Grove?"

"A danged uncomfortable buggy ride, if ya want t' know." Jaspar stepped deeper into the room. He found the odors offensive, but he tried to disregard them.

"What kin I do for ya, Jaspar?" Jim asked.

"I come t' pay ya a visit, Uncle Jim."

43

"I ain't never knowed ya t' come out here 'less'n there was a reason for it."

"My time is valuable, Uncle Jim. Naturally, I do whatever I do with a reason. I ain't got th' time t' pussyfoot around with thin's that ain't got no reason behind them."

"I kin see a lotta ol' Milton Callahan in ya, bo'."

Jaspar walked away from the old man. "Ya don't much like me, do ya, Uncle Jim?"

"I ain't never said that. Fact is, I never think much 'bout ya one way or t'other." Jim chuckled. "What's on ya mind?"

"Some ol' woman come askin' me t' give five hundred dollars t' Letty, that's what's on my mind," Jaspar snapped.

"That ol' woman 'parently never knowed ya very well, did she?" Again Jim chuckled.

"What would ya say t' th' fact that I bin thinkin' seriously 'bout doin' jus' that?" Jasper said as he took a magnanimous position.

"Plumb out an' give it t' her?" Jim questioned, unable to disguise the skepticism in his voice. "That'ud be mighty Christian a' ya."

"Ain' nothin' t' do with bein' Christian!" Jaspar fired back. "Well, th' fact is, I wasn't a-meanin' t' outright give it t' Letty. I was a-fixin' t' maybe loan it t' her."

"Loan it?" Jim scratched his head and aimed toward the spittoon. "I knowed ya wouldn't lend money if'n a person didn't put up collateral. Letty ain't got no collateral."

"Ya gonna leave Moss Grove t' her, ain't ya?"

"How'd ya-all find out 'bout that?"

"I know 'bout such thin's."

"Reckon ya make a point a' knowin', don't ya?"

"I'm a gambler, Uncle Jim. I make a point a' investigatin' thin's I gamble on. That's jus' good business sense. I actually would loan th' money t' you, Uncle Jim. An' if'n ya wasn't able t' pay me back th' five hundred dollars, ya-all could sell me two or three acres a' ya land. It'ud be a might expensive for land, but I'd do it for ya because ya're my kin."

"Two or three acres? Why don't ya jus' come out an' offer t' buy 'em t' begin with?"

"They ain't worth five hundred dollars, not even th' best a' them," Jaspar replied. "I'm only a-doin' this because that ol' woman come an' ask me to."

Jim thought a moment. "That's mighty generous a' ya, Jaspar. Well, it's some'un I'll have t' think 'bout, ain't it?"

"Seems t' me there's some urgency in gettin' th' money," Jaspar said. "I wouldn't think 'bout it none too long if'n I was you, Uncle Jim." He struck a match to relight his cigar. "Where's Letty now?"

"Reckon she's gone off with Jeremiah somewheres," Jim replied offhandedly. "She teaches that bo' how t' dance."

"Jeremiah? Th' nigra?" Jaspar looked alarmed.

"Th' same." Jim curiously watched his nephew's changed expression. "They done growed up t'gether."

"Letty's nigh on t' eighteen, ripe an' ready," Jaspar snorted, "an' ya let her go off with that young black buck?"

"Reckon neither a' them thinks a' th' other as either black er white."

"Well, they must think a' each other as male an' female."

Jim shrugged. "Doubt that ever much entered their minds. Jeremiah's a fine a young man as ya'll find, black er white. I ain't never give that much thought."

"Ya-all'ud better, Uncle Jim. Black or white, nature has a way a' takin' its course—an' a niggah is still a niggah. An' niggahs want revenge with our white girls."

"What're ya goin' on 'bout, Jaspar?" Jim questioned.

"I find out he ever—or if'n any black man molests a white woman, I'll personally see that he's strung up," Jaspar declared. "Ya-all remember what happened t' ya own mama, don't ya?"

"Reckon it ain't so much what th' niggah done t' her," Jim said, "as it was what her own people done by a-makin' her watch th' slave be hanged that made her lose her mind. Mama was made t' feel riddled with guilt."

"She was still had by a niggah man."

"An' Millijoy was th' result a' that," Jim added. "I d'clare, Millijoy was one a' th' most powerful Phenwick woman what ever lived. Mulatto or not, I loved her. An' ol' Adam Truff used t' say there weren't no better woman what ever lived."

"I don't know nothin' 'bout Millijoy Phenwick. I jus' know that if'n I ever hear a' anythin' happenin' between any niggah an' a white woman, well, ya jus' better believe I'll see that justice is done."

"Fear," Jim stated. "Fear. That's what it is, ain't it? Fear that th' black man is as much a human bein' as th' white man is, an' that someday them sold, beaten an' abused black men're gonna rise up an' take revenge for th' way they was treated. I don't have that fear, Jaspar, 'cause I always tried t' treat 'em like they was jus' as good as me—an' some a' 'em as better."

"Ya-all're a sick, disillusioned ol' man, Uncle Jim. An' ya jus' don't know how thin's really are." Jaspar fumed. "But, be that as it may, I ain't gonna make my offer a' money for Letty more'n once. Ya kin take it or leave it."

Jim glanced over at the rose which had been placed in a jar of water on the table. "Adam Truff."

"How's that?" Jaspar questioned.

"Nothin'. I was jus' a-thinkin' t' myself. I wonder."

"Wonder what?"

"D'ya mind givin' me a few minutes t' collect my thoughts?" Jim asked. "Why don't ya go say hello t' ya Aunt Mattie?"

"I'd rather take a whippin' than do that," Jaspar replied. "Ya know I cain't stand that ol' woman. An' th' sooner ya put her in th' crazy farm, th' better off ya-all'll be."

"I've heard ya opinions 'bout Mattie before, Jaspar. I consider th' source. Well, then, why don't ya jus' mosey 'round a little while I think?"

"I ain't got all night, ya know."

"Another fifteen minutes ain't gonna hurt ya none, is it?"

Jaspar made sounds of annoyance. "Well, fifteen minutes—an' I'm a-leavin'."

Jim chuckled to himself again as Jaspar strode from the room. Then he turned his attention and stared at the rose. "Adam Truff? Are ya somewhere in this room? An' if'n ya are, give me a sign if'n I'm t' accept th' money from Jaspar?"

As if he expected to hear some sort of answer, Jim sat in absolute silence. Only his eyes moved. He was about to give up on the situation when he became aware of a powerful fragrance coming from the rose. His eyes widened.

"Is that th' sign?" Jim asked.

"What do you want, a bolt of lightning?"

"Who said that?"

"You ask, I gave. What more do you want?"

The old man's eyes darted around the room. "Adam? Is that *really* you?"

Hollow laughter seemed to inundate the room.

"Does th' rose mean my Letty is meant t' be a Phenwick woman?" Jim asked.

"She is a likely candidate. I can tell you no more—"

"Adam—?" Jim suddenly had the feeling that whatever force had entered the room had as quickly left it. He would remain staring at the rose until Jaspar returned.

"Chances a' me a-goin' t' England're mighty slim," Letty said as she and Jeremiah made their way back through the woods. "But if'n I do go, I'll only be away a short time, Jeremiah."

"I'll miss you, I sho' will miss ya, Miss Letty." Jeremiah walked ahead and put his hand to his face, to his eyes, which had begun to become liquid with emotion.

47

When Letty caught up with him, he turned his head. "Ya cryin', Jeremiah?"

"Ain't a-cryin' none. Jus' got dust in my eyes, I reckon, an' they smart."

They were standing in a cleared area near to the old slave buildings. Letty stepped forward and put her hand to Jeremiah's face, forcing it toward her. "Ya are a-cryin', ain't ya?"

Jeremiah shook his head.

Quickly Letty threw her arms around him and pulled his cheek next to hers. "Jeremiah, I love ya as if ya was my own brothuh. Fact is, I could never love any a' my kin better'n I love you."

Jaspar was standing on the second floor veranda. "Lord-have-mercy!" he exclaimed as he saw the unmistakable display of affection. He recognized Letty and he could see that the shirtless man with her was black. Leaning on the rail, he watched as his blood pressure began to rise.

"Reckon I better git back t' th' house now," Letty said as she again hugged Jeremiah and kissed him tenderly on the cheek. "Ya practice them steps I showed ya, Jeremiah, an' we'll dance ag'in tomorra." She let her hand slip down the length of his arm and squeezed his hand before she disengaged herself and ran toward the mansion, carefree and happy because she had spent beautiful moments with her dear friend.

"Jeremiah James! Yo' gits yo' black se'f in dis house dis very minute!" Cissy called. "I's takin' a stick t' yo', yo heah?"

"What I done, Mama?" Jeremiah asked as he faced Cissy.

"I done seed yo' out dere wif Miss Letty."

"No, mama, don't hit him," young Pansy called.

"Yo' stay outa dis, chile!" Cissy replied. "Yo' drops yo' britches, Jeremiah, so dat it stings all de more. Yo' heah?"

"Ye-us, Mama. But sticks an' switches ain't gonna hurt me near as much as de hurt what I feels inside," Jeremiah sobbed.

Jaspar dashed into the house before Letty saw him. He made a bee-line for Jim's room. "I tell ya I seen 'em with my very eyes, Uncle Jim—Letty an' that niggah a-huggin' in broad daylight!"

"Jaspar Calhoun, ya done gotta evil mind. If'n they was doin' anythin' wrong, they wouldn'ta bin doin' it where ya-all coulda seen it. Now then, before ya bust one a' ya good blood vessels, I'll tell ya I'll accept ya proposition."

"Ain't so sure I want t' offer it anymore—not after what I done seen," Jaspar puffed.

"Jaspar—? You ever bin with a black woman?" Jim asked.

"A woman's a woman whatever th' color a' her skin."

Jim wrung his hands together. "That answers my question, an' it tells me a lot more 'bout ya. Well, maybe I'd better git that money an' send Letty off—for her own good. Don't ya think that's right?"

Jaspar sputtered. "Well, ye-us, I reckon as how." He wanted to say more, but thought better of it. "I'll git th' money t' ya tomorra. But I think ya-all had better keep a close eye on Letty an' that niggah. Good evenin', Uncle Jim." He stormed out.

Jim was laughing when Letty entered his room a few minutes later.

"What niggah was Jaspar Calhoun a-talkin' 'bout?" Letty asked, explaining that she had been standing outside the room and overheard the tail end of her cousin's remarks.

"Was you an' Jeremiah James a-doin' anythin' what ya shouldn'ta bin doin'?" Jim asked.

"Goodness, no!" Letty appeared alarmed, but not embarrassed. "I d'clare, what're ya talkin' 'bout?"

"Nothin', Letty, nothin' at all." Jim bit off a chew of tobacco. "It seems as how Jaspar is a-gonna put up th' money for ya t' go t' England."

Letty stared at her grandfather, but she could not speak.

Chapter Four

IT RAINED THE FOLLOWING DAY as Jaspar Calhoun rode out to Moss Grove. Not caring about his clothing, he protected the money and the papers he carried. The downpour stopped a mile before he reached his destination and the sweltering humidity that followed was almost unbearable. He wished that he had not decided to travel in the heat of the day.

Cissy James was in the main house where she had just finished cleaning after lunch. Pansy was with her mother and the two stared expressionless as Jaspar entered the house.

"Niggah woman, ya-all tell my uncle Jim that I'm here," Jaspar ordered.

"I only come in t' fix Mistah Jim's lunch an' Miss Mattie's. I ain't no regular maid," Cissy replied. Beneath her proud beauty was arrogance to match Jaspar's. "Reckon as how yo' knows yo' way about, Mistah Calhoun."

"Insolence!" Jaspar fumed. "Ya-all'd better learn ya place."

"I knows my place, Mistah Calhoun." Cissy put her

arm about Pansy's shoulders. " 'Scuse me." With that, she pushed the little girl toward the front door and started to leave.

"Since when does niggahs use th' front door?" Jaspar called.

"Since it was done proved dat we is real people after all," Cissy fired back and let the door slam behind her.

"Danged baggage!" Jaspar hollered before he climbed the steps to the hallway that led to Jim's room. He pushed the gaping door open with his foot and stood to observe his uncle sitting by the window going over figures in a book. "Uncle Jim."

Jim turned back and pushed an old pair of wireframed glasses down his nose. "Jaspar? I reckon I weren't 'spectin' ya so early in th' day."

Jaspar looked rumpled after his ride in the rain. He felt uncomfortable, and that did nothing to enhance his disposition. "I brung ya th' money an' papers t' sign. I got business t' attend t' back in town, so I ain't got time t' lollygag none." He produced the documents from his inside coat pocket and handed them to his uncle before he slapped the stack of currency onto the table. "Ya count it—five hundred. I would've come out before th' heat a' th' day, but I had t' wait for th' bank t' open."

Jim glanced at the handwritten papers before him, over to the money and then up at Jaspar. "Ya wasted no time, did ya, Jaspar?"

"Th' ol' woman what come askin' for th' money said it was urgent," Jaspar replied as he sauntered around the room while Jim examined the document. "It's all perfectly legal."

"I've no doubt 'bout that, Jaspar," Jim commented. "But a-bein' legal an' a-bein' fair is two different thin's."

"It's fair, Uncle Jim. Do ya think I'd try t' cheat ya?"

Jim swallowed his immediate comment as he reached to touch the stack of money. "Reckon not." The glasses were put back in place as he held the papers to good light.

Jaspar paced like a caged lion. As he gazed about,

looking at nothing in particular, his attention kept returning to the red rosebud that appeared to be as fresh as it had been the day before. "What's th' matter with that flower?"

"Huh?" Jim didn't turn his attention from the paper.

"It was jus' like that yesterday. Why don't it open up full in all this heat?" Jaspar asked curiously. He touched the rose. "I put a rose in my buttonhole of a Sunday, an' it's full-blown before th' sermon is done with."

"Don' know much 'bout roses," Jim remarked, "nor 'bout contracts. But I reckon this is good enough." He shuffled the pages and scanned the scribbled words.

"Where's Letty?" Jaspar asked a few minutes later. "How come I never see her 'round much?"

"She's off practicin' her dancin', I reckon," Jim said.

"She oughta be here t' witness ya signature, Uncle Jim."

"Horace James is down in th' kitchen a-cleanin' th' stove. He kin witness."

"A niggah?"

"He's a free man now, Jaspar. He kin witness as good as th' next person," Jim replied as he got up and went to the door. He called, "Horace! Ho-race! Ya come up here, will ya?" He turned back into the room and stared quizzically at Jaspar. "Ya up t' somethin', ain't ya, Jaspar?"

"Why ya say that?" Jaspar questioned, trying to assume an expression of absolute innocence.

"Ya're too eager t' lend money."

"I ain't eager. An' if'n ya think that way, I'll jus' take it back an' forget 'bout th' whole thin'." Jaspar fumbled in his pocket for a match to light the well chewed cigar.

"Ain't important. Ya do what ya see fit, Jaspar."

Tall, enigmatically handsome Horace stood at the door, holding to the straps of his overalls. "Yo' called me, Mistah Phenwick, suh?"

"I want ya t' witness my signature, Horace," Jim

said, then turned to Jaspar. "That is, if'n ya still want me to sign it."

Jaspar made a nondescript motion of his hand which was taken to be an affirmative gesture. "Go ahead, Uncle Jim."

Horace strode into the room. Although he was proud, he lacked the blatant arrogance that made his wife offensive to certain people. Glancing only briefly at Jaspar, he went to where Jim was seated again at the table and watched as he scribbled his signature.

"Ya jus' sign it there, Horace. That's all," Jim said.

Horace did as he was told.

Jaspar took the papers and examined the signatures. "Horace, ya seen Miss Letty around anyplace?"

"She was out a-dancin' like she always do," Horace replied. "She an' Jeremiah am always at it whenever they gits done wif di chores."

"Jeremiah?" Jaspar puffed deeply on the cigar. "Ya bo' Jeremiah?"

"Yassuh, Mistah Calhoun. I neber knowed dat bo' could dance like de way he do," Horace said. "He done lifts Miss Letty right off a' de ground an' spins her 'round above his head."

Jim noisily cleared his throat. "That'll be all, Horace."

"Yassuh, Mistah Jim. Reckon I best git back t' cleanin' dat stove." Horace edged his way from the room and moved faster than he usually did when he reached the door.

"Lifts her up over his head, does he?" Jaspar questioned.

"That worries ya, don't it, Jaspar?"

" 'Cause I wonder what else he does t' her, that's what!"

"Ya-all want t' believe what ya wants t' believe, Jaspar, which may er may not be what actually is an' what actually ain't," Jim said as he took aim at the spittoon. He reached for the money that his nephew had brought. "I spent time with my Uncle Joshua an'

Aunt Olivia in London onc't. Them was th' best a' all my mem'ries. Reckon Letty should have some pleasant mem'ries in her life. I look at thin's this way, Jaspar: life's got many different thin's t' offer, but less'n a body takes advantage a' 'em, they may as well not be there at all. If'n Letty kin know some happiness, then whatever th'price, I'll be pleased for her."

"Even th' price a' bearin' a mulatto child?" Jaspar snapped.

"Bearin' a—whatever ya talkin' 'bout, Jaspar?"

"Ya're ignorant, Uncle Jim, but ya ain't altogether dumb. Maybe ya-all don't see th' signs, but I do!" Jaspar exclaimed. "Well, we'll jus' see 'bout that, won't we?" He stormed toward the door.

"Ya runnin' off so soon, Jaspar?"

"Gotta git back t' town. Bye."

"Thank ya for th' money, Jaspar."

Jaspar did not reply. His heavy footsteps were heard going over the hallway and down the stairs. Moments later the front door was slammed.

Jim shook his head and counted the money.

Twelve-year-old Lucas James was swinging on a rope from a large magnolia tree, dragging his bare feet in the dust. He looked up when he heard the door slam.

"What ya doin'there, bo'?" Jaspar called.

"Nuthin' but a-swingin'," Lucas answered.

"Ya-all Jeremiah?"

"No, suh. Jeremiah's my brothah. He out by th' pond wit Miss Letty. Dey is dancin'. Lordy, how dey kin do all that jumpin' 'round in all dis heat sho' beats me."

"Do ya ever watch 'em dance, bo'?"

"I has sometime. Dey don't like me a-watchin'."

"What do they do when they ain't dancin'?"

"Dey rests, I reckon."

"Ya ever seen 'em restin'?"

"Dey jus' lays 'round on de rocks or in de shade. Dey chases me off. Why yo' asks, mistah?"

"Never mind, bo'. Go on with ya swingin'." Jaspar said. His impulse was to go out toward the pond and have a look for himself. The hour and the near suffocating heat made him think better of the idea. He glared at Lucas before he went to the buggy, where the black driver was nodding. "Let's git on back t' town as quick as possible! Ya hear?"

"Yassuh."

Jaspar stared at the plantation house as the buggy pulled into the road. His eyes scanned back to the trees beyond the old slave quarters as he seethed with anger.

Shortly after four o'clock that afternoon, Vladimir Popkin stumbled through the street near the courthouse. The heat augmented the usual effect of the liquor he had imbibed. One eye closed, he attempted to focus on his directions. Deciding that he wasn't fully able to navigate his way for awhile, he found a place in the shade near a bench.

"Mistah Popkin," a voice called.

Vladimir raised his hand to shield afternoon sun from his eyes. His vision was hazy as he perceived a slender man coming toward him.

"Ain't that grass wet, Mistah Popkin?" Todd Potter asked.

Vladimir remarked in Russian before he said, "No. Or if it is, I don't feel the wet."

"Mind if'n I join ya a spell?" Todd took a small bottle from his hip pocket. "I've got a taste I'll share with ya."

Vladimir closed one eye and stretched his neck forward before he recognized the man with whom he had drunk on several occasions. He motioned for Todd to sit beside him.

The two men passed the time of day in mundane, somewhat intoxicated conversation.

"I hear ya lady is a-goin' t' go off for a spell," Todd remarked after there was a lull in the conversation and Popkin appeared on the verge of losing consciousness.

"Madame Roselle is taking me with her," Popkin replied. "What would I do here without her? Fact is, what will I do with her?" He belched loudly. "In Russia I was a lady's man, as you would say. But now, I haven't much use for ladies. I only like to drink."

"Ya ever hear a' th' night riders, Mistah Popkin? That's somethin' t' do for excitement," Todd commented.

"Night riders? What're they?"

"They take th' law in their own hands when niggahs do what they ain't s'pose t' do with white ladies," Todd added. "Th' night riders are gonna ride t'night. An' if'n ya want a little 'citement, ya kin come along. I'll tell th' bo's."

"What kind of excitement?" Popkin's eyes widened as he attempted to focus fully on Todd Potter's face.

"Lynchin' probably."

"In Russia, the Czar—" Popkin's words trailed off. "Who are they going to lynch?"

Todd glanced about him to make certain they weren't going to be overheard, then he spoke in a whisper so that Popkin only heard part of what he said, but he managed to get the gist of what it was about.

Popkin shook his head and tried to push himself to his feet. "The old lady—" He fell and it took even more effort to raise himself again. "I got to get home. The old lady will be looking for me. I don't believe in lynching. No. I've seen too much violence."

"Ya-all want me t' walk a ways with ya, Mistah Popkin?" Todd volunteered.

"No, the old woman see me with you and she'll lay into you with the broom," Popkin replied. "I go alone." With that he lurched forward, made several false starts before he managed to head himself in the direction of Madame Ivanovich's house.

Todd Potter watched, scratched himself and went toward a place he knew several of his cronies to hang out.

"Look at you, Popkin!" Roselle exclaimed as the man lay on the floor of the large room used for a dance studio. "Just look at you!"

"I can't even see you, so how could I look at myself?"

Roselle got a bucket of water and threw it on him. "You're no good, not to me or to anyone, much less to yourself. I should kick you out. And the very idea of taking you to London with me is insane!"

Popkin smiled as he wiped the refreshing water from his face. "Then leave me here."

"You would starve to death before I returned," Roselle said, trying not to sound sympathetic. "I don't know what possesses you to drink as you do. Are you so bored with life?"

"I couldn't have put it better myself." Popkin made a regurgitating sound. He picked himself off the floor and staggered to a chair. "What is the use of life, anyway? I see no purpose in going on. I'd kill myself, but I'm too much of a coward to do that. Now, if I were black, I'd take a white woman and let the night riders come and lynch me. That would be terrifying for a while, but I would get over it."

"The night riders? Now what foolishness have you been listening to?" Roselle asked as she started for the kitchen.

"The night riders are going to ride tonight!" Popkin proclaimed, raising his hand in the air as if it held a sword. "Blood is going to be shed!"

"I don't want to hear of such things," Roselle exclaimed and went into the next room.

"Not even—" Popkin said a moment later as he stood at the door, braced against the frame, "not even if it concerned someone you know?"

"What *are* you talking about, Vladimir? You make no sense at all when you've been drinking. And since you drink most of the time, you never make sense. I don't know why I put up with it." Roselle checked a pot of beans simmering on the fire. She waited, thinking that Popkin would finish with his narration. Finally, she turned back to him. "*Whom* do I know?"

Vladimir shrugged and made an uncertain gesture with his large hands. "Who do you know, Roselle? Who is the one person in all Savannah you believe to have great talent?"

"Letitia Phenwick?"

Popkin nodded, making exaggerated movements of his head.

"What're you talking about, Popkin? Tell me."

Stumbling toward a kitchen chair, Popkin sat before he related what Todd Potter had told him. Although he was somewhat incoherent, Roselle was able to piece together the thread of his story. She had listened to Letty's praise of Jeremiah's talent as a dancer. Propriety, however, would not permit her to take the young black man on as a student. She didn't even want to see him dance, much less meet him. Still she knew that Letty believed in his ability.

Roselle had told herself time and time again that there was no place in the arts for Negroes. Not that she personally had anything against them, and in the past she had had several black friends in Europe. It might have been different, she thought, if she had known Letty while living in Paris and the girl had told her about Jeremiah. The entire social situation was different. But here in Savannah, she would only be asking for trouble to consider teaching a black student. Besides, even if he were the most talented dancer in the world, what future could he possibly have? Free or not, Negroes were still Negroes in Savannah, and if they didn't know their places, the whites would soon see that they found them.

"Was Jeremiah James's name mentioned?" Roselle asked when Vladimir slouched into a stupor. She shook him.

"What, woman?"

"Was Jeremiah James's name mentioned?"

"I don't remember."

"Was Letitia's name mentioned?"

"He said—he said—uh—Letty Phenwick."

Roselle got more water and doused Vladimir with it. "Sober up, you old fool!"

Vladimir waved his hand as if to shoo her away and dropped his head to the table.

Beside herself with anxiety, Roselle took part of the money sent her by Georges LeVeque and went to the stable to hire a horse and buggy. Unskilled at driving such a vehicle, nonetheless she determined that she could manage.

Nearly an hour had passed since Vladimir had lost consciousness. When she returned to the kitchen, Roselle warmed coffee left from the morning and, while it was heating, she again drenched the pianist with cold water.

"Wake up, you damned fool!" she hollered.

Popkin raised his head with a start only to be inundated by a second bucket full of water.

"What are you doing to me? If you want to drown me, why don't you just hold my head in the bucket? I promise not to resist."

"Here, drink this coffee," Roselle ordered. "I have a buggy waiting outside and you're going with me."

"To London?"

"No, to Moss Grove. Drink the coffee and no back talk." Roselle scampered about, adjusting a bonnet on her head and getting a scarf.

"I am sopping wet," Popkin complained.

"You will dry before we get to Moss Grove." She plopped his hat ungraciously on his head. "Finish that coffee and we will go. There is no time to waste. Even with two hours before dark, we will still be racing time. Hurry, Vladimir, hurry! It may be a matter of life or death!"

Her words aroused Popkin and he swilled the coffee as rapidly as he could, coughing only briefly in reaction.

Chapter Five

THE SUN WAS FAR IN THE WEST, sinking toward the horizon as Letty carried water to the topless wooden-walled structure which she had had Horace build especially so that she could drench herself with cold water after strenuous hours of dancing. The cold water tingled against her skin, naked in the privacy of the enclosure. The chill of it revitalized her as gooseflesh momentarily appeared.

Upon drying off, Letty skinned into a clean dress, faded but still with plenty of wear to it. Then as she towelled her hair she permitted herself to speculate about the adventure of going to England. She would personally go to thank Jaspar Calhoun for the assistance he had given before she actually left on the voyage. Yet she could not help but believe that he had some devious motive behind his generosity.

Her hair nearly dry, she was in the process of brushing it when she heard the rattle of the approaching buggy and the racing hooves of the horse. Concerned for the animal being driven at such a pace on that hot day, Letty ran shoeless toward the front of the house.

"Madame Ivanovich!" Letty exclaimed with surprise as she recognized the woman.

Roselle yanked on the reins with all the strength she had. "You stay here, Popkin," she ordered. "Mam'selle, give me a hand down, will you?"

"What is it? What's all th' excitement?" Letty asked.

"Come into the house with me," Roselle commanded. "I'll not waste my breath retelling the story over and over. Come."

Roselle took Letty's hand and pulled her toward the house, while Vladimir Popkin remained in the buggy, eyed the situation and returned to reclining in the back of it.

"You run and pack your things, mam'selle," Roselle said as she climbed the stairs with effort, "while I tell your grandfather what is happening."

"What *is* happenin'?" Letty asked innocently.

"Just take what you absolutely need, your best things."

"My best ain't very good," Letty protested. "Cain't ya tell me what this is all about?"

"Get your things, I'll explain on the way," Roselle said. She pushed Letty toward her room. "Time is of the essence."

Roselle went directly to Jim's room where he was napping. Her narration was jumbled and Jim did not at first comprehend what it was all about.

"There's a railroad stop in Hardeeville, South Carolina," Roselle said. "I had been there once. I'll drive Letitia and Jeremiah there, where they can catch a train heading north."

"Ain't ya bein' hasty 'bout all this?" Jim questioned.

"You know of the night riders, don't you?" Roselle returned.

"Ye-us."

"Well, they're coming out here to lynch Jeremiah James," Roselle stated plainly. "I don't believe anything immoral ever happened between the boy and the girl, but those cruel men want to think otherwise. Furthermore, from what I've gathered, you had best hide the rest of the James family. Send them into the woods or anywhere."

"There's a secret room down in th' basement what was dug out durin' th' War t' hide in," Jim commented, now beginning to catch some of the urgency which Roselle was projecting. "Reckon they kin go there."

"I'll assist Miss Letitia," Roselle instructed, "while you go get the Jameses. Get Jeremiah's best clothes, not so much that he can't carry them in an emergency. There's no time to linger. Hurry, Mr. Phenwick, hurry!"

Jim hobbled from the room. He knew only too well about the night riders and the fate of other Negroes who had been their unsuspecting victims. Beyond reason or rational thought, the old man went as quickly as he could, thinking only of the urgency of the situation and not the motives behind it.

Fear played terror in Horace James's face when Jim made the announcement. Cissy immediately gathered what she could for Jeremiah, tied it in a burlap sack and did her best to keep her composure while Horace rounded up Lucas and Pansy. Jeremiah stood in bewildered amazement as he watched, hardly able to change into a clean outfit of clothing as the panic surged through his family.

"What'd I do? What'd I do?" the handsome youth kept repeating.

"Ya done nothin'," Jim assured him, "but them night riders don't know that."

"Mama—" Jeremiah called as Cissy began hustling the other two children toward the main house. "Mama, I is scared."

Jim took Lucas and Pansy by the hands and pulled them toward the house while Cissy went back to Jeremiah.

"Yo' gots t' go, Jeremiah. Dey will hang yo' if'n yo' stays here," Cissy warned, trying to contain the panicky feeling that was driving her to the edge of hysteria.

Still she knew she had to be brave for Jeremiah's sake. "We kin't dawdle none, bo'. Dere ain't time fo' dat. Yo' understand?"

"I don't understand nuthin', Mama. Kin't I jus' hide wif de rest a' yo'?"

"No, no, Jeremiah, yo' kin't." She threw her arms around him and kissed him before the tears came.

Horace gently took Cissy's arms from about Jeremiah. "Yo' goes on wif de others, Mama, I sees t' Jeremiah."

"My baby! My baby!" Cissy screamed and sagged to the earth.

"Yo' grabs one a' her arms while I gits de other," Horace instructed Jeremiah. "C'mon, bo', do like I says!"

Father and son lifted the distraught woman to her feet and practically carried her to the main house. Again Cissy clung to Jeremiah, sobbing incoherently as Horace peeled her from him and guided her to the front porch.

"Mama—"

Horace hurried back to Jeremiah. "Yo' gots t' go now, bo'."

"D-daddy—?"

"I loves yo', son, an' 'cause I does love yo', I wants yo' t' go. Don't yo' understand?" Horace pleaded.

"Daddy—I doesn't want t' go. I doesn't!"

"It ain't what yo' wants, bo', it's what must be." He threw his arms about Jeremiah and hugged him as if he intended to crush his bones. "Now go."

Letty and Roselle appeared at the front door. Although she was herself confused, Letty had begun to perceive in part what was transpiring. She leapt down the steps and ran to where Jeremiah and Horace were standing.

"Come along, Jeremiah, there ain't no time for long good-byes," Letty said warmly, understandingly. She put her arm about the youth and led him reluctantly toward the buggy.

Jim leaned against the door as he caught his breath.

Roselle went to the buggy and used her cane to poke

Popkin. "Get up, Popkin. Mam'selle and Jeremiah will have to ride back there where they can be covered up, if necessary. You'll have to ride on the seat with me."

"Letty!" Jim called and managed to get down the steps before Letty ran to him. "Ya forgot th' money. Here, ya-all stick it somewheres it'll be safe. Don't keep it all in one place. Remember these names: Alexander Phenwick an' Daniel Charles Phenwick an' Joshua."

"Cain't ya come with us, Gran'daddy?"

"No, Letitia, I cain't. There's Mattie—an' I've got t' look after Horace an' Cissy," Jim said. "This ain't th' end a' ever'thin'. Ya-all'll be back one day."

"Mam'selle!" Roselle called after Vladimir had made an awkward attempt at helping her onto the seat.

"Go now, Letty."

Oh, Gran'daddy, Gran'daddy!" She hugged and kissed him.

"I want ya t' do somethin' for me, Letty."

"What is it, Gran'daddy?"

He took the rose from his shirt pocket. "I want ya t' become one a' th' greatest Phenwick women there ever was. That would make me proud. Don't forget ya rose. An' maybe ya kin write t' me sometime."

"Mam'selle, the sun has set."

As Jeremiah cowered in the back of the buggy, Horace reached over to pat him understandingly before he went back to Cissy.

"I love ya, Gran'daddy! An' I promise I'll make ya proud as daylight a' me," Letty said, gave the old man one final kiss and picked up her bag. "Ya take care a' yaself, ya hear?" She ran toward the buggy.

"My baby! My baby!" Cissy cried hysterically as Horace caught her in a substantial embrace.

"Don't, Mama, don't!"

Cissy became limp and collapsed in his arms. Tenderly he lifted her and carried her into the house.

Letty climbed in the back of the buggy beside Jeremiah. She held his trembling hand and let him lean against her as he cried uncontrollably as if he instinctively knew that he would never see his people again.

Jim waved as he leaned against the Corinthian column. Tears misted his eyes, too, but he stood brave and remained where he was until the buggy pulled through the entrance where gates once had been. Then, as the vehicle disappeared in a gust of dust down the road, he turned back and went to help Horace take Cissy into the basement with the other children.

"It'll be all right, Jeremiah, ya hear?" Letty soothed. "I just know it'll be."

Jeremiah sobbed and mumbled incoherently as wave after wave of terror went through him.

Letty didn't look back. She refused to allow herself to think of what might happen at Moss Grove, or about what the future would hold.

Chapter Six

"THAT HORSE'LL NEVER MAKE IT twenty miles," Popkin observed as the buggy reached the main road leading to Hardeeville, "much less get us back to Savannah."

"Do you remember how to pray, Vladimir?" Roselle asked over the clatter.

"I know the technique," the man said, still blurry-eyed and miserable with a piercing pain in his head. "I can recite the old prayers backwards and forwards; but I suspect essential faith is missing."

"Use the technique," Roselle responded, "I've got the faith."

The road was particularly bumpy in places. The ride was not only uncomfortable, but hazardous. Letty sat close to Jeremiah and continued to hold his hand, gently stroking it.

"Why is we a-runnin' away, Miss Letty?" Jeremiah asked. The tears had made furrows in the dust on his cheeks. His bewildered expression caused Letty to react with all the compassion within her.

"Don't think a' it as runnin' away, but as goin' on a' adventure," she said.

"I's too young an' scared t' go on a' adventure," Jeremiah replied. "Jus' walkin' into town's 'nuff adventure fo' me."

"Think a' th' bright side, Jeremiah."

"What am de bright side?"

Letty thought a few minutes before she smiled. "You'll see." She laughed and squeezed his hand.

Jeremiah appeared even more perplexed.

The gray sky in the west was quickly being overcome by the black in the east. The first stars had begun to twinkle, but most of the heavenly sparkle was obscured by dark clouds that had been drifting in from the ocean. The air was again heavy with moisture, sticky, hot humidity that seemed to accentuate the scents of the magnolias and wild honeysuckle. Crickets and frogs had begun their nocturnal serenades, creating an electric sound of buzzing suspense.

An owl hooted in a large maple and his call received a reply from another owl in a hickory tree on the opposite side of the old mansion. The frantic squeal of a jackrabbit pierced the night as sharp talons snatched it from the field. The dogs barked. Old Blue paced on the front porch and periodically looked up at Jim as he sat in the hammock, the shotgun across his lap. He had been watching one of the cats catch moths, leaping about in odd contortions.

The fireflies began to appear.

"Brothah! I gotta queer feelin', Brothah!" Mattie called from her room. "Ya hear, Brothah?"

Jim chose not to hear as was often the case when Mattie made sounds in the night.

As if on a given signal, all of the night sounds stopped at once. Blue raised his head, turned from side to side and ambled over to where Jim was swinging back and forth.

"What ya-all hear, Blue?" Jim asked. He patted the

dog's head. An apprehensive sensation came over him before he whistled to call the other dogs, who usually found cool places in the back of the house. Within seconds, five of the large hound dogs appeared, expecting a handout of some kind.

"Ya-all stay close here," Jim ordered. "Lay down an' wait."

Three of the dogs flopped on the porch while the other two stretched out on the ground just beyond. Blue scooted closer to his master as if he knew he was the favorite.

"Why'd them frogs an' crickets git so quiet?" Jim questioned aloud.

Blue barked and whined. He was suddenly to his feet as the other dogs began to take an interest. Blue went to the steps, barked again and whined in anticipation before he went back to where Jim was waiting.

"They's comin', ain't they?" Then Jim heard what the dogs had perceived, the sound of racing horses' hooves. He braced himself.

There was a tense, static moment of anxiety before one of the dogs in the yard began barking. The others joined in, leapt from the porch and ran to the old gate entrance.

Six hooded horsemen appeared and rode onto the property as the barking began to have a frantic tone to it.

"Ya stay here with me, Blue," Jim ordered. "Them others'll greet th' riders."

The horsemen didn't even slow as they passed the black shadow of the house and continued toward the old slave quarters. The dogs were in hot pursuit.

Three of the men circled the building where the Jameses lived, luring the dogs with them, while each of the others went to the buildings, kicked the doors in and entered without dismounting.

"Ain't no one here!"

"That's th' place where they live!"

Chickens cackled as their sleep was disturbed. A gaggle of geese came honking and hissing.

A shot rang out.

"Don't do no shootin', ya damn'd fool!" the leader of the group ordered. "Ya'll scare them niggahs off."

"I'm gonna shoot me a goose if'n he keeps bitin' at me!"

"Y'all ain't gonna shoot nuthin'!" the leader of the group hollered.

A bolt of lightning stabbed with electric brightness. The horses reared back and one of the men was thrown from his mount. Immediately the fallen man was charged by dogs and geese. He used his rifle, holding it by the barrel, to lash out at the animals.

"Ain't no niggahs here!"

The fallen man managed to scamper into the building and close the door behind him.

Thunder hammered with such ferocity that it sounded as if the entire sky was falling down on top of them. The geese scattered as huge raindrops began to fall.

"They's a-hidin' some'eres!" the man in the building called. "But they bin here not long ago."

"Set fire t' it, an' let's go t' th' main house!"

The dogs charged at the man as he came from the Jameses' lodging place, fire burning behind him. Gunshots were fired to scare the dogs, giving the man time enough to remount.

The downpour was intense as more lightning struck.

"Stay right here, Blue," Jim ordered as the horsemen came toward where he was still sitting.

As the men reined up before the house, Jim fired a shot into the air over their heads. "You-all git outta here. This is private property, an' ya' trespassin'!"

"It's th' ol' man."

"Call off ya dogs!"

"They'll leave ya be onc't ya' off my property," Jim stated.

"Where's th' niggahs?"

"Ain't here!" Jim called above the violent sounds of the rain. "They's gone!"

"Gone? Where?"

"None a' ya' damn business!"

"We'll search th' house!"

"Ya-all do, an' them dawgs'll eat ya alive!" Jim warned.

"Not after they's shot dead, they won't!" the leader replied.

"My nephew sent ya-all out here, didn't he?"

There was no reply.

"Or maybe one a' you hooded jackasses is Jaspar Calhoun," Jim speculated.

A dog nipped one rider's ankle. In response the man fired at him. The bullet barely grazed the animal, but he went howling off. The other dogs, discouraged by the deluge of rain, went for nearby shelter.

"Two a' y'all wait out here, while th' rest a' us go on in an' git th' niggahs!" the leader instructed. "Y'all keep ya guns aimed on th' ol' man an' th' dawgs."

With soaked hoods, and otherwise drenched, four of the men dismounted and stomped over the porch to enter the house.

"I tell ya-all, I'm here alone," Jim called. "Ain't no one here but me'n my crazy sistah!"

"Y'all jus' don't say no more, ol' man, 'cause I gots a' itchy trigger-finger."

Jim looked back to see that one of the slave buildings was on fire. "Ya-all set fire t' my place, didn't ya?"

"Reckon th' lightnin' did that."

"Lightnin' don't strike inside a house first," Jim commented.

The men rampaged about inside the plantation house for a good twenty minutes. During that time, the rain continued in a tumultuous downpour.

"What's a-keepin' 'em?" one of the two men remaining outside asked.

"Beats me."

"Reckon we better go take a peek?"

"Best not."

The loudest crash of thunder rumbled overhead.

One man poked the other and pointed in the direction of the slave quarters.

"Lookee there, Tom."

"Lord-a-mercy!"

Stalking toward them was a luminous figure of a man, well dressed and obviously not concerned with the torrential downpour.

"That—that ain't no human bein'," the more cowardly of the two declared.

Jim turned to observe and braced himself as best he could. "Reckon ya bo's're a-seein' my ghost," he said, trying to sound calm and collected, which was not at all the way he felt.

"G-ghost?"

"Let's git outta here!"

"We cain't run off on th' others. They'd a-tan us!"

"Wal, I'm a-scared as hell!"

Two of the four men who had gone into the house appeared at the front door.

"Ain't no niggahs in there?"

"Where they at, ol' man?"

"Bert, look yonder!"

"Reckon they went off t' Atlanta this evenin' 'cause th' woman's mammy's sick an' dyin'," Jim contrived.

"Off t' Atlanta?"

The other man touched the one who had just spoken and pointed toward the approaching apparition. Quickly both men ran to their horses.

"Her brothah come for her," Jim continued as if nothing was wrong. "They up an' left in a hurry."

The other two men arrived.

"Ain't no one in there but a' ol' crazy woman!"

"We-all gotta git out here. Look yondah!"

A moment later, as if he had been magically transported, the ghostly figure of the man appeared on the porch alongside the two who had recently emerged from the house.

Two of the men on horseback immediately raced away toward the road. Their departure coincided with a slash of lightning, which frightened the two horses waiting for riders. The men yelled. In the pandemonium that followed, the last two men scampered to catch the startled horses while the other two rode to the gate. The muddy, splashing scramble was humorous to watch amid swearing, terrified shrieks and angry calls of frustration.

The geese waddled toward the house as if they expected a reward for their part in the foray.

The rain suddenly stopped. The dogs slunk out from where they were hiding.

"Is that you, Adam?" Jim asked after what seemed to be an interminable pause.

The luminous figure before him dissolved into darkness.

"What d'ya-all make a' that, Blue?" Jim asked as he pushed himself to his feet.

Blue made a whimpering sound.

Light appeared inside the house as if a lantern were being carried toward the entrance.

"Dang fool, Horace! Ya-all git back down in that basement." Jim called. "Them men may be back."

To his surprise it was Mattie who stood in the doorway with the lantern. Her hair was wildly disheveled, which augmented the expression of madness in her face and eyes. The worn and soiled muslin gown was torn, ripped in several places and stained with blood. The lantern fell from her hand and Jim went to get it before a fire started.

As he looked up at his sister, Jim saw an expression he had never before seen in Mattie's face. It startled him.

"Th' Yankees done come ag'in, didn't they?" Mattie uttered as if the words were difficult for her to say. "They done come an' did t' me what they done did before." A bloodcurdling scream pierced the night air. She glared vehemently at Jim. "Ya-all damn' Yankee! I'll kill ya!"

"No, Mattie, it's me, ya brothah!" Jim shouted as he backed toward the hammock.

"Ya-all ain't my brothah! Th' Yankees up an' killed him." Mattie charged at Jim, who fell against one of the columns. She started toward him, thought a moment, and detoured to the hammock to where Jim had left the shotgun.

Mattie had raised the gun before Jim lurched toward her. There was no reasoning with insanity. He jerked the gun and attempted to dislodge it from her grasp. In the struggle the gun was discharged. Mattie stared incredulously at her brother, before her body sagged and she fell against the wall.

"Mattie!" Jim yelled. "Mattie!"

The madwoman was spastically jerking as she rolled on the floor.

In the panic of the moment, Jim ran into the house and down to the basement. Caution be damned, he had to have help. He stubbed his toe, stumbled and fell before he reached the secret entrance to the place the Jameses were hiding.

"Horace, Cissy, come help me, quick!" Jim called.

"Am de night riders gone?" Horace asked.

"They've done gone," Jim assured him. "Ya-all better send th' children t' th' kitchen while ya come an' help me with Mattie. She's bin shot—an' Lord knows what them men did t' her."

Cissy took Lucas and Pansy to the kitchen while Horace went with Jim.

"She jest done bin hit in de shoulder," Horace said after he examined Mattie, "but she's a-bleedin' badder'n anythin'."

"Let's get her inside where there's light," Jim instructed.

By the time they managed to get Mattie to the parlor and stretched out on the sofa, Cissy arrived and took charge.

"Lordy! Her body am a mass a' scratches an' bruises what weren't dere before," Cissy stated after she had examined Mattie. "Dem mens done had dey way wif her, dat's what dey done."

Mattie had fortunately lost consciousness so that they were able to carry her back to her room without too great a struggle.

"Ya-all'll have t' stay in th' house here t'night," Jim said a short while later. "They done burned ya place."

"Why'd dey done did dese terrible thin's?" Horace asked a short while later as he and Jim went to sit on the hammock.

"Ignorance, I reckon, fear, lack a' understandin'," Jim replied. "I reckon I don't right know all th' reasons—if'n there was any reasons worth mentionin'. Th' War's done bin over nigh on t' fifty years or more, an' they still fightin' it."

"Mistah Jim, d'yo' thinks my Jeremiah done did some'un what he neber should a' done wif Miss Letty?" Horace asked.

Jim shook his head. "Letty loves Jeremiah like he was her brothah, an' I reckon Jeremiah loves her like she was his sistah. Seems they jus' growed up without noticin' th' color a' each other's skin. Jeremiah's a good bo', Horace. An' ya-all kin jus' bet that Letty'll take care a' him."

The crickets and frogs had begun their nocturnal din once more. The clouds were drifting over and stars appeared. Only the victims knew that it was a night different from any other at Moss Grove.

Chapter Seven

THE TRAIN WHISTLE'S DESOLATE CRY pierced through the heavy humid midnight air. The clacking wheels slowed, steam escaped, cars rattled and made lurching sounds as they came to a halt. Voices called out, yelled back and forth. Everything was routine. Very little excitement happened at Hardeeville Station that hour of the night,. rarely were there passengers. A slow train, it had fifteen- to twenty-minute holdovers at each stop. The two passenger cars carried few travelers, mostly railroad people who were going from one place to another. One car was reserved strictly for whites while the second car had a section in the rear where Negroes could ride.

Exhausted, muscles aching and on the verge of collapse, Roselle Ivanovich sat on a hard wooden bench inside the small stationhouse, desperately attempting to maintain a cheerful face and not to show the fatigue that had overtaken her from the long drive from Savannah. After Letty and Jeremiah vacated the rear of the buggy, Popkin crawled into it and went to sleep.

Jeremiah wasn't permitted to sit in the same section

of the station that Letty and Roselle sat. He huddled in a corner and did his best to control the emotional reaction he could not escape. Heavy-eyed, he watched Letty. Few incidents in his life had ever caused him to have the apprehension that now went through him. He had lived a sheltered existence on the old plantation and rarely had he encountered anyone away from it. His life was simple, or at least it had been. Letty often told him stories and filled him with dreams of what the "outside" world was like. And he would often escape into the fantasies, attempting to imagine what any other way of life could possibly be like. A natural dancer with an innate sense of rhythm, he had easily grasped what Letty had taught him; but it was all a game to him and he enjoyed it.

Always aware of Jeremiah's presence, Letty tried not to stare at him. Her attention went to strangers, especially those who entered the small stationhouse. Yet, since the trip from Savannah, while uncomfortable, was without incident, there was little reason to be so apprehensive. Still that uneasiness prevailed.

"You will count the days, mam'selle," Roselle instructed, sighing between every other word. "When ten days have passed, you will meet me at twelve noon near the large clock in Grand Central Station. I don't know how, but I will manage to get money. You will have to use part of what you have just to live during that time—but you must be extremely frugal."

"What is to become of Jeremiah?" Letty asked.

"If I can raise sufficient money, the boy will come with us," the older woman replied. "The attitude toward black people is entirely different in Europe. And if he has the talent that you claim he has—well, we'll just have to see about that, won't we? In the meantime, although I realize it will be a gigantic task, I want you to try to teach yourself to speak less like a Southern person and more like a Northerner. And, for that matter, you would do well to teach Jeremiah to speak as well as he possibly can. As I say, it will be a tremendous task, but a major accomplishment if you succeed."

"Why is that necessary?"

"Just trust me that it is. You have a good ear. There have been times when I've heard you mimic me," Roselle went on. "I do speak with a slight European accent, but I've worked to rid myself of it. You must learn to do the same concerning the way you speak. It won't happen overnight, but you can begin—and the same applies to Jeremiah."

"All'board for th' train t' Richmond an' transfer t' Washington, D.C. an' points North!" the conductor called.

"Jeremiah," Roselle said as the three walked out to the platform, "you take care of yourself and do exactly as Letitia says. And if the conductor tells you to do anything, you do it without question. Just pretend that you've taken this trip a dozen times or more."

"Yes'um, I try dat, but I ain't sho' I kin do it none," Jeremiah replied.

Letty threw her arms around Roselle and hugged her tightly. "Now ya-all git some rest, Madame Ivanovich."

"Say that again, mam'selle. This time properly."

"You-all git some rest."

"Leave off the 'all.' And the words is 'get,' not 'git.'"

Letty laughed awkwardly. "I'll try t' remember."

"Try *to* remember," Roselle corrected.

Letty kissed her on the cheek. "I'll do my best, you-all—I mean, you will see."

The conductor directed Jeremiah to the rear of the car where he was to sit. Fortunately the seat in front of him was vacant in the "white section." Letty took it.

"Y'all travelin' with th' niggah?" the conductor asked.

"I'se her servant," Jeremiah volunteered with a wide, toothy smile.

The conductor chuckled. "Ya runnin' away from somethin'?"

"No, suh, I ain't," Jeremiah lied. "I'se a-goin' wif Miss Letty up t' New York." His smile didn't diminish until the conductor left. Then he sagged and tried to get comfortable.

After reassuring Jeremiah that everything was going to be all right, Letty made herself as comfortable as possible and tried to get some sleep. Still the events of that day replayed over and over again in her mind. She was still very confused and did not completely grasp the full impact of the situation.

Madame Roselle Ivanovich watched until the train was out of sight. There was no way humanly possible that she could drive the buggy back to Savannah that night. Although it seemed a bit risky, she decided that she would let Popkin take the vehicle back and she would return by the morning train. She sat up in the station after she had purchased a ticket and did not rouse Popkin until about four o'clock the next morning to give him instructions.

"Where's Letty?" Jaspar Calhoun demanded to know of his uncle.

"Reckon she ain't here, Jaspar," Jim replied as he stared up at his red-faced nephew who was sucking on an unlit cigar.

"Well, where's she at?"

"She said five hundred dollars jus' weren't enough for what she needed, so she went off t' Atlanta when Cissy's people come t' fetch her last night," Jim contrived. "Reckon she'll be leavin' right from Atlanta."

"Ya-all let her travel with them niggahs?" Jaspar questioned. "Ya ain't right in th' head, ol' man."

Jim glanced at his nephew before he got up and went to the window. "How'd ya know Letty weren't here, Jaspar?"

"What? Well, I never knowed she weren't here," Jaspar sputtered. "But when I come a-lookin' for her, she was gone."

Jim stared out the window at the old slave quarters. "Jaspar, ya-all got a sickness what I see in lotsa folks here in Savannah."

"I ain't sick!"

Jim tapped his head. "Ya are up here. Reckon ya-all ain't got th' sense ya was born with. Oh, ya got a business sense, all right, an' a sense a' how t' cheat an' swindle an' do underhanded thin's an' ya got sense enough t' pretend t' be religious an' all that, but ya ain't got basic good sense none."

"What you goin' on 'bout, ol' man?"

"I got eyes in my head, Jaspar, an' I got some pretty good notions 'bout what's goin' on," Jim stated as he turned to observe his nephew. "Them men what ya sent out here last night burned one a' my buildin's."

"Have ya gone daft, Uncle Jim?" Jaspar was suddenly on the defensive. "D'ya think I sent them men out here?"

"All three a' them," Jim baited.

"Three? What happened t'—? He stopped.

"What was ya gonna ask, Jaspar? What done happened t' th' other three?"

"Now look here, ol' man! I don't know what ya're 'sinuatin', but I don't like it none," Jaspar countered, his voice getting out of control.

"They wasn't men—they was heathens, plumb animals, that's what they was. They done worse t' ya Aunt Mattie than them Yankee soldiers ever did," Jim said. "Why don't ya go yondah t' her room an' see what's become a' her?"

Trying for a look of innocence, Jaspar asked, "Was Aunt Mattie threatened?"

She was attacked, maliciously attacked, Jaspar," Jim replied. "Reckon I'll have t' put her up in th' crazy house now." He moved back to the rocking chair. "Seems t' me ya owe me far more than that five hundred dollars ya loaned me for damages t' my property. I'll jus' let that be on ya conscience. As for ya Aunt Mattie—well, I reckon ya'll jus' have t' go t' ya grave with how she was treated."

"I didn't tell them t'—" Jaspar's face became a fiery

red. "Ya don't know what ya' talkin' 'bout, ya damn fool!"

"Don't I, Jaspar? Well, maybe not. But I reckon you do."

"I ain't gonna stand here an' hear this."

"No one's askin' ya t' stay, Jaspar. Go on with ya. Ya-all may have a streak a' Phenwick blood in ya, but there was Phenwicks who wasn't th' most upright people in th' world. An' as for th' Calhouns—well, I ain't gonna say no more."

"An' I ain't a-gonna hear no more, ol' man!" Jaspar wanted to retaliate with more threats, but he decided against it. Without further comment, he stormed from the room and out of the house. Even as he went, vindictive thoughts for revenge were forming in his mind. The one thing he hadn't realized was the intelligence of his uncle. And he wondered how many other tricks the old man might have up his sleeve.

The train arrived in Richmond the following afternoon. There was a four-hour wait for the one going to Washington, D.C. During that time Letty and Jeremiah were unable to communicate with each other. Jeremiah was forced to sit with the other colored people in the waiting room designated for them. He kept to himself and spoke with no one, yet he constantly held his eyes on Letty.

Letty tried to maintain a position where she knew Jeremiah could see her. She had not realized that there was such overt antagonism toward the blacks. Finding a newspaper, she scanned it. then took time to read each word as it was spelled, sounding every letter.

Jeremiah did not ride in the same car with Letty from Richmond to Washington, D.C. since a car was reserved strictly for Negroes. It was a difficult time for him, and the first time that he felt truly alone. Never before had he associated with other blacks with the exception of his own family, so he had had little experience with the white attitude toward colored. He longed to be back at Moss Grove and to have things as they had been. Deep in his heart he knew that those days were gone forever.

Putting dark thoughts from her mind as best she could, along with worries about Jeremiah and his well-being, Letty concentrated on pronouncing words. An older woman sat beside her and, after they had struck up a conversation, she helped Letty as best she could.

Although it was generally frowned upon, Letty and Jeremiah were permitted to sit together after they had changed trains in Washington, D.C. During that ride Letty began to teach her friend to speak as she was learning. By teaching, she was taught, and she was remarkably surprised to see how rapidly Jeremiah picked up what she told him. She had always known him to be a fast learner when it came to dancing; now she was amazed at his sense of comprehension and the sharpness of his ear for being able to grasp sounds and repeat them.

"Why's we a-doin' dis?" Jeremiah asked.

"Why are—" Letty corrected before he interrupted.

"I mean why are we doing d—uh—th-this?"

Letty laughed. "Because we're going to learn to speak properly, that's why."

"Oh. Don't we now?" Jeremiah questioned.

"Uh-uh. Madame Ivanovich said people are judged by the way that they speak," Letty replied, enunciating each word precisely. "Think of it as a game, Jeremiah. It will be something we will learn together."

Blacks as well as whites frowned on the two young people. Suspicions were aroused, but no one said anything to them: they were north of the Mason-Dixon line.

The train was scheduled to arrive in the early morning, however there were two major delays which kept it from reaching Pennsylvania Station before noon.

"I feel like I would like to just get out and leap, skip

and hop," Letty exclaimed. "Don't you feel like dancing, Jeremiah?"

Jeremiah shook his head. "I doesn't—I mean, I don't feel like doing much of anythin'—anything but sleeping."

"You'll feel more like dancing once you get to moving around and get all of the kinks out of you," Letty commented with a laugh. "Oh, Jeremiah! Somehow I feel we are both suddenly free at last."

Jeremiah wasn't so certain about that. He had no idea what the future held in store for him, and it frightened him to think about it.

Chapter Eight

SWELTERING HUMIDITY! Despite the high ceiling of Pennsylvania Station in New York City, the enormous main area of the depot lacked air circulation. The worn and disgruntled travelers, weary from their long journeys, moved like sluggish machines of discontent. Tempers erupted over minute inconveniences as a general ambience of irritation prevailed.

Pretty ladies, normally cool under most circumstances, displayed annoyance. Fanning themselves, dabbing lace handkerchiefs over perspiring brows they had become wilted and wrinkled in their stylish cotton dresses, which all the more added to their states of discontent. One lady in particular, collapsed parasol in hand, fumed as she looked about for a porter to assist with her luggage. Laura Donnally—Mrs. R. Pruman Donnally—raised her hand several times to wave for attention. Her frantic gestures were ignored.

The woman of obvious means, charm and perfected social graces was the epitome of elegance and fashion, and considered by many a ravishing beauty. She always attracted attention except when she wanted it most at such a time as this. Why hadn't she brought along a traveling companion or a servant?

"You, young man!" Laura called. "Forgive me for prevailing upon you, but I am desperately in need of assistance. Would you like to earn a dollar?"

Jeremiah James stared curiously at the lady. "Was yo'—I mean, *you* talkin' to me, miss?"

"I was. I can't seem to find a porter. And all this dreadful heat is about to reduce me to hysteria," Laura replied.

"I'se—I mean, I am waitin' for my friend," Jeremiah articulated slowly, making a point of remembering what Letty had taught him.

"You have a friend? Good. I'll give each of you a dollar. I've several pieces of luggage. My husband always says I travel with too much baggage. I could have done without the portmanteau, but one never knows how much one will require on a trip."

"Miss Letty—"

"Miss Letty?"

"My friend."

"Oh. I thought you meant a male friend." As Laura spoke she glanced up to see Letty approaching them. Despite the faded, countryish appearance of her attire, the woman perceived a stately self-awareness about the girl.

"There you are, Jeremiah. I told you not to wander off." Although she still spoke with a noticeable trace of a Southern drawl, she too was precise in her pronunciation.

"I neber—uh—never wandered none—least ways not much," Jeremiah returned. A look of relief came over his face upon seeing her. "This lady wants me to tote her bags for her."

"I had offered him a dollar," Laura interjected.

"A dollar apiece," Jeremiah corrected.

"That was before I realized your friend was a young lady," Laura stated.

"A dollar?" Letty blinked. "I'm strong as a' ox. I can tote most anything for a whole dollar."

Laura found her statement amusing as she looked from one to the other. "Where are you young people from?"

Letty nudged Jeremiah. "From—Atlant—Atlanta, Georgia. We just arrived in New York."

"Is someone meeting you?" Laura asked, taking a curious interest in the girl, who was both bright and personable.

"In a few days they will," Letty answered.

"Oh." Laura thought a moment. Her husband had often criticized her impulsiveness, but she still had an innate, perceptive way of discerning a person's character upon first contact. There was something very magnetic about each of the young people's personalities that appealed to her. "Obviously you two are not related—I suppose that goes without saying. And, since you came from Atlanta, it strikes me as peculiar that a girl and boy of—well, of two different races should be traveling together. Unless—Oh, dear!"

"We's good friends," Jeremiah assured her.

"Jeremiah!"

"We *are* good friends," he corrected himself.

"Jeremiah and Letty," Laura mused as she glanced from one to the other. "My husband, Mr. Pruman Donnally, says that I'm impetuous by nature. And since my father has said the same about me for as long as I can remember, I suspect it is true."

"Impetuous?" Letty asked.

"I do things on the spur of the moment. But, the fact is, I'm generally right about first impressions. I have a feeling about you two—and don't ask me why that is, because I can't for the world explain it. I've taken a suite of rooms at the Waldorf-Astoria—extravagant of me, but I've always been extravagant, so it's expected of me. Is New York your destination?"

"It is for a week," Letty returned.

"And what are you doing for the next week?" Laura persisted.

"We don't know," Letty said. "We're waiting for someone."

"What is your last name?"

Letty quickly scanned their surroundings as she thought, and, without flinching, said, "Porter."

Jeremiah became wide-eyed until he saw the sign above the porter's stand.

"Letty Porter?" Laura questioned. "A very pretty name. But you can't both have the last name."

"King," Jeremiah said.

"King?" questioned Letty.

"King. I like that name," Laura remarked. "There is a certain kingly quality about you, Jeremiah. Well, let me see. I would judge that you are about the same size as I am, Letty. I must have an old frock you can wear. I don't mean to criticize your clothing, but it is a bit— well, faded and not in the least stylish."

"I never had any fancy clothes," Letty explained. "My people are poor."

"Would you like to work for me for a week?" Laura asked. "I know this all seems terribly strange and Mr. Donnally would surely complain about my impulsiveness, but it seems to me that we could be of service to each other." Laura pointed to a suitcase. "Can you carry that one? There's a dressing room downstairs. You must think me terribly eccentric, which my brother has always insisted that I was—and I'm the first to admit it."

Letty picked up the suitcase, still confused about what was transpiring.

"Jeremiah, you will have to remain here with the luggage," Laura gushed excitedly. "We'll see to you later."

Jeremiah stood gaping as Laura whisked Letty away in the direction of the ladies' room. He had never before in his life encountered such a person; little did he realize that very few others had, either. While he waited he observed the people passing by. Blacks mingled with whites, chatted and laughed. The black porters were not like the people of his race he had known in Savannah. They moved about with assurance and even talked back to their white customers. He was in another world from what he had known, and it fascinated him.

Nearly twenty minutes later, Jeremiah gawked incredulously as the lovely young lady in the green and white striped gown came toward him, hair in an upswept arrangement. Jeremiah wasn't the only one who stared.

"Is my eyes playin' tricks on me?" Jeremiah questioned.

"Do I look so different, Jeremiah?" Letty asked.

"Miss Letty, am dat you?"

"Is that you?" Letty corrected.

"It's me, all right, but is it you?" Jeremiah returned.

Laura came up to where the two were standing. "She's a real beauty, isn't she, Jeremiah?" She laughed. "Now it's your turn to stay with the luggage. Oh, I just love being impetuous like this! Come along, Jeremiah. There's a shop just outside of the station."

Letty enjoyed the attention she was receiving. A refreshing wash-up and the donning of fine apparel did wonders to bolster her spirits. While changing, she had told Laura Donnally about her interest in ballet, only to discover that the woman was a reputed patron of the arts—all the more reason to take Letty under her wing. Letty had also informed her that she believed that Jeremiah had tremendous talent. Laura was impressed by her devotion to the youth.

Jeremiah's transformation was equally as dramatic, if not more so than Letty's. He had never before worn a dress suit. The white heavy cotton outfit with matching white shoes was impressive and underlined his amazing handsome features.

"Am dat you, Jeremiah?" Letty asked, mimicking the way he had reacted upon first seeing her.

"I don't believe it," Jeremiah replied. "I done looked at myself in a mirror, and I thought somethin' was wrong with the glass." He smiled broadly. "Is we dreamin', Miss Letty?"

"I would say that we were, except that everything around us seems to be very much real," Letty commented. She turned to Laura. "I never knew ladies like you existed in the whole world, Miz Donnally."

"I've been told by my husband that he wished I were more conservative," Laura replied. "The fact is, I was born into wealth and I've always had it at my fingertips. I like doing extravagant things. And doing things for others always makes me feel so much better. Let me be extravagant and enjoy it. Now then, we'll just gather up the things and catch a cab to the Waldorf-Astoria."

Jeremiah carried the bulk of the baggage, while Letty took the hatboxes and a small valise. Eyes watched as the three grandly paraded to where they found a vehicle waiting.

At the hotel, Laura tried to arrange to get a three-bedroom suite. There were none available. In which case, she arranged to have a private room for Jeremiah, explaining to the doubting desk clerk that the young man was an internationally known artist, and that she, Mrs. R. Prúman Donnally, was a patron of the arts, who—incidentally—tipped lavishly for special favors. The clerk complied with her wishes and arranged for Jeremiah to have a room on the same floor as hers.

Once they had settled into their rooms, Laura ordered a luncheon to be brought up to her suite.

"Why've you done all of this, Miz Donnally?" Letty asked before Jeremiah arrived.

"Done all of what? Oh, you mean following my hunches," Laura exclaimed. "Although I live in a most conventional society, I've not always been a conformist, much to the annoyance of my husband, my father and my brother. My father, for instance, is a staid and proper judge, the family patriarch, and about as proper a gentleman you would hope to find. My husband comes from a long line of extremely proper and conservative Bostonians, who shriek with dismay over some of the things I do. Fortunately my brother is not quite as hidebound and seems to finds my adventures amusing. I know all three of these very important men in my life love me, so they tolerate my predilections. Oh, there was a time when I tried to be more of a conformist than I am now. It was boring. I believe life is to be lived and enjoyed, and to me, enjoyment comes from giving to others. Philanthropy has always been my strong point. I must say I've never before so brazenly scooped up two young people, practically urchins of the street, as I've done with you and Jeremiah. Still I believe you are both basically trustworthy and that I can place confidence in you."

"But what if we weren't trustworthy, Mrs. Donnally —not that we aren't."

"One has to come to trust an inner depth reaction," Laura replied. "I can usually sense if a person is honorable or not. One develops that ability after a while. If I have any talent at all, it's an awareness to know people. If I feel comfortable with you, and I do, then I believe I've taken the first step to getting to know you. On the other hand, if an uneasiness came over me while in your presence, then I shouldn't want to know you."

"I confess I don't understand much about what you're saying."

Laura observed Letty as she sat in a comfortable chair. "This is all very alien to you, isn't it? Even as I listen to you speak, I perceive that you are making every effort to speak properly, as if to do so was not natural to you."

"I am making an effort to use the right words and to speak correctly," Letty admitted.

"Let me guess about you," Laura continued as she studied the girl. "You were raised in the country in a rather plain and simple environment. Yet you somehow had a brush with culture—perhaps through your desire to dance. Am I mistaken?"

"You are right." Letty stood and raised to her toes as if it were a natural reaction. "I've wanted to dance for as long as I can remember. It just seemed that my body wanted to move, to express itself as a dancer. I've never seen much dancing, certainly I've never seen a ballet, yet, for as long as I can remember, I've wanted to dance. Just by accident I heard of Madame Ivanovich. She tried me, and I've gathered eggs and sold them to pay for lessons. I can't explain why I have such a persistent urge to dance."

"It was something you were born with," Laura said, somewhat guardedly, "just as singers are born with a desire to sing, or actors to act."

"My granddaddy says I'm a dreamer," Letty commented. "He's old, a widower and lonely. I've lived with him most of my life."

"I could be lonely, too, if I permitted myself to be so," Laura remarked. "But I do not choose to be either lonely or unhappy. Although I must admit I was beginning to feel a little sorry for myself traveling alone from Philadelphia, where my sister-in-law lives. As I was beginning to sit on my pity pot, I suddenly shook myself out of the doldrums. Usually, if I find myself in such a state, I find that something unusual is about to happen, so I begin looking forward to what that will be. And, as you see, I've met you and Jeremiah. You can be my companion for this week and, who knows, I might be able to assist you in more ways than you can imagine."

Letty was bewildered. In all her dreams she had never imagined anyone like Laura Donnally existed.

When Jeremiah arrived, the three visited until the luncheon was served. It was a time of getting acquainted. Letty began to regret that she had deceived the lady by telling her that her name was Porter and she realized that she was really being overly cautious needlessly. Still the damage was done, and to explain that her name was actually Phenwick might cause Laura to distrust her. Both she and Jeremiah would have to live with that lie.

Chapter Nine

THAT EVENING LETTY AND JEREMIAH were left alone while Laura went to visit with her brother and his wife. Exhausted from the travel, both young people wanted only to retire early.

"I'se lonely for my people, Miss Letty," Jeremiah moaned before he left for his room.

"I am lonely for my family," Letty corrected, saying each word with precise diction.

"Are you, too?"

"No, I was telling you what you should have said," Letty replied. "But now that you mention it, I do miss Granddaddy. But I can't think about that, can I? Who would have dreamed that things would have turned out this way?"

"It only for a week," Jeremiah sighed.

"It's a beginning, Jeremiah, and a new direction," Letty said optimistically. "We must do whatever we can to make Miz Donnally like us. I believe there's a reason—a very good reason—why we met her."

Jeremiah yawned. "Can we talk 'bout it tomorra? I'se—I am sleepy."

"You go on to your room, Jeremiah. Sleep well. Good night."

" 'Night, Miss Letty."

Donning a gown Laura had lent her, Letty stretched out in the warm room and listened to the noise of the city. For the first time she missed the familiar night sounds of the country, the crickets and frogs, even the owls. It was as if she had suddenly come into a new world, a world that would somehow evolve into the fulfillment of at least some of her dreams.

Laura's brother had admonished her for taking in Letty and Jeremiah, especially the latter since he was both male and black. Laura assured him that she had taken them on as a challenge and they were just the kind of stimuli she needed to perk up a seemingly dreary summer—at least a week of it. She, however, accepted her brother's warning and promised to proceed with caution.

The following day Laura took Letty and Jeremiah shopping and bought them each ballet tights, shoes and accessories, as well as two other complete outfits of attire apiece. While they had slept the night before, Laura had examined their pitiful belongings and decided that none of their things was in any condition to keep. Buying for them gave the woman tremendous pleasure, especially when she observed their admiration of the nice new things and warmly expressed their appreciation to her for buying them.

"I was to have met my cousin for supper tonight," Laura announced when they returned to the hotel. It was an uncomfortably hot day and the shopping had wearied them. "I called her and asked that we make it another time. I have other plans for the evening. We are going to the ballet."

"To the ballet?" Letty questioned, suddenly revitalized with excitement.

"We are going. And tomorrow, I will arrange for you and Jeremiah to use a practice studio where you may get back to your dancing. Besides, I want to see just how good you are."

"Jeremiah's never had any lessons but what I've taught him," Letty said.

"If there is talent there, it will show. Now I suggest you each rest for an hour or so, then we will have a pleasant little repast and prepare to go to the ballet." Laura felt pleased with herself. She couldn't remember when she had gotten so much enjoyment.

Letty's long hair was fixed in a bun at the back of her head. The lovely curve of her face was elegantly beautiful, her entire appearance stunning. Her gown was lemon yellow, floor-length and she wore white gloves and a few pieces of Laura's costume jewelry at her wrists and around her neck and in her hair. Laura's gown was icy blue and she wore real diamonds. The two women attracted tremendous attention alone, and, with Jeremiah vibrantly tall and handsome clad in white, eyes followed them with admiration as if they were celebrities. Laura had advised the young people to be aloof, not to stare or look curious.

"Ah, Madame—uh—Madame Pruman!" a man exclaimed in the lobby of the theater, a heavy accent surrounding his words.

Laura glanced over toward the sound and recognized a familiar face, yet she could not quite place where she had previously seen it.

"Madame Pruman! Allow me!" the round-faced, extremely handsome man said as he came up to her, took her gloved hand and grandly kissed it. As his moustache brushed over her hand, Laura remembered that she had seen the man in Boston at some social function or other. She couldn't recall exactly where they had met. "Did I get it correct? I do not always have ease with the English language. Or is it Madame Truman?"

"It's Mrs. R. Pruman Donnally," Laura said. "I don't believe I recall your name, sir."

"Ah, but of course, it was so long ago. I am Signor Tiziano Spolini."

"Maestro Spolini?" Laura questioned. "But of course I should have remembered you from Boston."

"This lovely cannot be your daughter, Madame," Tiziano exclaimed. "You are far too young to have such an outstanding daughter. But such a gorgeous family resemblance."

Laura nudged Letty slightly. "My distant cousin from Atlanta, maestro. She is a budding ballerina. May I present Miss Porter? And this is my protégé, Mr. King. He is also an aspiring dancer."

"Signorina Porter," Tiziano said as he bowed to kiss her gloved hand. He stared eagerly into Letty's somewhat amazed expression. "It is an honor, signorina." He turned to Jeremiah, a look of tremendous admiration as he gazed at the youth's handsome face. "Signor King, it is my pleasure."

Tiziano Spolini was in his thirties, admirably handsome with a lithe body and agile movements. He had the classic appearance of the artist, the eccentricity of one who is proud of his talent, yet who is driven toward creative artistic endeavors. "I am with a party of several others, my friends, but I look forward to speaking with you during the intermission. *Ciao,* for now."

Laura watched as the distinguished-appearing man made his way through the crowd. Many people recognized him and several spoke. "I recall him now. He is a conductor composer with a ballet troupe that was in Boston. He composes special music for the ballet. How could I have forgotten Signor Spolini?"

"You know many famous people, don't you, Miz Donnally?"

"I do. But you must call me Cousin Laura now after what I told Signor Spolini."

"Why did you say I was your cousin?" Letty asked.

"I don't know. It just seemed the thing to do at the moment. No harm is done. The art world is full of pretense. Come along, we must find our seats before the house lights go out."

During the performance both Letty and Jeremiah sat entranced. The ballet was far more spectacular than Letty had ever imagined it would be from the descriptions of it Mádame Ivánovich had told her. It was beyond Jeremiah's most remote imagination. A world of fantasy, color, exotic movement, dramatic music, grace, beauty, an experience that was so overpowering that they were both left speechless.

Tiziano Spolini was with a party of three other distinguished-looking men. All four made a point of seeking out Laura during the first intermission.

"Will you join us after the performance for refreshment, Signora Donnally?" Tiziano asked.

"Just us?"

"There will be two of the ballerinas with us," Tiziano hastened to add. "Perhaps even more. It will be a celebration. Ah, excuse me, máy I present Signora Donnally, her cousin, Signorina Porter, and her protégé, Signor King? This is Signor Madison Davis, Signor Worth Bassett, Signor Brian Coleman and Monsieur Georges LeVeque, the impresario from Paris."

"Mr. Davis and I have met," Laura said. "You're the playwright, aren't you?"

"How clever of you to know!" Madison Davis, the tallest of the four men introduced by Tiziano Spolini, exclaimed. "So few people know of playwrights unless one is a Bernard Shaw or an Oscar Wilde."

Letty recognized the name and she diligently tried not to stare at Georges LeVeque, aesthetically attractive with a definite artistic posture.

"Will you join us in our box?" Georges LeVeque asked.

"I think not, thank you," Laura replied. "I find sitting center orchestra gives me a far better perspective of what I am viewing. We will be pleased to join you, however, after the performance."

They all chatted briefly. An exceptional amount of

curious interest was shown to Jeremiah, who became very confused by all of the attention.

The bell rang for the performance to continue.

"She is very wealthy, Georges," Tiziano said in French. "You would do well to cultivate the Donnally woman. And there is money on both sides of the family—extreme wealth; so I presume the cousin is equally affluent."

Georges LeVeque made a flip of his wrist as if to pretend not to be overly impressed.

By the end of the performance both Letty and Jeremiah were completely overwhelmed, stunned by the magic that had happened before their eyes.

"Oh, Cousin Laura," Letty exclaimed, unused to calling her that, "I declare I'm speechless. Never in my life have I seen anything like it. One day—"

"Yes?"

"Oh, I'm such a dreamer at times," Letty confessed. "Still I could just imagine what it would be like being up there dancing. And I will be someday, you'll see."

"I'm certain I shall, Letty. That's a very strong feeling I have," Laura said. "Now I must warn you, if we go with the gentlemen, that you are liable to see and hear things you've never heard before. Artists are a breed unto themselves, flamboyant, eccentric and most unconventional. Be warned."

The private backroom of a nearby restaurant had been booked for the celebration. Over thirty people were present, including several of the principal dancers.

At first Laura acted protectively toward Letty and Jeremiah. Then she realized that it was far better to let them find their way among the guests, but she kept a watchful eye out. Letty was singled out by several of the men and especially by Madison Davis. Tiziano Spolini and Worth Bassett took extraordinary interest in Jeremiah, and tried to draw him out, but the youth remained awkward and tongue-tied.

"Blacks in Europe, especially talented blacks," Worth

97

Bassett said, "are treated far differently than they are in the States, don't you know. Here the Negro is considered as common, ordinary, a thing to be looked down on, while there—because one sees so few—they are novelties, unique and quite adored by many."

"With whom have you studied, Signor King?" Tiziano asked.

Jeremiah shook his head. "I ain't—I mean—Miss Letty's what has taught me."

"Ah!" Worth exclaimed as if he were impressed. "And with whom does Miss Porter study?"

"I doesn't—I don't know. Madame Roselle, I reckon." Jeremiah felt himself breaking out with perspiration under the men's intense scrutiny.

"Roselle? Do you know the name, Tiziano?" Worth asked.

"Roselle? Roselle?" The Italian shrugged. "The only Madame Roselle I've ever heard of is Madame Roselle Ivanovich. But no one has heard of her in years."

Jeremiah nodded his head up and down.

"Is it Madame Roselle Ivanovich?" Tiziano asked.

"Yes. She done—I mean—yes." Jeremiah glanced around to see where Letty was. "Excuse me."

"A strange one, that," Worth commented. "Yet so very young."

"Do you find him interesting, Worth?" Tiziano inquired. "So do I. If he has talent and/or exceptional potentialities, there is no end of possibilities."

Georges LeVeque had been standing nearby. "Did I overhear you mention Roselle Ivanovich?"

"It seems Signorina Porter studies with her," Tiziano said.

"But didn't you say Mam'selle Porter was from Atlanta?"

"That is what I understood."

"Impossible! Roselle has been teaching in Savannah," LeVeque commented. "I suspect there is deceit somewhere. I looked for Roselle like for a needle in the straw before I located her. I know she is in Savannah.

But she will be coming here to travel with me to London. She's not aware that I am in New York. It is to be a surprise."

"I say, old man," Worth said, "have you had any luck with Mrs. Donnally?"

"There is time, Worth . . . sufficient time," Georges replied. "She is in New York to attend the wedding of her cousin, which does not occur until next Saturday. I will arrange to have lunch with her."

"And the black boy?"

"He has a most impressive appearance, and, if he has talent—well—time, Worth, time." Georges LeVeque turned his attention to other of the guests and excused himself.

"I've always been highly interested in all forms of art," Madison Davis remarked as he stood beside Letty at the side of the large room. "Unfortunately, I only have talent as a writer. Or perhaps it is fortuitous that I only have talent in one direction. The poor devils who are multi-talented diversify their efforts and never seem to get anywhere with any one aspect of what they have."

"I know little about such things," Letty managed to say.

"Ah, well, then I suppose you haven't heard of Miss Phyllis Burdick," Madison continued. "She's one of my very best friends—and I might add, the leading actress in my current play. She is about to diversify her talents and play the role of mother—a part, I suspect, which she is not particularly suited for. Alas!"

"Phyllis Burdick?" Letty questioned.

"Actresses should never have children. They get caught up in living life and stop pretending it," Madison commented. "Have you ever heard the name Phenwick?"

"What?"

"Phenwick. With a P-H, not an F."

"I don't understand."

"P-H-E-N-W-I-C-K."

Letty felt as if she had grown a bright scarlet. "I don't believe—"

"Phyllis Burdick is married to Simon Phenwick," Madison explained.

"Excuse me, Mr. Davis, I must see what has become of Cousin Laura," Letty said and quickly darted away.

"What is it, Letty?" Laura asked a few moments later when the girl stood beside her.

"I'm very tired, Miz Donnally," Letty said. "I would like to go back to the hotel."

"Yes, by all means. This sort of thing can become exhausting rather quickly. We'll gather Jeremiah and leave."

As she was saying good-byes, Laura told Tiziano Spolini that she was staying at the Waldorf-Astoria.

Eyes were held on both Letty and Jeremiah as Laura ushered them from the private room.

"We both enjoyed the ballet very much tonight," Letty said later that night after Jeremiah had retired and she was preparing for bed. "One of my dreams was to see a ballet. Another dream is to dance in a performance."

"If you have talent, dear Letty, you will dance." Impulsively, Laura went to the girl and hugged her. "I can't explain why I feel so close to you, but I do. It's as if you were the answer to one of my prayers. You see, I've never been able to have children of my own and I—well, just leave it at that. Sleep well, Letty—and pleasant dreams."

Letty wanted to laugh, but she didn't.

Chapter Ten

Only the soul of an artist can know the agony of the tedious striving toward perfection in creative expression. Only one driven to the ultimate quest for beauty, and a search for the Infinite in human existence can appreciate the interminable hours required to fulfill even the tiniest realization of the truth in art. All artists are scientists at their core, discovering the laws of nature and defining them in finite terms. Without art all hope for humanity is lost. Misunderstood, persecuted, condemned for his unconventional nature—that which is far from and above the petty mundane inanities of basic necessity—the artist has the obstacle of the abbreviated concepts of race-mind to overcome. The poet is the sensitive, whose inner ear has been stimulated by the touch of God. If the artist's nature seems perverse, it well could be that the perversity is actually in the critic, or the observer who cannot see what the artist sees.

Whether beauty is painted with a brush, the mystical written word, the melody of romance, the godly grace of the human form in motion, whatever the *creative expression, there is reflected on earth a minute glimpse of eternity and the vastness and order of the universe. Like all great artists, the dancer punctuates the very essence of beauty with the most transient forms of expression—and leaves behind only a memory shadow of those few moments of achievement and artistry. Yet as with all aspects of creative art, the dancer is thrust forward with an insatiable compulsion to express that purpose for which he was born to this earthly sojourn. The true artist is born, but an appreciation for the arts is learned.*

Tiziano Spolini glanced up from the essay written by Madison Davis. He penciled out a phrase or two and added a word here and there before he put it aside. A brooding mood had come over him that morning and had lingered through the largest part of the day. Glancing again at Madison's essay, he pondered a particular line that stood out in his mind. He had lived among artists in the world of creativity for as long as he wanted to remember. A man of fashion and distinction, he was accepted wherever he went, looked upon by many as a genius, and placed on a modest pedestal as one who had acquired moderate fame.

The doorbell sounded. Moments later, Fazio, the muscular servant with remarkable Mediterranean beauty, appeared to announce the arrival of Mrs. R. Pruman Donnally.

Tiziano was standing at the mirror, meticulously checking his appearance when Laura Donnally entered, clad in summery yellow and white cotton and appearing remarkably cool and content considering the heat and humidity.

"Ah, Madame Donnally!" Tiziano exclaimed upon seeing her reflection through the mirror. "What a pleasure it is to greet you again!" He turned to go to her and kiss her hand as he bowed with aristocratic poise, as if he had spent much time among royalty.

"Signor Spolini, it is good of you to see me," Laura replied, a bit more formal than she usually was. However, when in the company of persons such as Tiziano Spolini, her admiration and awe was difficult to contain. "You will forgive me for bursting in on you this way."

"I don't feel that you have 'burst in,' Madame, not in the least. Fact is, I am honored by your presence," Tiziano replied with a flourishing gesture that appeared as if he were doffing a feathered hat. "Have you come alone?"

"Quite alone," Laura replied as she glanced about at the grandly artistic sitting room, artifacts and mementos placed in strategic positions and in fitting settings. "I shall come to the point of my visit, if I may."

Tiziano directed her to a comfortable chair and took one opposite her. He offered a cigarette. When Laura declined it, Tiziano asked permission to smoke in her presence. "Now then, how may I help you, Madame Donnally?"

"As you know, Signor Spolini, my husband is enormously wealthy," Laura confided. "We are childless. And there comes a time in life when, if one has no children of her own, she finds it difficult to contain a natural maternal compulsion. My brother and his wife are expecting a child, but to this time I haven't even a niece or nephew upon whom to dote. Mr. Donnally travels extensively so that we have our own individual interests."

"Why precisely are you telling me these things?" Tiziano asked as he held the cigarette between thumb and index finger and reached to put it into a holder.

"I shall come to that," Laura replied. "Let me add this: I myself come from more than substantial wealth. My family is one of the most affluent and influential in Boston. I have always been interested in cultural matters, although I have little or no creative talent; still I have a deep appreciation for the arts."

"Madame Donnally, are you suggesting that you

wish to become financially involved with the arts?" Tiziano asked, trying not to sound too eager.

"In a sense, yes; perhaps even in a far greater aspect at a later time," Laura returned, smiling sweetly. "I do not presume to be a judge of great talent, nor do I understand the technical side of artistry. Still I know what impresses me."

Tiziano decided it would be wise to listen without interruption. "Go on, Madame Donnally."

"Up until recently," Laura contrived, "my cousin Letty Porter was a virtual stranger to me. And I did not previously know Jeremiah King. They first appeared to me as waifs, confused and adrift in New York. I quickly developed a fondness for each of them. Shortly thereafter I arranged for them to practice their dancing—the girl was professionally taught, and she, in turn, taught Jeremiah. When I saw them dance in that hot, sticky rehearsal studio, I could hardly believe my eyes. As I say, I'm no judge of talent or artistic ability, still I know what moves me—and I was deeply impressed by what I saw. I would be honored if you would come and have a look at them. Surely, your opinion is by far superior to mine in such matters."

"You flatter me, Madame."

"I am honest, Signor Spolini."

Tiziano sat back and studied the woman for several moments as she searched for additional thoughts. Principled, yet an opportunist, he cogitated upon the situation.

"Letty is to meet her teacher here in New York," Laura finally said. "They're to travel together to London. There is some confusion here, and I've not yet been able to sort it out and discern what is at the back of it."

"Confusion?"

"As near as I can piece bits together, Letty and Jeremiah left their homes in the South rather rapidly and under extenuating circumstances," Laura replied. "As I say, it's not all clear at this time. Jeremiah was being pursued by notorious men who were suspicious of his relationship with Letty—which I have been assured was perfectly innocent and beautiful under the circumstances. They love each other as good friends, completely oblivious of the fact that they are of different races, and, for that matter, of opposite genders. You can imagine the horror they must have endured from the accusations of such racist men. It's deplorable!"

"Madame Donnally, you confuse me, not about the story you are telling, but as to what your purpose is in telling it, and as to what you think I may be able to do to assist you," Tiziano said thoughtfully, snuffing out the cigarette to return to a position with his arms folded.

"First, I seek your unbiased opinion about their talent," Laura stated. "I will gladly pay you for your services."

"If I tell you they have no talent whatsoever, will you seek another opinion?" Tiziano asked.

"Probably."

"Good! I would want that, even more so if I conjectured that they had the greatest talent in the world," Tiziano said. "But if I, and others, think Letty and Jeremiah, either one or both, had enormous talent, what then?"

"I haven't fully decided where to go from there," Laura answered. "Still I've toyed with the idea of patronizing their careers—if careers are foreseeable."

"Ah! Now I comprehend!" Tiziano smiled broadly.

"My brother thinks me quite mad for even contemplating such an action. He is an attorney who is involved in theatrical matters. I might have gone through his connections, but I wanted to do this myself. I just have a feeling about those children. My father would probably sentence me to the life of a recluse in a straitjacket if he knew I was even contemplating such a thing. And goodness knows what my husband will think, although I suspect Pruman will be supportive if I properly manipulate him."

Tiziano laughed. "You are deeply influenced by the three most important men in your life, aren't you, Madame Donnally?"

"I must be. These men are my life."

"Are they the *only* men, Madame?" Tiziano asked with a twinkle in his eye.

"Sir?" Laura reddened before she looked down as she picked at her fingers. Slowly she shook her head. "I try not to feel guilt-ridden. I love my husband dearly, I really do. But there have been other men who were— well, more than merely passing acquaintances." As she looked up, she stared deeply into the sparkling eyes before her where she perceived an undeniable invitation. As if held by a magnetic attraction, she could not move her gaze from his.

"My dear Madame Donnally, you are a paradox, are you not?" Tiziano spoke kindly, sympathetically. "Ah, but then, so am I! Perhaps I am far more a paradox than you. I am an artist, Madame, and I travel exclusively in art circles. I have preferences, but I have an ambivalent nature, one which is adaptable to most situations." He rose and stepped toward her. "I would be honored to view and appraise the talents of your young protégés. As to anything more, I am humbly at your service." He held his hand toward her.

Slowly, Laura stood and stared even more deeply into his nearly hypnotic expression.

"May I call you Laura?" Electricity shot from his hand into hers and she had begun to tremble.

"Yes, you may."

"And you may call me Tiziano."

"Tiziano . . ."

The following morning, after Letty and Jeremiah had spent an hour in limbering-up exercises and *barre* work, they were startled by the arrival of Laura and Tiziano. Their new tights and leotards were saturated with perspiration and strands of Letty's hair had fallen from the bun in which they had been woven. Red-faced from the heat and the exertion, Letty blushed even more when she recognized Tiziano Spolini.

"Will you dance for me, mam'selle?" Tiziano asked in a soft authoritative voice. "And you, monsieur, will you dance?" His eyes stared deeply into Jeremiah's nearly black eyes. The youth nodded. "Very well, shall we begin. What, no music?"

"We just do it to the count," Letty replied.

As the two young people began dancing, and within moments Tiziano obviously became impressed, the maestro gravitated to the old upright piano and began to improvise appropriate sounds to accompany the steps. He turned his head to watch them as well as their reflections through the wall of mirror.

Unbeknownst to Laura, Tiziano had invited his colleagues, Worth Bassett and Georges LeVeque to join them at the studio. The two men appeared shortly after Tiziano had sat at the piano. Nodding to his friends, he watched as they observed; then he motioned for Worth to take his place at the keyboard, a transition that took place without missing a beat.

Georges LeVeque had agreed under protest to be present; however, upon seeing Letty and Jeremiah perform a few steps, there was no disguising the interest he had suddenly taken.

When the dance was concluded, all three men applauded encouragingly. Jeremiah doubled over to catch his breath and Letty leaned against the ballet *barres*.

"You have not merely discovered two dancers, *bella mia*," Tiziano exclaimed after he exchanged glances with his colleagues, "you have found two precious diamonds in the rough—priceless gems! Don't you agree, Georges?"

Georges LeVeque nodded as Worth came to join the men.

"The boy is marvelous!" Worth declared. "I've never

seen the like of him. I say, and the girl, what a lovely flower. Of course they must go to London. Negroes simply aren't appreciated here in America. I suppose it's that old slave thing all over."

"Do you really think they have such potential?" Laura asked as she went to where the men were standing.

"Madame Donnally," Georges LeVeque said through his heavy French accent, "Pavlova and Nijinsky might well be outshone by the potential of these talents. I am sincerely impressed."

"I suggest you take these talented young people to bathe and become refreshed, rest and dressed to meet us for dinner by seven o'clock sharp," Tiziano instructed. "It will be a quiet affair at my apartment. But I must suggest that they be prepared to dance for my guests."

The men left after thanking Letty and Jeremiah for allowing them to watch their dancing. Laura remained, having difficulty containing the tremendous excitement that had been generated by the experience.

"They like you and your dancing," Laura said, trying to be as casual as possible under the circumstances. "I had promised my cousin I would have dinner with her tonight, but I can put that off—or—well, I don't know."

"What is it, Laura?" Letty asked.

"My cousin is very much involved with the arts, quite a grand lady, to say the least," Laura replied. "I wonder if I should take the liberty of inviting her to join us tonight. I'll have to think about that. Come along. I know it's far too hot for either of you to catch chills, nonetheless you've got to get out of those things and relax."

When Georges LeVeque got back to his hotel, he was surprised to see a familiar face waiting in the lobby. "Vladimir? Is it you, Vladimir?" he asked in Russian.

"LeVeque!"

"Vladimir Popkin! After all this time. Is Madame Ivanovich with you?" Georges asked.

"We have taken an inexpensive room in a disreputable-appearing hotel," Vladimir replied. "Roselle is economizing—but when isn't she?"

"I must see Madame as soon as possible," Georges said. "Where is she now?"

"Resting. The trip was difficult for her. Then, too, there were problems in Savannah before we left," Vladimir remarked. "It was all very tiring."

Georges LeVeque stood back and appraised Popkin's appearance. "Vladimir, old friend, things have not been going well for you and Roselle, have they?"

"Have you ever been in Savannah, Georges?"

"Never."

"Don't go. You won't like it."

"You will forgive me for saying this, but your clothing is badly worn," Georges commented.

"And these are the best I have. There hasn't been money. Roselle wrote to you in Paris, hoping that you could help us with more cash. But, since you are here, it is no wonder she didn't hear from you." Popkin looked sad.

"I will take care of that. Come, my friend, this is deplorable! And here, only moments before, I was so elated." LeVeque put his hand to Popkin's shoulder and led him toward the front desk.

"Paging Mrs. Thomas Phenwick!" the boy called as he circulated through the lobby. "Paging Mrs. Thomas Phenwick!"

"Phenwick?" Popkin questioned. "The great pianist?"

"Mrs. Phenwick is the singer," Georges corrected. "Tommy is the pianist. He'll be at the dinner tonight. Why do you look so strangely, old friend?"

"That girl, Roselle's prized student—"

"What is it?"

"Nothing. Only a queer thought. Coincidence seemingly happens too often without my going out of the way to look for it," Popkin replied as he observed an attractive woman hailing the page boy.

LeVeque withdrew money from the hotel safe. "Here,

you are to take this to Roselle with instructions that she is to purchase herself a grand gown for a dinner party tonight. You must also buy a fine suit for yourself and wait for it to be altered, if such work is necessary."

The page boy pointed in the direction of an elegantly attired lady with a large hat. Evelyn Phenwick thanked the boy and immediately went to where the woman was waiting. "Peggy! Is it you, Peggy?"

"Clever of you to have recognized me, dearest Evelyn. I love your perfume. Roses, isn't it?"

"My perfume? Roses? The scent must be coming from somewhere else," Evelyn replied. The two embraced and kissed each other on the cheeks.

While Georges LeVeque attended to another matter with the hotel clerk, Popkin wandered near to where the attractive ladies were standing. He tried not to be obvious in his appraisal.

"I beg your pardon," Evelyn said as she observed him.

"You are Mrs. Evelyn Phenwick, aren't you?" Popkin asked.

"I am." Evelyn wanted to dismiss the shabby-appearing man with a glance.

"I am Vladimir Popkin, seemingly the late Vladimir Popkin," he stated. "I once accompanied you at the piano—in Paris, many years ago."

"Vladimir Popkin?" Evelyn questioned. "My husband usually—ah, of course, Monsieur Popkin! How could I forget? May I present my cousin, Mrs. Peggy Phenwick of San Francisco?"

Peggy didn't voice the question, but she wondered why she perceived that the scent of roses lingered around the man called Vladimir Popkin.

Chapter Eleven

"WHAT DOES YO' MEK OB DEM MENS what come t' see us dance?" Jeremiah asked later that afternoon as he sat uneasily in the sitting room of the hotel suite.

"What do you make of the men who came to watch us dance?" Letty enunciated slowly, correcting him.

Jeremiah repeated the question. His ear was good and he was quick to learn.

"I think they were impressed with what they saw," Letty replied. "They watched me with interest, but they stared at you as if they thought you were someone special."

"I ain't—I mean, I'm not special. I'm just me," Jeremiah said, forming each word. He sat sullenly for a few seconds. "I sure do miss not being home."

"Jeremiah, what was can never be again," Letty stated. "The past is over. Things and people change. Madame Ivanovich once told me that a person has to get rid of old things to make room for the new to come in. Maybe we've both outgrown Savannah and the way of life we used to know."

"I'll miss it. This city scares me. Everyone moves so fast, and there's so many of them."

"You'll learn, Jeremiah, you'll learn."

Their conversation was interrupted by Laura's vibrant entrance. She was glowing and felt as if she blushed when her eyes met those of the young people.

"I trust you two have rested after your strenuous morning," Laura remarked as she removed her hat. "I must recline for a short while." She moved about the room. "You'll wear the white suit tonight, Jeremiah. It makes you look marvelously handsome. And I've purchased new tights for both of you. You will be expected to perform for Signor Spolini's guests. You must think of it as a performance and not merely an audition. Many very important people will be present. Oh, I'm so excited." As if floating on a pink cloud, she drifted into her room.

Letty followed Laura.

"May I come in?" Letty asked as Laura began the process of disrobing.

"You may assist me out of my things. I need a leisurely bath and at least an hour flat on my back in bed."

"Have you had a pleasurable day, Laura?" the girl asked, unable to decode the whimsical expression in the lady's face.

"I've had a perfectly marvelous day. So exciting," Laura commented as she slipped out of her dress. "I've been to New York any number of times, but never have I enjoyed it so much. Maybe it's because I feel as if I'm actually doing something constructive." She slipped into a dressing gown. "Life has been too easy for me. I've never really had to worry about much of anything. Oh, there was the time when my mother was ill for a long period of time. I did fret about her. She's gone now. And I do get concerned from time to time about my father. But, you see, Letty, I was born to wealth and I've always had whatever I wanted. Sometimes I wonder if that is why I've never really accomplished anything of particular note: there was nothing to motivate me to improve my circumstances. They couldn't have been better. Listen to me just rambling on. Was there something you wished?"

"No. I just thought I might have been able to help you," Letty replied. "Perhaps Jeremiah and I will go out for a little stroll while you're resting."

"Very good idea. But don't get yourselves exhausted," Laura called.

"We won't." Letty sauntered back into the sitting room. She looked around before she turned her attention to Jeremiah. "She is such a sweet person. I'm sorry we deceived her."

"Done—I mean, *did* what?"

"Lied to Mrs. Donnally about our names," Letty returned.

"Why did we?"

"Out of fear, I reckon," Letty said, her soft Southern drawl not completely disguised. "We left Moss Grove so hastily that I feared someone might have followed us and could have overheard us."

"But you said everything would be all right up here," Jeremiah stated. "The white people don't look at me the way they done down home."

"Did."

"Did."

"Well, we can't tell her we lied now," Letty said. "Come along, Jeremiah, let's go for a stroll."

"I don't much feel like walking none," Jeremiah returned.

"Well, then, you just go to your room and wait until I come back. I won't be but an hour."

The afternoon heat was more uncomfortable than Letty had imagined that it would be. Still she moved gracefully through the crowds of milling people. Periodically stopping to windowshop, she saw two hats that attracted her fancy and tried to imagine herself wearing either one of them.

"The white hat is you, Letitia, but not the gray one."
Letty turned to the sound of the voice. "Mr. Truff?"

"I thought you were going to call me Adam."

"What are you doing way up here in New York, Adam?"

"Just browsing. I must say there has been quite a transformation in you. I simply wanted to let you know that I was nearby."

"I want to ask you about that rose—"

"What rose is that? Oh, the one in your egg basket."

"Did you put it there?"

"Things are not always as they seem, Letitia. That rose may have only been an illusion."

"How could it be? Granddaddy saw it. And I still have it."

"Things of the spirit never die. Do not concern yourself, simply enjoy."

Letty looked back at the hat in the window. She was aware of seeing the reflection of people passing on the street—but Adam's reflection wasn't there. She quickly turned around to look to see if he had gone.

"What is it, Letitia?"

Letty's mouth gaped for a moment. "I thought you had left."

"I'm still here."

"But your reflection—?"

"What reflection?" There was laughter.

"What are you anyway?"

"I've told you. Now I must go. Why don't you go in and purchase the white hat with the cabbage roses?"

"I can't spend the money."

"Don't worry about it. See, isn't it a beauty?"

"It would be one of my most treasured possessions," Letty exclaimed. When she turned back to ask another question of Adam, he was gone. "My goodness." She looked both directions down the street.

Peggy Phenwick was seated before a mirror in the millinery shop, trying on a hat. She caught a glimpse of Letty through the glass as she entered. "No, I don't like this one," she told the prissy salesman. "It makes my face look too round. Let me see the white one with the cabbage roses on it in the window. That's what attracted me here in the first place."

Letty watched as the salesman removed the hat from the display window, fluff the roses and carry it gingerly back to Peggy. She gasped as she saw him hand it to the woman. Inching closer, Letty stood where she could watch Peggy try on the hat and smile. Letty shook her head until her eyes met Peggy's.

"Don't you like it on me?" Peggy questioned.

"I'm sorry," Letty said as she averted her glance.

"No-no, I want you to give me an honest opinion," Peggy returned, adjusting the hat slightly. Then she glanced sharply at the salesman. "Did you spray perfume on these artificial roses?"

"No, of course not, madam."

"Well, I distinctly smell the aroma of roses. And if anyone is familiar with that particular fragrance, it's me," Peggy assured him. She glanced again at Letty's reflection. "What do you think?"

"I definitely smell roses, madam," Letty said.

"Hmm." Peggy removed the hat and put her nose to the roses. "I was right."

"Perhaps the hat is not meant for you, madam," Letty suggested.

"Not for me? You think not? Well . . . maybe you're right. It's more for a younger lady. And, although I hate to admit it, I am becoming more mature with each passing day." She considered the matter. "Here, you try it on, young lady."

Letty suppressed a smile before she reached for the hat.

"Sit beside me," Peggy ordered, "where you can get a good look at yourself."

Letty sat and put the hat on her head.

"Perfect!" Peggy exclaimed. "It's you, my dear! And it *is* far too youthful for me. Let me see the gray one that's in the window."

"I can't really afford this," Letty said as she examined the price tag. "I was just browsing."

Peggy inhaled deeply. "If it is perfume, it's extremely good. They'll do anything to sell hats today. The very idea!"

"No, I can't afford this at all," Letty admitted.

The salesman had returned with the gray hat and placed it on Peggy's head.

"Yes, this is more like it," Peggy said. "It was a toss up between the two. I was simply trying to pacify myself by thinking the white hat would look well on me. Alas!"

Letty removed the hat and handed it back to the salesman. "It's lovely, but thank you, anyway."

"Do you really like it?" Peggy asked as she turned to the girl.

"Oh, yes, very much."

"Good, then I'll take it," Peggy stated.

"Which one, madam?" the salesman asked.

"Why, the gray—" She stopped and stared curiously at Letty's forlorn expression. "That is, both of them. I'll write you a check."

"But I thought—" Letty appeared dejected. "I mean, I was going to ask my—uh—my cousin if she would purchase it."

"She needn't purchase it for you now, my dear," Peggy said. "I've already done it."

"I'm such a dreamer and so impractical at times," Letty confessed. "Excuse me." She started to get up.

"Where are you going?" Peggy questioned.

"I must go now."

"Aren't you going to wait for your hat?" Peggy asked.

"My—my hat?"

"I purchased it for you. I'm impulsive and act on a whim. My husband says I'm notorious for doing such things," Peggy exclaimed. "But I do them, and I enjoy doing them. Besides, your forlorn expression would haunt me for days to come. Consider it a gift."

"But I'm a stranger to you," Letty protested.

"Giving to strangers always brings me pleasure," Peggy replied.

"Oh, thank you, madam, thank you!" Letty exclaimed. "I want to kiss you!"

Peggy held her cheek. "What is your name?"

"Letty." She kissed Peggy.

"Letty? A lovely name. I'm Peggy. No last names since we will probably remain strangers," Peggy said. "You may take your hat and go."

"Oh, thank you again, Miss Peggy."

Letty was beside herself with joy. She all but danced from the shop.

"Are you always so generous, madam?" the saleman asked as he handed her the hatbox.

"Not always. It does make my heart feel good to do for others less fortunate."

"Thank you, Mrs. Phenwick," the salesman said. "And do come and visit us again."

"May I wear it tonight?" Letty asked after modeling the new hat for Laura.

"By all means." Laura stood back and admired the beautiful young lady's appearance. "I find it difficult to believe that a woman—an absolute stranger—was so generous to you."

"You were generous, Laura."

"So I was. There must be something about you, Letty, that attracts good people to you," Laura observed. "My father says that giving is a wonderful trait—giving in all things; but he also adds that receiving is far more difficult. He also says that people must be open to receive as if they magnetically draw things to them. I suspect that is the case with you."

Letty smiled. She wished she could tell Laura about Adam Truff, but she had doubts that he actually existed.

"You had better see if Jeremiah is ready," Laura instructed. "We don't want to be the first to arrive, but it wouldn't do for us to be too late. I have a feeling about tonight. There are going to be important influential people there."

Letty had stepped into another world, quite apart from the one in which she had lived her entire life. Yet she realized that Laura Donnally's cousin was to be married in two days and that she would be returning to her home and husband. That realization brought with it a note of despair, which she quickly managed to replace with a thought of happiness as she viewed her reflection in the mirror and again admired the hat.

Someone had told Letty years before—she couldn't recall precisely who it was—that she should never dwell on a problem and the negative aspects of it; rather she should consider the solution and what positive results could grow out of it. Her faith in God as an omnipotent force, all-seeing, all-knowing, gave her the strength to simply plan the plans and let that Higher Power take care of the results. At first it was considered naïve of her to have such blind faith, but too often had the theory proved to be workable and accurate for her to in any way diminish her belief. Where had it begun? How had it developed and progressed over a period of time? She could not define the process. Although she was a dreamer in the actual sense of the word, yet as such dreams were molded into logical thoughts, and she believed they could actually materialize into realities, her faith went to work and she trusted in that Higher Power to bring them into form.

As such thoughts occurred to her, and she attempted to analyze them, Letty wondered if some spiritual force—that nebulous entity she knew as Adam Truff, perhaps—was somehow behind them. She had tried to imbue Jeremiah with such philosophy; and, while he could grasp in part, he had not as yet developed the faith she had.

"Something wonderful is going to happen," Letty said to her reflection as she stared deeply into the likeness of her eyes. "I just know it is!"

Chapter Twelve

THE ADDRESS WAS BEEKMAN PLACE, an enormous apartment building with spacious individual units. Tiziano Spolini could trace his ancestry back to Italian, French and German royalty, although he never presumed to take a noble title himself. He was in a lineage of wealth and at the very end of two extremely affluent families. The Beekman Place residence was surpassed only by the one Spolini maintained in Hyde Park, London, neither of which were as modest as the one he kept in Paris. Yet, with all of his extravagance, guardianship financial restrictions were kept on him, which made it constantly necessary for him to seek outside backing for his various projects.

Staffed with four servants, two of which traveled with him from residence to residence, Tiziano opened his homes to friends and as often as not had one or two guests staying with him most of the time. Still, he had his privacy. To him a small intimate dinner party was no less than twelve and as many as twenty-five, after which it became a large dinner party. Although not of the affluence of Spolini, Worth Bassett maintained an apartment on a lower floor of the same building, where the British playboy often threw his own parties. The two men had been close friends for years.

The two friends invariably wagered small bets as to who would be the first to arrive. Often they were mistaken, but it had become a game with them. To their mutual surprise the first to arrive was Mrs. Donald Phenwick—Peggy. The grand lady was attired in a silver gray gown, white accessories and the newly purchased hat.

"I'm so glad you were in town," Worth Bassett commented after the initial greetings were exchanged.

"Being fashionably late has never appealed to me," Peggy commented, "since I can't abide the habit in others. If the truth were known, I come early because I don't want to miss anything."

Worth Bassett and Peggy had been friends for several years, and it was he who had been instrumental in cultivating her interest in the art world.

"I suppose your husband isn't traveling with you, as usual," Worth commented.

"Poor Donald has undergone surgery on his leg several times over the years," Peggy related as she looked admiringly about at the decor, "but as he gets older, the old lameness has come back. He is not comfortable traveling, nor does he have the interest in the arts which I do." She went to examine an original Van Gogh painting and took the opportunity to survey several other handsomely-framed works by other well-known artists.

Other guests arrived. A flurry of excitement and chatter followed. At first Peggy began to think that she was destined to be in the company of strangers that evening; but she aggressively made acquaintances in a way that gave others the impression that they had known her for some time.

"You'll know at least two of the guests," Worth commented, when Peggy remarked about the lack of familiar faces. "Tommy and Evelyn will be here, of course."

"Yes, so I understand. But they're family," Peggy said dryly. "The most well known of the Phenwicks, I might add. I knew Evelyn was to be here, but I didn't tell her that I was to be in attendance. Ah! There's a familiar face."

Madison Davis had made an imposing entrance, making loud exclamations as he went to greet old friends.

"Madison can sometimes be a bit of a fish out of water, don't you know," Worth remarked as he watched the flamboyant playwright.

Peggy excused Worth to go speak with new arrivals while she went toward where Madison Davis had positioned himself among a group of three admirers. She found him amusing, his tall, lank figure towering above the heads of the others. Her attention went with Favio, the servant, as he stepped toward the front vestibule. Like many of the guests, she was boundlessly impressed by his extraordinary appearance, so classically godlike that it was startling.

"That hat!" Peggy exclaimed to no one in particular as Favio reappeared behind Letitia and Jeremiah. She frowned slightly at the boy's dark skin. Although she tried to be extremely broadminded, and she wasn't particularly prejudiced, a twinge of alarm rang through her whenever a person of the Negro race mingled with predominately Caucasian people.

Tiziano immediately interrupted his conversation and went to greet the two young people. "Ah, Miss Porter and Mr. King! I am so pleased you made it. But where is Mrs. Donnally?"

Letty explained that Laura would be along shortly and that she had sent them on ahead.

"I trust there was no problem?" Tiziano commented.

"No. She was simply delayed," Letty replied.

"Come, then, you must meet my guests."

"I thought it was to be a small dinner party," Letty said, momentarily terrified at the sight of so many guests.

"I confess that I get carried away from time to time," Tiziano explained. "The fact is, I was so impressed by your dancing today—both of you—that my enthusiasm became uncontained. Come along."

Jeremiah wanted to retreat. He was noticeably trembling.

"You've nothing to fear," Tiziano said gaily. "And if you're worried about the color of your skin, I've no doubt that you will soon find yourself a unique celebrity in our midst."

Letty practically pulled Jeremiah forward. Then she stopped cold when her eyes met Peggy's.

"Ah, you are fascinated by my friend," Tiziano commented as he observed the exchange of glances between Letty and Peggy.

"We ran into each other earlier today," Peggy said.

"Miss Peggy purchased the hat—" Letty returned.

"At the same millinery store that Miss Letty purchased hers," Peggy interrupted. "Are these the young dancers Worth was going on about?"

"The same." Tiziano beamed. "Mrs. Phenwick is quite a patroness of arts."

"Phenwick?" Letty questioned.

"I'm Mrs. Donald Phenwick," Peggy interjected. "Why does that alarm you?"

"Uh—alarm?"

"You've suddenly become quite pale."

"Miss Porter is not accustomed to meeting persons of your stature, Mrs. Phenwick," Tiziano said. "Excuse us."

"It's just a coincidence that her name is Phenwick," Letty whispered to Jeremiah as they followed behind Tiziano.

"I knowed it was a mistake."

"You knew it was a mistake, Jeremiah. Be very careful with your speech. Remember. Maybe it was a mistake not to give our right names, but I never dreamed things would happen the way they did."

"I can't stop shaking," Jeremiah confessed.

"You will. Just breathe deeply and pretend you really belong here. Remember what Laura said. These people want to like us."

"I'se plumb scared."

"You are plumb scared, Jeremiah. I am. Remember, I am."

"You, too, Miss Letty?"

"And don't call me Miss Letty. We're in the North now."

Although his hair had become partly gray, Tommy Phenwick was still a magnificent figure to behold. Age had coarsened his features, but he was as remarkably handsome as ever. After years of notoriety, fame, success and the darling of the social set wherever he went, he strode with self-assurance, yet with a humility that made him appear tremendously gracious. People were magnetized to him wherever he went. Likewise, Evelyn Phenwick was a celebrity in her own right, although she often stopped just outside of the limelight when in the company of her famous husband. Yet she was recognized and engaged in conversation by those who had heard her sing in concert.

Tommy, standing tall and glowing with an aura of success and fame, smiled benevolently as he reached to shake Jeremiah's hand. He seemed more impressed with the boy than he was with Letty. When he could, he drew Jeremiah aside.

"Forgive me for being so blunt, Jeremiah," Tommy said as he glanced about to see that they were not being overheard. "Do you know if you're a full-blooded Negro?"

Jeremiah had difficulty controlling his shaking. "Both my mama and daddy are mulatto."

"I thought as much," Tommy said with a broad smile. "Can you keep a secret?"

"Yes, sir."

"I'm mulatto, too," Tommy explained, hoping that it would make Jeremiah feel less ill-at-ease. "My grandmother was pure Caucasian, but the man who sired my mother was black—although I suspect that he, too, was mulatto, or my mother wouldn't have been able to pass for white through her life, nor would I, for that matter. My daughter is much darker-skinned than you are. Where are you from, Jeremiah?"

He looked around as fear again trembled his body. "Savannah."

"What a coincidence! My mother was born in Savannah," Tommy returned, putting his arm fatherly about the boy. "We must become better acquainted."

"Well-well, Tommy," Worth Bassett remarked as he arrived at the place the two were talking, "you certainly let no time pass."

"Worth Bassett! Whatever are you going on about?" Tommy asked.

Worth winked. "And you haven't even seen him dance. You've a treat in store for you, old man. But I'm going to steal Jeremiah from you. I've others for him to meet."

Completely confused by what had happened, Jeremiah simply went with Worth and only once glanced back at Tommy Phenwick. It wasn't until he moved away that he began to wonder if the great pianist was related to the Phenwicks of Savannah.

Evelyn and Peggy were conversing when Laura Donnally entered. Their attention went to her.

"Laura's certainly looking radiant tonight," Peggy commented. "I suspect all this intrigue she's been going on about has to do with a man."

Evelyn didn't comment, but went to greet Laura. Peggy was a short distance behind.

"There she is," Laura stated after she had hugged the two women and they had exchanged small talk. "The girl in the white hat with the roses. That's Letty."

"Of course it's Letty," Peggy returned. "She practically snatched that hat out of my hands at the millinery shop."

"Are you the one who purchased it for her?" Laura asked. "What a small world it is, after all."

"Perhaps even smaller than we know," Evelyn added.

"Meaning?"

"Just a thought," Evelyn replied. "I've come to believe, and not without good reason, that nothing happens really by accident. I'll say no more."

As Laura stepped to where Letty was being introduced to a group of people, Peggy and Evelyn followed.

"Letty, dear," Laura called, "may I speak with you?"

"Yes, Laura." Letty excused herself.

Laura looked back at Peggy and Evelyn before she pulled Letty aside. "I may have made a mistake introducing you to Tiziano as my cousin. The fact is, my real cousins are here tonight. It could be a bit embarrassing. I had no idea they would be here." She indicated Peggy and Evelyn.

"The Phenwick ladies?" Letty asked.

"Yes. Peggy told me about the hat."

"I didn't know you were a Phenwick," Letty said.

"My father is Judge John Phenwick of Boston. Why do you have that strange expression?"

"Do you know a Alexander Phenwick or a Daniel Charles Phenwick?" Letty questioned. Now she was beginning to tremble.

"They're distant cousins. Do you know of them?"

Letty frowned.

"What is it, Letty?"

"Did you ever hear of a person—no, not a person, but a—well, did you ever hear of Adam Truff?" Letty asked.

Laura shook her head.

"What was that?" Peggy asked. She had been straining her hearing as she inched toward where the two were standing. "Did you say Adam Truff?"

Letty's face grew red as she turned away. She nodded.

"Who is this girl, Laura?"

"I'm Mrs. Donnally's cousin from Savannah," Letty stated.

"If you're Laura's cousin, you must be our cousin, too," Evelyn commented. "I didn't realize."

"Nor did Laura," Letty replied.

"Now what is that all about?" Peggy asked, curiously staring at the girl.

"What's going on over here?" Tommy questioned as he moved to where the ladies were. "You Phenwick women get together and you neglect the rest of the company." He eyed Letty. "Miss Porter, you must forgive my wife and cousins."

"I must ask their forgiveness, Mr. Phenwick," Letty said. "My name isn't Porter. It's Letitia Phenwick."

"Now, Letty, you don't have to—" Laura interrupted.

"But it's the truth, Laura. I am Letitia Phenwick. My granddaddy is Jim Phenwick of Moss Grove in Savannah."

"Jim Phenwick?" Tommy questioned. "Mother used to speak of my Uncle Jim in Savannah. He was really a half-uncle, my mother's half-brother."

"Granddaddy's mama was named Harriet," Letty went on.

"My grandmother was named Harriet—Harriet Pettijohn," Tommy stated.

"Yes, that's it, Pettijohn—Harriet Pettijohn," Letty brightened.

"And I've heard of Moss Grove," Tommy said.

"As unusual as it seems," Tiziano exclaimed, as he went to where the Phenwicks were in conversation, "I've planned an enormous feast, and I think it would be only fair to our special guests to let them dance before we dine. Tommy can play the piano on a full stomach, but dancing is quite another thing."

"That young lady," Peggy stated a short while later as Letty went to join Jeremiah to prepare to dance, "is, without a doubt, destined to be a Phenwick woman."

"How's that, Peggy?" Laura questioned.

"Just take my word for it. I should know."

Chapter Thirteen

"POPKIN! VLADIMIR POPKIN!" exclaimed Tommy Phenwick, who had a roaring quality to his voice when he wanted to project the otherwise soft melodic tones of it. He held his long arms out, stretching those great agile fingers as if he intended to clutch as much of Vladimir Popkin as he possibly could.

"You recognized me after all these years," Vladimir replied as he wrapped his arms about Tommy in a Russian bear-hug that might have snapped bones of a less sturdy individual. Europeanlike, the men planted kisses on each others' cheeks and remained embraced as they each appraised the physical features of the other.

"How could I not recognize you, Popkin?" Tommy continued, oblivious to the fact that the two were attracting the attention of the other guests.

"Ah, but you have gone on and on with your fame," Popkin commented with a sigh, "while I have merely gone on and on in my usual infamous way."

"Has Tommy taken up wrestling in public?" Peggy questioned aside to Evelyn.

"That is Tommy's customary way of greeting old friends," Evelyn said. "My husband has never done things halfway. He is very much like his mother in that respect. And everyone remembers what a flamboyant individual Millijoy was. I've purposefully cultivated a sedate manner to offset my husband's boisterousness."

Roselle Ivanovich stood quietly in the doorway. The diminutive woman had a way of making herself unobtrusive. It pleased her to see Vladimir and Tommy together because she realized that Vladimir was back in his element, and she had long known that the isolation of being closeted in Savannah had greatly contributed to his excessive drinking. An artist in an inartistic ambience could well suffocate and/or turn to any means of escape he could find. Hadn't she felt the same restrictions, the same confinement?

"Madame Ivanovich!" Georges LeVeque cried as he spied the woman and went dashing toward her.

"Monsieur LeVeque," Roselle acknowledged as he bowed to kiss the back of her hand. "Popkin told me you were here."

"You are looking marvelously well," Georges commented as he gazed deeply into her weathered face. "It is good to see you again. How could you have stood being buried in Savannah all these years? It must have been impossible for you."

"I have endured, Monsieur LeVeque. I have endured," Roselle sighed. "Yet among all the weeds in that banal place, I discovered one precious flower, one talent which is still a damond in the rough—relatively speaking—who shows tremendous promise. That discovery alone made my stay in Savannah bearable. I am to meet her here in New York and, with your benevolence, she will travel to London with us."

"This seems to be a time for discovery all around," Georges commented. "Madame Donnally has uncovered two potential diamonds, as you said. They are preparing to dance for us now—before supper. I will want your opinion of their talents, naturally."

Fazio had moved among the guests as he gently urged them into the large room known as the music chamber where needlepoint-covered chairs had been arranged near the box grand and a cleared area for performing. The Phenwick cousins sat together while Tommy joined Popkin and Roselle Ivanovich in the company of Georges LeVeque and Madison Davis. Worth Bassett sat at the piano, and felt inadequate in the presence of Tommy Phenwick and Vladimir Popkin.

Tiziano Spolini simply announced that they were to be entertained by two young dancers.

"I doesn't think I can do it," Jeremiah moaned as he stood with Letty just outside of the room.

"You don't think you can do it, Jeremiah, not doesn't," Letty corrected , "but I think that you can—I know that you can. Just remember, this could be one of the most important moments of both of our lives. We've got to be perfect."

"I ain't—I mean, I'm not close to perfect," Jeremiah said. "I'm trembling too much."

Roselle gasped when she recognized Letty and Jeremiah. LeVeque reacted to her quick inhaling of air, but she managed to pass it off as inconsequential. Yet as she watched, she became absolutely fascinated by Letty's stage presence and technical ease and skill. Although the teacher had several comments to make along with corrections, she was more than adequately pleased with the performance. More important, she was absolutely overwhelmed, as was everyone else in attendance, at the sheer grace, beauty and natural talent of Jeremiah. It amazed her to think that Letty had been able to teach him so much. True, he was far from being technically perfect and he made several awkward moves, still his promise was so obvious that even the most severe critic had to respond favorably.

Tears were streaming Roselle's cheeks by the time the pair concluded their dance. And it was all she could do to contain the depth of emotion that wanted to respond with crying when the audience vociferously applauded and rose in a standing ovation. She was the last to rise, leaning heavily on her cane and using Georges's arm to pull herself up.

"My cousin is sensational!" Tommy exclaimed.

"Your cousin?" Roselle questioned.

"Letitia Phenwick is my cousin," Tommy replied before he stepped to join the others who had clustered around the two panting young people.

Roselle dug strong fingers into Popkin's arm. "My prayers are being answered, Vladimir. I know they are being answered."

The enthusiastic commotion that followed was both exhilarating and confusing. Ultimately the Phenwicks surrounded Letty, while Worth Bassett, Tiziano and other men of artistic temperament circled Jeremiah. Uncertain of what to make of the excitement and the barrage of compliments being fired at him, Jeremiah remained speechless and searched for an avenue of escape.

"Dear friends," Tiziano managed to say above the cacophony of praise, "you must let the young people prepare themselves for supper. You will have the rest of the evening to lavish them with adulation."

When Letty arrived in the room where she was to bathe and change, Roselle Ivanovich was waiting for her. Speechless, the girl ran into her mentor's arms and the two stood in silent embrace for several moments.

"I don't know how you managed to do it, mam'selle," Roselle said at last, "but you have certainly proved yourself. It was far from perfect, but it was adequate and most impressive. Only I can know that your greatest display of genius was depicted in Jeremiah's performance. Even now Worth Bassett and Tiziano Spolini are fighting over which of them will have the privilege of sponsoring him."

"Was Jeremiah really that good?" Letty asked as she peeled out of her wet costume.

"You have trained him well," Roselle replied, "but he still has much to learn and his technique is a long way from being perfected. Yet, as an audition, he—you—both outshone yourselves. It was a display of promise, and that in the world of art is far more important than the finished product at the stage where you both are at this time. Isn't it ironic? In Savannah Jeremiah would simply go unnoticed as another black person; yet in the artistic world, and especially in Europe, he is certain to be unique, a special attraction because of the color of his skin—as well as his natural dancing ability. I am impressed."

Supper was held until Letty and Jeremiah had freshened themselves and changed into their party attire. The conversation that followed their performance was completely centered around them.

"I swear I didn't know that Letty was a Phenwick," Laura said to Evelyn and Peggy, and she explained the circumstances under which she had met the young people. "Is it fate? I wonder."

"Dearest Laura," Peggy remarked, "there seems to be a strange mysterious force that surrounds the Phenwick women, call it spirit guidance, if you will. It's inexplicable and doubtlessly incomprehensible to persons who do not have the distinction of being Phenwick women. I don't mean to make you feel uncomfortable or neglected, Laura dear, but it is a fact."

"My mother had the dubious distinction of being known as a Phenwick woman," Laura remarked, "and I don't see that it ever really made a difference in her life."

"But it did, perhaps only in an oblique way," Peggy returned. "Isabelle endured much, yet she always seemed to have that spiritual guidance that protected her from extreme adversity. I suspect that you were never singled out as a Phenwick woman, although you were born a Phenwick—as were many others who were not chosen—because your life is practically devoid of any major crises. Whereas, we who are known as Phenwick women have all suffered our moments of terror, rather like the heroines in gothic novels. I suppose that doesn't make much sense, but that seems to be the way things are."

"Are you suggesting, therefore," Laura asked, "that if Letty is indeed intended to become a Phenwick woman that she will have experience terrifying events?"

"That seems to be the fate of Phenwick women," Evelyn concluded. "I speak from experience." She glanced away, uneasy with the trend of the conversation. "It's been a long while since I've seen Tommy so enthusiastic about talent. Of course, he has always enjoyed the ballet, but rarely has he doted over a performer as he is doing with that young black man."

"Perhaps he feels a distant kinship," Peggy suggested without sounding judgmental. The secret of his background was no longer a mystery and the facts of it were accepted by the Phenwicks.

"Possibly." Evelyn raised an eyebrow and excused herself.

"Are Evelyn and Tommy having problems?" Laura questioned when Evelyn was out of earshot.

"I suppose they, like all of us, have had our little problems from time to time," Peggy speculated. "Evelyn's career is waning, while Tommy's is on a spiraling upswing. Naturally, at Evelyn's age, her voice isn't what it used to be. It must be distressing. She has spoken to me of retiring and perhaps teaching. That is liable to separate her and Tommy for greater periods than they've been apart in the past—and that could cause certain complications."

"Does your long periods of separation from Donald cause complications in your marriage, Peggy?" Laura questioned without facing her cousin.

"Donald is most understanding," Peggy replied. "I spent so much of my youth in confinement, a self-imposed prison, as it were, that I require freedom of movement."

"Does that imply that you have affairs on the side?"

Peggy stared curiously at Laura. "I am a vital woman, Laura. I enjoy life and all aspects of it. Are you asking if I am promiscuous? I can only say that I am discreet— and you may read into that anything you wish. However, I find the question, mixed with your present attitude, curious. It seems to me that you are away from Boston more than usual—away from Pruman for prolonged periods. I won't ask the obvious question. And, quite frankly, if you are indulging in such activity, I don't wish to know about it. We can always chat together, Laura. Shouldn't we see what these other interesting people are up to?"

Because of his tremendous inheritance from Millijoy, and the wealth he had accumulated from his extensive concertizing, Tommy was among the richest of the Phenwicks. Philanthropic and a backer of worthy causes, he used his wealth to encourage other promising artists. It was not unusual that he felt he wanted to be supportive of the careers of both Letty and Jeremiah, especially the latter, the rationale being that Letty was a Phenwick and others, such as Peggy and Laura, would see to financial support for her.

As the evening went on, Tommy found himself in the library with Worth Bassett, Georges LeVeque and Tiziano Spolini. They smoked and sipped sherry.

"You three are far more involved in the world of dance than I am," Tommy stated. "True, I've financed in part a couple of ballets that Fokine has done with Diaghilev, only out of friendship. Still I don't consider myself an expert from a technical aspect about ballet."

"You are one of the most world-renowned musicians, Monsieur Phenwick," Georges LeVeque remarked. "Surely, your artistic eye tells you much."

"My artistic eye tells me that both my cousin Letitia and Jeremiah are exceptional talents," Tommy returned, looking from one man to the other.

"I would like to propose that Jeremiah be given special instruction with Fokine himself—since you are a friend of his," Worth Bassett suggested. "He has the potentials of another Nijinsky, and the added attraction of being black. I can foresee a tremendous future for him."

"And for my cousin Letitia?"

"In this case, she has the misfortune of being Caucasian," Worth continued, "ergo, there is not the novelty about her appearance that can be capitalized upon. Therefore, if she were to develop into a marvelous technician and an extraordinary performer, I might project that she could have an excellent career and achieve stardom. Europe, London, Paris, Moscow, those are the places she will have to prove herself, not in the United States. To have such exposure, there would have to be sufficient financing behind her."

"Very well, since my mother and Letitia's grandfather were half-brother and sister," Tommy said after a pause for consideration, "I will see that she has backing. And since my cousins are so impressed with Letitia's ability, I suspect they will willingly add their support, especially Laura Donnally, who believes she discovered Letitia's talent. But I do not underestimate Peggy Phenwick, who very much reminds me of my own mother in many ways."

"So much for Letitia," Tiziano inserted. "What about Jeremiah?"

"Gentlemen, this may come as a surprise to you," Tommy said, "but I am myself part Negro, several generations removed."

The men murmured among themselves.

"The child born to my wife and I," Tommy continued, "was born quite dark. My mother tried to disguise the truth by having a white child substituted for my own, and I raised him lovingly as my own son. Years later, when the truth was revealed and my black daughter was made known to me, I learned the truth about myself. I've tried to make up to her for the deceit.

Ironically, the boy I raised as my son, Gordon Thomas, fell in love with my daughter, Lanny, and they married. Maybe I have a distant feeling of guilt because of the unfortunate way Lanny was treated as a child. At any rate, I would like to contribute to Jeremiah's education and eventual career. Will you gentlemen help me?"

Tiziano became all smiles, as did Georges LeVeque, but Worth frowned, uncertain quite how to react to Tommy's statement. Tiziano raised his glass and proposed a toast. Worth drank, but he did so with reservation.

Chapter Fourteen

BEFORE RETURNING TO EUROPE and their home near Zürich, Tommy and Evelyn made a trip to Savannah to visit Jim Phenwick. Tommy especially was shocked to witness the dilapidated condition of Moss Grove. With Evelyn clinging to him, they entered the old plantation house after no one responded to Tommy's call.

"The place seems deserted," Evelyn remarked. "Maybe it has been abandoned."

"I think not," Tommy replied. "There were chickens picking around and dogs." He paced around in the downstairs rooms. "Mother used to speak of this place as if it were an opulent mansion. Look at it."

"It must have been fifty years since she was here." Evelyn ran her finger across a dusty tabletop. An eerie sensation came over her, the kind that comes when one perceives they're being stared at. She went to where Tommy was standing. "Tommy, I feel uneasy here."

"I shouldn't wonder. Well, I'll have a look upstairs, and, if I find no one, we'll go back to town."

There was a sound of footsteps from the area of the kitchen. Evelyn nudged her husband and nodded her head in the direction of the sound.

Cissy James appeared in the doorway, a kerchief wrapped about her head and wiping soiled hands on her faded skirt. "What yo' folks a-lookin' fo'?"

"Ah, excuse me," Tommy said. "I was wanting to see Mr. James Phenwick."

"Mistah Jim's upstairs. He's poo'ly. What yo' doin' here?" Cissy asked.

"We're Mr. and Mrs. Thomas Phenwick," Tommy explained. "Mr. Phenwick is my Uncle Jim. The door was open, we simply came in."

Cissy eyed them curiously and motioned with her head to indicate the stairs leading up to the second floor. Then she watched as the well-dressed pair climbed them and went toward Jim's room.

"Who—who is it?" Jim asked feebly from his bed. He was shirtless and only a thin soiled sheet covered his body. "Reckon I don't know ya-all, anyway."

"Are you James Phenwick?" Tommy questioned as he moved into the room and Evelyn lingered at the doorway, repulsed by the strong aromas that came from the room.

"What if'n I am?"

"I'm Thomas Phenwick. My mother was Millijoy, your half-sister," Tommy said, going closer to the bed so the old man could get a good look at him.

"Millijoy's boy? Land alive! Yo're dang-near as handsome as Millijoy was pretty," Jim commented as he raised himself to get a better look. "Ye-us, I kin see ol' Millijoy in ya face, bo', I sure as dickens kin." He chuckled.

Tommy stepped to the bed and reached to shake hands with the old man. "Uncle Jim."

"Millijoy wrote a time er two t' me," Jim said. "I believe she mentioned you a coupla times."

"Are you not well? The servant woman said you were poorly."

"Cissy? Reckon she'd know. Actual', I'm jus' a-ling'rin' around a-waitin' t' die," Jim stated. "I git some good days, but most times I don't feel like a-doin' much a' anythin'. Had t' put my only livin' sistah in th' crazy farm after she got shot an' got so sick. An' now that Letty's gone, I ain't got much t' live for. I've done enough livin', anyway."

"I saw Letitia not more than three weeks ago in New York," Tommy said, "when she sailed for England in the company of my cousins. You would remember Alexander Phenwick, wouldn't you, Uncle Jim?"

"Xan? Land, ye-us!" Jim chuckled. "Does that mean that Letty found him?"

"Letitia found a lot of the Phenwicks."

Tommy, Evelyn and Jim visited for two hours. Tommy told the old man about the turn of events in New York and how both Letty and Jeremiah were going to Europe to study their dancing. Then Jim explained about the situation in Savannah and of the contriving machinations of Jaspar Calhoun.

"How much do you figure Moss Grove is worth, Uncle Jim?" Tommy asked after he had heard the details.

"I couldn't rightly say, Tommy. It ain't worth much a' nothin' t' me," Jim said. "But I reckon as how ol' Jaspar's got his eye on th' property. Why'd ya ask?"

"Because I want to buy it," Tommy stated.

"Tommy, you don't!" exclaimed Evelyn.

"My dear, you heard what I said."

"I kin't sell it out from under Horace an' Cissy an' th' young uns," Jim said. "'Sides, if'n I did, where 'ud I go?"

"To Boston," Tommy replied. "And, as far as that goes, you can take the Jameses with you. Unless I'm very much mistaken, they will have cause to be very proud of their son Jeremiah one of these days. I haven't formulated any plans, but rest assured I'll take care of arrangements. Leave it to me."

Jim was confused, but a glimmer of hope came to his eyes.

Tommy and Evelyn had taken a hotel room in town. The place left much to be desired compared to the way they were accustomed to living. Still they were comfortable.

The following day, Tommy called at the office of Jaspar Calhoun after first visiting the assayer's office.

"I don't know no Thomas Phenwick," Jaspar Calhoun belched when Todd announced him.

"He says he's ya cousin from Boston, Massachusetts."

"My cousin? Ain't likely. Still—" Jaspar went to the door and peeked through the crack of it. "What's he up t'?"

"He never said."

"Well, show him in, but ya keep ya ear t' th' door, ya hear?"

"Yes, sir, Mistah Calhoun."

Jaspar wore his best righteous smile when Tommy entered.

"Well-well, so ya're my cousin from Boston, huh?"

Tommy extended his hand. Jaspar looked queerly at it before he condescended to shake it.

"Uncle Jim Phenwick was my mother's half-brother."

"You th' one what is part—uh—well, part—uh—"

"I'm part pianist and part businessman," Tommy filled in. "I'll come directly to the point of my call, Cousin Jaspar. Uncle Jim signed a paper with you when you loaned him five hundred dollars. I wish to redeem that paper."

"Redeem it? What fo'?"

"For five hundred dollars and whatever interest on the loan you feel is right and fair."

"Why ya want t' do that?"

"Because I intend to purchase Moss Grove, and I want it clear from debt," Tommy said forthrightly.

"That property ain't worth nothin'."

"It is to me for sentimental reasons," Tommy assured him.

"Sentimental?"

"I have a sentimental streak."

"Ya ain't never lived out at Moss Grove."

"No, but my mother had stayed there."

"Sentimentality is one thin'," Jaspar allowed, "but good business is another. That Moss Grove property ain't worth foolin' with. 'Sides, I thought Uncle Jim was a-leavin' it t' Letty."

"Maybe I'm purchasing it for her," Tommy suggested. "The fact is, it really isn't important why I am intending to buy it, is it? I have my reasons, whatever they may be. I've simply come to you to redeem the note Uncle Jim signed."

Jaspar thought a minute. His eyes squinted nervously and he drummed his fingers atop the desk. "Well, I'll have t' have fifty dollars interest for it."

"Fine." Tommy took cash from his pocket.

"Reckon ya got plans for th' place, ain't ya?"

"Not yet. But I well may in time. Of course, that will have to be up to Letitia."

"Where'd Letty git th' money?"

"You might say I'm lending it to her." Tommy put the money on the desk before Jaspar. "The paper, if you please, Cousin Jaspar."

"Th' paper?" Jaspar stared quizzically at Tommy, hesitating before he pulled open a drawer and shuffled through papers. "It's a dang waste a' money, that's what it is." He tossed the paper toward Tommy.

"One other thing," Tommy said after reading the paper and pocketing it. He stood until he was certain he had Jaspar's full attention. "If I ever hear of night riders again going out to Moss Grove, I will contact friends I have in the federal government and make certain that the invaders are brought to justice for trespassing."

"Ya needn't threaten me with ya high falutin part-niggah ways, Tom Phenwick!" Jaspar barked, his face a bright crimson.

"Excuse me, Jaspar. I believe our transaction is completed." Without further word, Tommy strode from the office and did not look back.

Jaspar cracked his knuckles and beat his fist against the top of the desk. Then he reached for a cigar, and after several attempts, he managed to light it.

With the deed for the property in hand and the transaction finalized in every legal aspect, Tommy returned to Moss Grove with Evelyn. He had left instructions with the Jameses to pack whatever belongings they needed, as he had done with Jim Phenwick. Upon arriving, Tommy announced that he had made arrangements to have all of their things shipped to Boston.

"What a' Mattie?" Jim asked. "I kin't jus' go off an' leave her in th' crazy farm."

"Aunt Mattie is beyond help, Uncle Jim," Tommy said kindly, sympathetically. "You said yourself that she doesn't know you."

"But she is my sistah."

"I'll take you to see her before we leave, Uncle Jim," Tommy said. "We have to drive into town, anyway, to take the luggage to be shipped. There won't be room in the limousine to carry it all."

Mattie Phenwick's condition had worsened. Her arms had to be tied about her and she had to be restrained from violent actions. When Jim and Tommy were taken into the room where she was kept, Jim gasped before he rushed to her and kissed her. She spat at him.

"Mattie, why'd ya go an' do that?"

"Damn Yankee! Damn Yankee!" Mattie shrieked.

"Aunt Mattie, I'm your nephew Tommy."

"Let me outta here, ya hear?" Mattie yelled. "Let me out!"

"Ya-all kin't git out no way, Mattie," Jim soothed.

"Then I wanta die, I jus' wanta die!"

Tommy led Jim from the room. "You see, it's no use, Uncle Jim. There's nothing can be done for her. She doesn't know you, nor does she know what she's saying or doing. Believe me, it is best to leave her here. I'll make special arrangements for her care."

Tears streaked Jim's face. "It'ud be humane t' put a gun t' her head like they do with sick animals, wouldn't it? But ya jus' kin't do that, kin ya? Ya're right, Tommy, there ain't nothin' we kin do for her now."

The limousine Tommy had purchased for the trip to Savannah was loaded to capacity. The James family sat in the back while Jim rode in front with Tommy and Evelyn. As the car pulled through the opening between the gateposts, Jim looked back, watery-eyed.

"Reckon I'll never see ol' Moss Grove ag'in," Jim moaned. "But I reckon maybe I seen enough a' it already. Oughta take a match an' set fire t' it, that's what ya oughta do. But years an' years a' memories kin't be burned up, kin they? They'll still go on burnin' right here in this ol' head, won't they?"

Horace James put his hand to Jim's shoulder and patted it.

Alexander and Ursala Phenwick, the newlyweds, spent considerable time with other members of the family during the ocean crossing. A good many years older than his new wife, and never the great romantic, Xan took time to become acquainted with Letty and Jeremiah. Ursala, too, made special effort to get to know Letty, since they were relatively close in age. They would become good friends.

"I dearly love Mr. Phenwick," Ursala confided in Letty. "In many ways he's the father I lost when I was so young. Still he's very nice and considerate, and I find him very enjoyable to spend time with. Like with his late wife, he wants me to have interests of my own—which suits me well."

"I've never really thought much about love and marriage," Letty confessed. "I suppose it will happen someday—but I'm not eager to be anything but a good dancer at this time. Later—well, we'll see what happens later."

"I hope you won't think it indiscreet of me to ask," Ursala said, her pretty face changing from vivacious animation to sullen concern, "but I'm curious about your relationship with Jeremiah."

"With Jeremiah?" Letty blinked. "I love Jeremiah like a brother. We grew up together. I'm proud of Jeremiah and the way he has learned to dance."

"But he is a male."

"What is that supposed to mean?" Letty asked innocently.

"And you're a female."

"I'm well aware of that."

"Opposites—like Mr. Phenwick and me," Ursala batted her eyes. "Jeremiah is really quite handsome, even for a black man."

"Jeremiah's only a boy. He's younger than I am. I don't understand what all the fuss is about," Letty commented. But she had been made more and more aware of the fact that her friend was of the male gender, and it had occurred to her that her closeness to him could lead to a more intimate relationship—if she were to allow it, or if he was so inclined to pursue such a thing. While in New York, she had observed couples of mixed races. True, they were few and far between; nonetheless, they did exist. She refused to ponder the idea and quickly managed to change the subject.

Still there were moments when Letty was alone aboard ship, when she strolled the deck, or sat quietly in the shade watching the passing sea, when she couldn't help consider thoughts that had been planted in her mind by others concerning Jeremiah. Why couldn't two people just be two people, never mind the color of skin or the gender? Admittedly she knew little or nothing about romantic relationships. There had never been anyone to tell her about such things.

Worth Bassett had taken a deep interest in Jeremiah and had assumed the role of tutor in various areas of his need for learning. No white man had ever attempted to be the boy's friend in the past, and Jeremiah was somewhat overwhelmed by the attention and interest shown him by Worth. Letty observed and felt grateful that someone else had wanted to help her friend. Worth could do far more for Jeremiah than she could. Still she perceived a sense of jealousy come over her whenever she saw the two together and seemingly enjoying themselves. She wanted to be happy for Jeremiah. Feeling somewhat left out, she began spending more time with Ursala.

Chapter Fifteen

THE THREE YOUNG MEN WAITING at the gate of debarkation in Southampton, England, looked enough alike to be identical triplets. The eldest of the handsome youths had auburn red hair and the youngest had lighter, nearly orange-colored locks, while the middle in age possessed a hue in between his brothers'. Distinguishingly good looking, with sculptured features of artistic proportions and bodies so idyllic in beauty that it seemed only a great artist could have created them, they caused a sensation wherever they individually went; but when they appeared together as a group, traffic stopped and stunned observers gawked as if they could not believe their senses. The sons of Daniel Charles Phenwick II and the former Louise Ornby pretended not to enjoy the attention they attracted, which was why they rarely were seen as a trio in public.

The eldest, Charles Ross was twenty-nine; the next, Augustus Miles, was fourteen months younger, while Timothy James was twenty-four-years old. They were each within a half-inch of being the same height, which was close to six feet tall, and all three possessed nearly the identical shade of lavender blue eyes. The bachelor, playboy sons of the wealthy Phenwicks were considered to be the prize catch among the elite of London society.

Stately, sedate, it was not difficult to see that the younger Phenwicks had inherited their looks from Daniel Charles II and beautiful Louise, who had become the reigning society queen of the London Phenwicks. The five stood in a group as if they were posed for a family portrait as they awaited the arrival of their kin from the United States. Both parents doted proudly over their sons.

Xan was the first to spot his half-brother, Daniel Charles II, and pointed him out to Ursala. "There's my brother and his family. Wave."

Ursala slightly lifted her raised parasol and nudged Letty to turn her attention in the direction of the waiting family.

A short while later the entire traveling part was introduced to those who had come to meet the ship. Kisses and handshakes were exchanged. It was arranged that Xan and Ursala, along with Laura and Tiziano Spolini would ride in the limousine with Daniel Charles and Louise, while Letty, Worth Bassett, Georges LeVeque, Jeremiah, Roselle Ivanovich and Vladimir Popkin squeezed into the other automobile with the three Phenwick sons. Charlie drove.

The elegant house in Hyde Park was spacious with an abundance of varnished oak and white marble. Crystal baubles hung from chandeliers and wall fixtures. Fine Wedgwood porcelain and brass statuary were in abundance along with several fine oil paintings from the 17th and 18th centuries. The household staff was efficient and proper. It was the grandest house Letty had ever been in.

"Times are few and far between when my brother visits me," Daniel Charles said when Xan suggested that he and Ursala take a hotel suite. "I won't hear of you staying elsewhere."

Louise was the gracious hostess and insisted that the entire party stay for tea before Spolini, Bassett and LeVeque went to their respective apartments.

"I have arranged for Jeremiah to take one of my guest rooms," Worth Bassett mentioned. "I plan to personally see to his training."

Georges LeVeque had arranged for an apartment for Roselle and Vladimir near his home. "Naturally Letitia will study at the Academy, and it would be best if she were to maintain residence there. I wish for her to take an accelerated course this summer in hopes that she will be able to perform during the autumn season."

"Don't you think that is rushing it, Georges?" Roselle questioned. "Doubtlessly she has fine talent, but it does require perfecting and polishing."

"Agreed. We will simply evaluate her progress by September," Georges returned, "and make the final decision about her performing then."

"And what of Jeremiah?" Letty questioned.

Georges frowned before he smiled broadly. "Jeremiah is to be Worth's protégé. Since he has not had a formal education in dance, but he does show remarkable potentialities, his learning procedure will have to be different from Letty's."

"Actually, don't you know, I plan to take Jeremiah to Moscow in the next week or so, and on to Kiev," Worth informed them. "I know some perfectly marvelous miracle workers in the field of ballet. I don't dare to hope that he will perform this coming season, but when he does make his debut, I promise it will be spectacular."

During the conversation, the three Phenwick brothers sat in straight-backed chairs in rigid attitudes as they followed the remarks being exchanged. When Daniel Charles suggested that he and Xan adjourn to another room for a gentleman's conversation, Charles and Augustus asked if they could be excused. Timothy remained and boyishly grinned as he listened.

"How did you get mixed up with all of these dance people, Xan?" Daniel Charles asked.

"I'm *not* mixed up with them," Xan assured his brother. "Circumstances were such that their crossing coincided with ours. Ironically, we had reservations on the same ship."

"But Cousin Laura is involved, isn't she?"

"That's another matter," Xan replied. "I'm happy to see Laura taking an interest in someone other than herself. Pru Donnally at first objected to his wife coming to England, but Simon came to his sister's rescue—as he always has—and Pru relented. I feel the change will be good for Laura. And perhaps the absence of his wife will cause Pru to change his attitude about several things."

"I see. And how is Donald's health holding up?" Daniel Charles questioned as if inventing topics to avoid the subject he wanted to broach.

"Our little brother has become quite lame," Xan replied. "And, although Peggy is not aware of it, Donald confessed to me that the sight in his one remaining eye is failing."

"Ah, wonderful Peggy, I love her dearly." Daniel Charles offered a cigarette. "I regret that we were unable to attend Richard's funeral. That was a shocker, wasn't it?"

"Brother Richard had been going off the deep end for some time," Xan explained. "I couldn't help entertaining the feeling that something drastic would happen to him—and it did."

"Polly, Albert and their family are all well, I suppose."

"Yes." Xan cocked his head and peered curiously at his older brother. "You've something on your mind, haven't you, Daniel?"

"Why, whatever—?"

"Although we don't see each other often," Xan replied, "I know how you are. You're curious about my marriage to Ursala, aren't you?"

"Curious? I suppose you might say that." Daniel Charles, modest and reserved, felt as if he were blushing. "She seems terribly young, you know."

"She is. And I worry about that a little. Such a vast difference between the ages of a husband and wife can present problems. Yet basically, I feel we each have a definite need for the other," Xan said. "Of course I don't have the energy or the enthusiasm of a man closer to her age, and, as you well know, I've never been much of a romantic—certainly not in a physical way. Still, if she is dissatisfied, she has never mentioned it and she worships me as if I were a king. Our marriage has rejuvenated me in quite an extraordinary way."

"Hmm. Yes, I can see that in your attitude, Brother dear," Daniel Charles stated, but he could not disguise his tone of skepticism. "What happens after the honeymoon is over and the novelty is gone?"

"That will be what we will have to face at that time, won't it be?" Xan replied. He laughed. "In the last years of our marriage, Yvonne and I were husband and wife in name only. We each went our separate ways. It was my daughter Katherine who encouraged me to remarry. I had reservations, of course. Still I did become quite fond of Ursala."

"Quite fond and being in love with are two different things, Xan. Surely you know that."

"I do. And in all honesty, I must admit that I am truly very much in love with Ursala. My feelings for her are far greater than they had ever been for Yvonne, who, as we both know, was a colossal opportunist. I always had tremendous respect for Yvonne, and she is the mother of my child. But we've been over this before."

Daniel Charles put his hand to Xan's shoulder. "I am pleased if you are happy, Xan, you know that. I only pray that you will always be as content as you are at this moment."

Xan sighed. He wanted to change the subject of conversation. "How is it that you still have three

149

grown sons living at home? And here, Charles is nearly thirty and Augustus not far behind him."

"Charles Ross has been twice engaged, and each time the marriage was called off at the last minute," Daniel Charles informed his brother. "Both he and Augustus are finishing medical school, so I'm just as pleased that neither of them have married before finishing their education. As for Timothy—well, Tim is still in the process of finding himself. I have three devoted sons, both to Louise and me as well as to each other. They're quite close."

"Two physicians—and what does Tim plan to do?" Xan questioned. It was a topic he had brought up before since he felt a closer affinity to Tim than to the two older of his nephews.

"Tim seems to have developed a singular interest in the arts," Daniel Charles explained. "Louise has encouraged him, no doubt. Now that he's finished at Oxford and is considered a scholar among the top of his class, I imagine he will accept a professorship at a university somewhere."

"I see." Xan reserved comment. "There is one other thing I must discuss with you." He glanced about secretively to make certain they were not being overheard. "I'm also in London on official business with the U.S. government. It has to do with all this political and economic business with Germany and Kaiser Wilhelm. I suspect President Wilson is rightly concerned about the trend of what is happening in Europe."

"Are you doing investigative work for the government now?"

"I was called to Washington, D.C. just prior to my marriage. It seems I was recommended for some special investigative work. As a result, I will be away for some time in a few weeks. Naturally, I will wish for Ursala to remain here."

"Ah, I see."

"No, I don't believe you do, Daniel. I can't divulge even to you the intricacies of my mission. Fact is, I've not been advised fully of the details," Xan explained. He poured himself a glass of brandy. "In three weeks, our cousin Oliver will be arriving in London, Luke's son. I must ask your assistance in dealing with a most delicate matter, Daniel. . . .a matter of vast international importance."

"You make it sound terribly serious."

"It is—most serious. I can tell you no more at this time. But not only will I require your cooperation, I will also presume upon your hospitality. It will be necessary for Oliver Phenwick to stay here for a few days as a visiting cousin."

"Oliver is still in his teens, isn't he?" Daniel Charles asked.

"He will be nineteen in October." Xan drank. "I really can't tell you more now, Daniel. Perhaps I can in a week or so."

"It all sounds so terribly mysterious and fraught with intrigue."

"It is—believe me, Brother, it is."

After Tiziano Spolini and Georges LeVeque left for their respective London homes, Letty asked if she could speak privately with Jeremiah before he went off with Worth Bassett. Worth remained to chat with Louise and Laura.

"We haven't had much opportunity to speak for the last few days, Jeremiah," Letty said after they had gone into the garden which was relatively small, but magnificently laid out. "Mr. Bassett has been occupying much of your time."

"I like Worth very much," Jeremiah replied. Under Bassett's tutelage his speech had vastly improved. "Already he has taught me much, and not only about ballet."

"Worth?" Letty questioned.

"I think of him as a good friend," Jeremiah replied, avoiding looking directly into her eyes. "My skin will never change color, but Worth treats me as a white man."

"He encourages you to dance?"

"Yes."

"And he wants to take you to Russia?"

"Yes, Letty, he does. He says I will learn much faster there," Jeremiah replied. "I will train with other boys. Worth says that only a man can teach me to dance like a man should, not a woman. I believe him."

"Do you want to go with him?" Letty questioned, unable to analyze the expression in Jeremiah's face.

"I do. But I will miss being with you, Letty."

"And I'll miss you, Jeremiah. Yet, what you say is true, Madame Ivanovich told me that you should study dancing with a man teacher."

"Yes, I spoke with Madame Ivanovich, too."

Letty took his hand. "Already you sound so different, Jeremiah."

"Worth says that I learn fast. He makes me work at speaking properly, much more than you ever did."

"I'm glad to hear that." Letty looked away, dropped his hand and turned slightly from him. "It's not because—I mean, you're not going with Mr. Bassett because I'm—well, I'm white and a girl and you're —well, black and a male? I mean—"

"You are my best friend in the whole world, Letty, and I love you," Jeremiah replied. "Mrs. Phenwick did have a talk with me about that, so did Worth. I understand now."

"Which Mrs. Phenwick?"

"Mrs. Peggy Phenwick."

"Oh, God, why should we be separated after all we've been through?" Letty questioned, no longer able to contain the emotion she was feeling. "What business is it of Cousin Peggy?"

"She told me and I understand, but I don't think I can explain it to you," Jeremiah replied. "And Worth —well, I've learned much from him."

Letty ran to Jeremiah and threw her arms about him, hugging him as tightly as she could. "Why is it wrong? *Why is it wrong?*"

Jeremiah was unable to reply. Slowly he allowed his hands to touch her back and almost immediately pulled them away. "Worth will be wanting to go soon, and I mustn't keep him waiting."

When Letty looked up into Jeremiah's face, tears were streaking down his cheeks. He quickly turned his head away and went toward the house.

Letty ran to him and addressed him from behind. "Why?"

"We'll always be good friends, Miss Letty—always."

Letty could no longer contain the tears when Jeremiah went into the building. She remained in the garden, sobbing, crying, giving vent to the emotions that had been building yet had not been known to her for a long time. Although she knew they would always be friends, somehow she knew that their relationship would be different from that day forward.

A long-haired, gray and white cat brushed against her legs. Letty stooped to pet it, then picked it up and held it cuddlingly in her arms. A warm breeze came up and rustled through the bushes. She sat on the ground as she held the animal to her face.

"I see you and old Ned have become friends," the genteel voice said from behind her. The high baritone was warm and friendly. "But don't consider that you're getting preferential treatment. Ned makes up to everyone, don't you know." Pause. "Are you all right, Cousin Letitia?"

Letty nodded her head without turning back.

"I passed Jeremiah on the way. He appeared to be a bit distraught. It was an emotional parting, wasn't it?"

Letty was aware of trouser legs before her. She looked up into the compassionate, handsome face of Timothy Phenwick. In the next moment, Tim was seated on the grass beside her. He reached to stroke Ned.

"He's a good puss. Aren't you, Ned?"

"Are you—?"

"I'm Tim, the youngest. It must be a devilish time for

153

you sorting the three of us out. Everyone says we look ever so much alike." Tim laughed. Then his expression changed as he reached his hand to brush the tears from her cheeks with his fingers. "I understand, Letitia—at least I want to understand."

"Do you?"

"Mother said I was to come and see if you were holding up," Tim remarked. "The fact is, actually, I wanted to get to know you better. Do you mind?"

Letty forced a faint smile as she dried her eyes and attempted to be pleasant. "Have you always lived in London?"

"I was born in Vienna, where my grandfather, Dr. Augustus Ornby, has his practice," Tim replied.

"I met old Dr. Joseph Ornby in New York," Letty explained. "He stayed there for a while after coming for Xan and Ursala's wedding. He is quite an impressive person. I confess, it was difficult for me to think of him as my distant cousin."

"My brothers and I were once permitted to visit Uncle Joseph in Boston," Tim said. "He's my grandfather's brother. The two of them have done quite a bit of experimental work together over the years in psychological studies. Grandfather was more deeply into the subject, don't you know, than Uncle Joseph. My brother Charlie plans to become a general practitioner in medicine, but I believe my brother Augustus wants to follow in my grandfather's footsteps."

"And you?"

"I'm not the scientific sort," Tim admitted, a large friendly grin lighting his face. "My preference is the arts. I would like to do extensive traveling before I settle down to a profession."

"Travel? To where?"

"Different parts of the world. I want to go to the United States, particularly to San Francisco where there is a most successful Medallion company belonging to the Phenwicks."

"Cousin Peggy spoke of it, since San Francisco is her home."

"I've met Cousin Peggy. She is really quite a lass, don't you know. I say." His boyish qualities could not be disguised. "I've attended several ballet performances here in London. And while I was in Paris, I was introduced to the great Nijinsky by the impresario, Diaghilev. I wish I had been exposed to ballet when I was younger, perhaps I might have had a go at it, or at least given it a try. You probably know that my mother is involved with various of the performing arts, opera, the theater and ballet. I suspect I get my interest in the arts from her. Listen to me just running on this way."

"I enjoy hearing about you, Timothy."

"Do you care for opera?"

Letitia blushed. "I fear I don't know anything about it. Madame Ivanovich several times mentioned that she had danced in ballet sequences in operas, but I've never attended one."

"I say, that is jolly. I mean, perhaps you would consider attending Covent Garden with me," Tim suggested.

"Is Covent Garden the name of an opera?"

Tim laughed. "No, no, it is an opera house. You must let me take you on a tour around London. I would enjoy that, and I'm certain you would. It's such an historic old city, you know."

"I'm to begin lessons tomorrow at the Academy— whatever the Academy is," Letty said. "I may not have much time to myself."

"We'll find time, I'll see to that—that is, if you would care to accompany me," Tim stated. "Then, too, I would like to take you to Buckingham Palace and the castles and Westminster Abbey. There is so much to see."

"I appreciate your enthusiasm, Timothy," Letty replied, "but, as I said, I do begin studying and I expect to have a schedule of long hours every day."

"But there will be time for a holiday here and there,

won't there? They can't expect you to dance unceasingly," Tim commented.

"I've decided to devote my life to ballet." Letty got a far distant look in her eyes. "Really, I seem to have an extraordinary compulsion to dance. Sometimes I wonder why that is. I can only conclude that there is something deep within me that wants to be expressed through dancing."

"But even dancers have social lives. All work and no play, don't you?" Again Tim laughed in a playful way. "My father has often accused me of being devoted to all play and no work."

"Are you?"

"Not actually," Tim replied. "What is work for some people is actually play for others, and the opposite also holds true. Father has little room for criticism, since he hardly ever seems to work. Oh, he does, but he uses his mind and he has multiplied his fortune several times over by shrewdly investing his wealth. I fear I have no mind for business. As I say, I will probably end up with a professorship somewhere and devote my years to scholarly pursuit. In time I will probably marry and settle down to raising a family, live in a country cottage and become a landowner."

"That does not sound disagreeable," Letty said.

"Not disagreeable, but some people would think it terribly banal and unexciting," Tim returned.

"Excuse me, Cousin Timothy, I don't understand your words. I've had a limited education. Most of what I know, I've taught myself."

"Marvelous! How wonderful! I say, I can't conceive of doing that myself—I confess I wouldn't know where to begin. You are a wonder, Cousin Letitia." Tim stared deeply into her face and the broad smile began to fade from his lips before he caught himself and repositioned the smile.

Letty turned her head so that she wouldn't have to face him. "I also taught Jeremiah how to read. Fact is, several years ago I trained myself to speak properly, not as an uneducated Southerner. That was after I began studying ballet with Madame Ivanovich. I tried to teach Jeremiah to speak properly, too. He couldn't see much need of it until we left Savannah, then we both forced ourselves to learn quickly. Madame Ivanovich always said that speaking incorrectly was like wearing a label of ignorance."

"I could never think of you as ignorant, old girl," Tim said. He paused to gather his thoughts. "Well, I *do* want to show you around London. Promise that you will find the time for me."

"The time for you?"

"To show you about London."

"Oh." Letty smiled at him before she moved toward the door leading into the house. "Maybe we should get back and see what is planned. I really want to take time to relax. The sea trip was restful, but I still seem to be a little fatigued. Are you coming in, Cousin Timothy?"

"I say, yes, of course. Shall we?" He wanted to reach to take her hand, but he restrained himself.

Chapter Sixteen

THE DANCE ACADEMY WAS A PRIVATE establishment which operated in conjunction with the Conservatory of Music, the whole of which was simply called the Academy, if one was a dancer; the Conservatory, if one was a music student. A large, sprawling mansion in Somerset had been converted into the school with a limited amount of space for on-campus residents. Other students took rooms in nearby private homes where space was available to rent out.

Letty's arrival at the Academy coincided with an opening in the housing located within the school itself, a room which she would share with another young lady. Tommy had made the financial arrangements, which represented the combined support of several of the Phenwick family members.

In the meantime; Worth Bassett hustled Jeremiah off to Moscow, and Madame Ivanovich and Vladimir Popkin accompanied Georges LeVeque to Paris where work was in progress for the fall ballet season.

Under the pretense of wanting to be close at hand, but not always in evidence, Laura Donnally took a small apartment in Kensington Gardens. She claimed she was there to assist Letty as best she could, but her real motive was to be close to Tiziano Spolini, who milked her romantic interest in him for all of the financial support he could get. Basically, Tiziano was not unscrupulous, only slightly deceptive, since Laura was the one who blindly rushed into the situation and allowed herself to be used.

Letty's room was shared with a Czechosovakian dance student named Alexandria Muzakova, a talented young lady with an exotic, somewhat mysterious beauty. Her dark hair, deep brown eyes and Slavic features were remarkably haunting and appealing. Her expression was serious, but her lips were formed in a natural smile that almost appeared paradoxical. Her English was imperfect, and she welcomed the opportunity to share with an English-speaking person.

"I have studied dancing since I was five years old," Alexandria informed Letty after introducing herself. "Dancing is all I've ever known."

"You are far more fortunate than I," Letty replied in her soft Georgian tones that had only a hint of a drawl to them.

"My mother had always wanted to be a dancer," Alexandria continued. "By the time she learned how to earn money, she was too old to study dance seriously."

"Did your father object?"

"My parents were married only a brief time before my father was killed during a political uprising," Alexandria stated. "At first my mother was in the employ of several wealthy men."

"Several? As a domestic?"

Alexandria smiled enigmatically. "My mother was young and beautiful, and she knew what pleased men. Ultimately she met one man who kept her as his mistress. He was much older than she, and jealous. It was a good arrangement, and he left her financially taken care of when he died."

Letty had never heard anyone speak so bluntly about

such things, and she found herself shocked by the disclosures. Still Alexandria spoke with such straightforwardness and honesty that Letty found what she had to say fascinating. Not to show her ignorance in such matters, she merely listened and grasped what she could. The fact is, she knew little about intimate relationships, since she was totally inexperienced in that direction.

Despite Alexandria's cold facade, her inner warmth and sensitivity were projected to Letty and the two were destined to become close friends. Letty told of Moss Grove and the way of life she knew in Savannah, which struck Alexandria as being primitive and quite different from what she had imagined.

"I was largely raised in Paris," Alexandria recited in the continuing story about her background, "but I only lived with Mama until I was eleven years old, when I was put in a private *académie* for what you would call talented children. Mama and I saw each other regularly, but I know she was kept from doing what she wanted to do by the responsibility of having me live with her. I understood." A pouty expression came to her face. "Yes, I understood."

"Did you, really?" Letty asked.

Alexandria shot her a sharp look. "Do you question me?"

"Only because your face tells me you didn't really understand."

"That is not true. My devotion was to my dancing, nothing more," Alexandria said coldly. "I could not have danced if my mother hadn't done what she had done. I accept that as fact. One must be realistic."

There were other questions Letty would have liked to ask of her newfound friend, but she thought better of doing so. She realized that there was much she could learn from Alexandria Muzakova and she wanted to develop a tight closeness with her.

The week after Letty had begun her intensive course of study at the Academy, she was visited by Timothy

Phenwick to who she introduced Alexandria. The reason behind his visit was to invite Letty to a special party his parents were giving wherein there would be several international guests. He took it upon himself to extend an invitation to Alexandria to attend.

"I've missed not seeing you this past week," Tim said when he was alone with Letty and they strolled to the shady bank of a river that meandered not far from the school.

"That is kind of you to say, Timothy," Letty returned. "I've been far too occupied to really miss anyone—not even Jeremiah."

Tim looked crestfallen. "I say, that was not the reply I had hoped to receive."

"Surely you must understand that my studies occupy all of my time." Letty smiled sweetly, but she realized that Tim was displeased. "My day starts early and ends late. Practically my only means of relaxation is to listen to daily recitals given by the instrumental students. And even that is to acquaint myself with certain musical appreciation. Only when we are physically weary do Alexandria and I collapse in our room and indulge in conversation. Usually I fall asleep listening to her, or sometimes it's the other way around."

"Is such a rigorous routine so essential?" Tim asked, covering his disappointment with a congenial smile. "I muse about you quite often. I believe you know you've made an indelible impression on me, rather."

"My principal interest in the world right now must be my education. Alexandria has been dancing since she was a small child. Although I had a marvelous teacher in Madame Ivanovich, I've still so many technical things to learn. I sometimes feel inadequate when I see how accomplished she has become."

"I am not at all unsympathetic to your cause, Letitia." He motioned to a fallen log upon which they could sit. "But, don't you know, I'm a bit impetuous and patience isn't always my best quality. I simply pray that it will not disturb your artistic progress if I come

161

to visit you regularly and we can have pleasant moments like this."

Letty laughed because she couldn't think of anything else to do. "I enjoy your company, Timothy."

"And I very much enjoy yours." He sighed. "I didn't tell you the latest news in my life. I've received a teaching assignment in a private institution for young gentlemen. I'll be teaching the classics and art appreciation. Which I believe is a ruddy good show, don't you know. I consider myself most fortunate."

"How wonderful for you!" Letty exclaimed, pleased that the conversation had turned to Tim. "Will you be teaching in London?"

"Not far from London. It's in the country, remote and in a lovely setting. Once I begin teaching, you must come and visit me. I fell in love with the place. And the students come from extremely well-to-do families. I can share an identity with them."

"We had better get back soon," Letty said. "I've another class this afternoon."

"Doesn't all that dancing exhaust you physically?" Tim questioned.

"Very much so, but I love it. Yet the more I dance, the greater endurance I develop and the greater my strength becomes."

The following Saturday afternoon Tim drove out to Somerset to pick up Letty and Alexandria and, after a slight delay, they motored back to London. Because the roadster was open, conversation was difficult. But Letty sat close to Tim and that made him happy.

Louise Phenwick greeted Letty and Alexandria and immediately whisked them away from her youngest son, who stood gawking after them and did his best to overcome any feelings of resentment.

"Since you girls share a room at school," Louise said as she led them to the second floor, "I'm certain you won't mind sharing a room here. We have far more house guests than I had initially planned on, and with

Oliver arriving, I have to have a space for him."

"Oliver?" Letty questioned.

"Oliver Phenwick. Your young cousin from Denver, Colorado. He's a distant cousin, nevertheless a Phenwick," Louise informed Letty. "I've never met him, nor has Daniel Charles. Still, I've no doubt that there are many Phenwick cousins I've never met. Charlie and Augustus have gone to meet him in Southampton. You and Alexandria will have to sleep in the same bed, but it's large and comfortable."

"We'll manage," Letty assured her, "won't we Alexandria?"

"I have learned to sleep anywhere," Alexandria replied.

"But, not I trust, with just anyone," Louise interjected.

Alexandria batted her eyelashes and smiled as she bit her tongue from saying the first thing that came to mind. "I am a ballerina, Mrs. Phenwick, not an adventuress."

Louise blushed, became apologetic and found an excuse to leave the girls to their own devices.

"If there is time, I should like to purchase a new pair of gloves before the party tonight," Alexandria said after the girls had unpacked and put their things in the closets.

"You should have said something to Cousin Louise," Letty commented. "She probably has an extra pair."

"No. I don't like to wear anything belonging to anyone else," Alexandria returned. "It will only take a short while for me to shop."

"Shall I go with you?"

"No. Thank you anyway, Letitia, I prefer going alone," Alexandria said mysteriously.

Although Louise offered to have the chauffeur drive Alexandria into the shopping district, the young lady insisted she could find her way and that she was quite familiar with London and getting about in the city.

Letty decided she would do well to rest while Alexandria was away. The drive from Somerset had caused her to become heavy-eyed and drowsy. Consequently she put all thoughts from her mind and almost immediately fell asleep.

Oliver Phenwick was tall, well-proportioned and stoically handsome. Golden blond hair glistened in the sunlight and vivid blue eyes sparkled. He had been accompanied by his Aunt Peggy Phenwick, who not only doted on him, but used his trip to London as an excuse to travel there herself.

Peggy had recognized the Phenwick brothers, Charles and Augustus, who enthusiastically greeted her.

"I'm a bit stiff from lounging about aboard ship," Oliver said as he got into the limousine. "My body is simply crying for exercise. You'll forgive my frankness, Aunt Peggy."

"I quite understand, Oliver."

"I say," Augustus suggested, "why don't we drop off Peggy and take you to our club. We've excellent facilities and a suitable swimming pool. Charlie and I go there regularly, and chances are we'll encounter Tim there, too."

"A marvelous idea," Charlie joined in. "And it will give us all the opportunity to get to know each other better, don't you know."

That decided upon, Peggy was deposited at the Hyde Park residence along with the luggage and the three young Phenwick men went off to the club.

"My first governess was a German woman," Oliver related as he and Charlie sat resting after a vigorous workout before going to swim. "I learned the German language fluently almost before I acquired a suitable vocabulary in English."

"My brothers and I have studied French, Latin and a smattering of Spanish," Charlie said. "I was never much into foreign languages, but Augustus is."

"For a time I wondered why I was given so much German," Oliver went on.

"You have a bit of a German look about you."

"So I've been told. I suppose there may have been a Prussian or two in my mother's background. We're not certain." Oliver laughed. "Hopefully I will be able to travel to Bavaria and up into the region where I can use my knowledge of the language."

"You'd bloody well better be careful there, the way things are going with Kaiser Wilhelm and that lot."

"I'll take my chances. Come along, let's swim."

"Bloody Americans," Charlie muttered as he lifted himself from the lounge and followed the athletic body of his cousin.

After a rigorous hour of swimming, far more than either Charlie or Augustus could endure, Oliver got from the pool and showered before he was given a massage.

"I say, you and Letitia are two of a kind," Augustus remarked as they were leaving the club.

"Letitia? Oh, yes, the dancer," Oliver remembered. "Aunt Peggy mentioned her to me while we were crossing."

"She seems to have inherited the same physical stamina that you have. It must run in the American side of the family," Charlie commented. "I suppose it's an admirable trait, but I can't for the life of me think of why it should be."

Xan was waiting at the house and after the introductions were made, he quickly ushered Oliver into the library where he closed the door firmly behind them. He stalked about the room to ascertain that no one was present.

"You're aware that this is not going to be easy for you, aren't you, Oliver?" Xan questioned as he stared deeply into the youth's sharply handsome face.

"So I've been led to believe."

"I have reservations about this party tonight," Xan continued. "Too many people will be here, most of whom I don't know. You must keep yourself as inconspicuous as possible—which, I might add, could well be an impossibility, as devilishly handsome as you are."

"Should I not attend?"

"No, you must. However, I hope that Baron von Klootz will arrive early, so that you can be introduced, escape the throng, and—well—become acquainted."

"It all sounds quite intriguing," Oliver acknowledged as a singular sensation came over him.

"Do you want to back out now? You can if there's any doubt in your mind," Xan said.

Oliver doubled his fist, but he did not hit it against the table. "No. I want to go through with it."

"Good boy." Xan extended his hand and shook Oliver's, then he clasped him about the shoulders. "I have faith in you."

Oliver smiled, but a feeling of uncertainty came over him that he could not shake for some time to come.

Chapter Seventeen

CONRAD VON KLOOTZ WAS A BARON of the Hapsburg lineage, a man of distinction and prestige. His was the posture and self-assurance of a Prussian military officer, yet he possessed the charm and manners of one who knew his way about royalty and court life. A slight limp marred his stately appearance, but it was hardly noticeable. A large reddish-gray mustache dominated his face and he wore a monocle that caused him to twist his features into a severe expression. Tall and impressive, his appearance could not go unobserved.

One of the servants presented the baron's card to Xan, who immediately interrupted his conversation with Daniel Charles and went to greet the guest.

"Ah, Baron von Klootz!" Xan exclaimed, but not loudly enough that it could be heard over the other party sounds and the music of the string orchestra playing in the background.

Conrad von Klootz glanced around, and made a scowl before he shook the hand extended toward him. "Herr Phenwick, how do you do? I had hoped that our meeting would be in less ostentatious surroundings."

"I'm afraid we Americans are not as—what shall I say—secretive about certain things," Xan returned, smiling pleasantly in an attempt to lighten the baron's disposition.

"Do you know all of these people?" Conrad asked, again glancing about.

"I've met most of them," Xan returned. "My brother, Daniel Charles, knows them all. They're his friends."

Conrad von Klootz made no comment as he made a sharp scrutiny of those in attendance. "I have risked my life, Herr Phenwick, in coming here. Is the boy here?"

"Yes. Shall I get him?"

"Not until you show me to a private room where I will not be disturbed," von Klootz replied.

"Certainly. Daniel Charles specifically designated a chamber for your meeting with Oliver." Xan led the way to the second floor via the back stairway. Once he had shown the baron to the room, he went to fetch Oliver.

Alone in the room Conrad von Klootz made a thorough search of it to determine the security and to assess whether there was any chance that they might be overheard. Satisfied that the small room was safe, a sort of study used by the Phenwick boys when they were growing, the Prussian noble took a cigarette from an engraved gold case and lit it. Still, an uneasiness came over him, the sort one gets when things aren't altogether proper. The cigarette lit, he examined the windows and looked out each of them to ascertain that there was no way an intruder could hide there.

"Baron von Klootz," Xan said as he returned with the boy, "may I present my cousin, Oliver Phenwick?"

Conrad von Klootz clicked his heels and held the cigarette between his thumb and middle finger as he squinted to examine Oliver. He muttered an exclamation in German. The monocle fell from his eye as he raised his eyebrows. "The similarity is extraordinary, quite amazing!"

"I beg your pardon, sir?" Oliver said in German.

"And you speak with hardly a trace of an accent," Conrad added. He reached to shake hands. "A strong grip, not unlike Frederick's." He switched to English. "You must forgive us, Mr. Phenwick. I am impressed."

"In that case, I will excuse you to get better acquainted," Xan replied as he went toward the door. "I'll return in an hour."

Von Klootz circled Oliver, appraising him up and down. "You will have to have a scar here." He pointed to Oliver's cheek. "It will only be momentarily painful. Do you know what this is all about?"

"Xan told me very little," Oliver replied as they both spoke in German.

"I will briefly tell you what I can," von Klootz said. "I am of the House of Hapsburg, wealthy and influential. From all outer appearances I am sympathetic with the cause of Kaiser Wilhelm—which is not necessarily the case. Fact is, although I am aware of what the Kaiser is doing, I believe he may be going about it in the wrong way. But I doubt that you know much about the politics of my country."

"I have studied a little about them," Oliver returned, standing stiffly erect as one does while being inspected. "As I am also a student of American history and economics."

"Ah, economics! Well, that is what this is largely about," von Klootz went on. "You'll have sufficient time to learn the details. Let me tell you, first, about myself. Six months ago my only son, Frederick, was killed in a hunting accident. That is, it was assumed to be an accident and I have no proof to the contrary, much less anything to support the fact that his death might have been brought about for another reason. Frederick was my only child, my sole heir. I lost my wife two years ago. Frederick was all I had in the world."

"I am sorry to hear that, sir."

"Your sympathy is unnecessary, Herr Phenwick. I must explain that Frederick was involved in an anti-Kaiser movement," von Klootz continued, "as I, and I say this in strictest confidence, as I am. Frederick had undergone certain specialized training of a subversive nature. That is why there may just be a possibility that his death was not accidental. Chances are, however, from all indications, that death came by accident with no plot behind it. I was called to the hunting lodge by the owner, an old and trusted friend, and arranged for a private burial for Frederick in a crypt belonging to a distant cousin in Hamburg. One day I hope to have the body returned to Munich and placed in our family crypt. But that may be a long time away."

"May I ask why you were so secretive about your son's death?" Oliver questioned without showing emotion.

"Because it is essential that my son still be alive," von Klootz replied enigmatically. "Frederick had a mission which must be carried out to completion. I will tell you the particulars of this at another time."

"And what is to be my role in all of this?"

"You, Oliver Phenwick, will become Frederick von Klootz, if you agree to play the part," von Klootz replied. "It may well involve intelligence work, espionage and—well, I don't wish to inundate you with negatives. Six months of Frederick's work has been lost— precious time when all hell is about to erupt."

"Xan hinted at such," Oliver said, unruffled by Conrad's statements. "I am not a mercenary, but I have been raised to expect to be remunerated for service rendered."

"Ah, yes, that! To be sure!" Conrad took another cigarette and offered one to Oliver, who declined it. "As I said earlier, Frederick was my only child and heir. There is no one else with the exception of a foppish nephew, whom I disinherited years ago. If you take this position and in essence become my son, it will be put in legal writing that you will be my heir, inherit my fortune as well as my lands. Even if certain of my property is lost, I have a small fortune deposited in foreign banks, jointly in my name and in Frederick's. There will be tremendous risk in what you will have to do, inconceivable danger. And you may face death many times; but if you are clever, as I believe you must be, you will overcome the obstacles."

"I am an adventurer, Herr von Klootz," Oliver said. "I was raised in Denver, Colorado, where there are still remnants of the Wild West. Part of my life was sheltered, but I was somewhat a renegade, much to my mother's horror, and went out of my way to court danger. I'm an expert horseman—and I say this in all modesty—an excellent marksman, an athlete of unusual skill and, I suspect this is most important to you, I am a gambler."

"A gambler? How so?"

"I am willing to chance anything if the stakes are high enough," Oliver replied. "I'm quite unlike other members of my own family—at least the Phenwicks. I know little about the Calders, my mother's side of the family, except that I know they had pioneer spirit. And way back a century or two ago, there was an indomitable woman by the name of Augusta Phenwick—the first Augusta—who was more of a man than most men who lived during her time. I like to think I've inherited my spirit from her."

"You're an amazing young man, Herr Phenwick," von Klootz commented, "and not greatly unlike my Frederick. Will you accept the position as my son, with all the ramifications involved therein?"

"Do I have time to consider it further?"

"Time? The world may erupt in a holocaust at any moment and you're asking for time?"

"The world?"

"If it is not averted, this madness that is going on," von Klootz replied, "it could well include the entire world. I have been privy to certain plans that are being made. God help me if my true sympathies are discovered! I can say no more about it until you give me a definite answer and commitment."

"May I have an hour?"

Von Klootz sighed. "Only an hour. But you must speak to no one about this."

"Not even to Cousin Xan?"

"Only insofar as it concerns your own family matters," Conrad replied.

"And what if I were to speak with others?" Oliver questioned.

"You force me to disclose something I had not wished to," von Klootz returned. "I am armed and I would risk my own life to see that what I have told you is not divulged—certainly in regard to the death of my son. Please do not take this as an idle threat, Herr Phenwick. I confess that I like you very much and I am certain that we would get along well together—as father and son—but you must understand my position."

"Your threat convinces me all the more of your integrity, Baron von Klootz. I'm certain, put in the same position, I would have to do the same." Oliver smiled warmly. "My esteem for you has risen."

Baron von Klootz remained isolated in the small study while Oliver went to speak with Xan. They, too, spoke in private.

Letty and Alexandria mingled with the guests as Laura and Peggy took turns introducing them to various people. Laura knew fewer than her illustrious cousin because she had not spent as much time in London as Peggy had. Still, there were family members present. Laura soon left the introductions to Peggy and went to join Tiziano Spolini with whom she had arrived.

Since many of Louise Phenwick's friends were involved in one way or the other with the arts, she managed to be at the hub of several small groups of fine art enthusiasts. She had hoped that Tommy and Evelyn Phenwick would have been there, but at the last minute they had sent their apologies. While Daniel Charles enjoyed different art forms, he allowed his wife to be the active member of the household in creative circles.

Louise insisted that Tim be dragged into several different conversations with his erudite knowledge. The youngest of her three sons was noticeably her favorite, primarily because he had always shown an interest in what she did. One wonders if his interest was innate, or whether it was learned through his association with his mother.

"I say, I thought I'd never be able to shake myself free of Mother, the old dear," Tim explained when he finally joined Letty and Alexandria, who likewise had been able to disassociate themselves from Peggy.

"I've met so many people tonight," Letty complained, "that my mind is a sea of names and faces, none of which go together."

"I didn't realize that Mother was making such an affair of this," Tim said as he looked admiringly at Letty. "I greatly admire Mother's enthusiasm, but it can get a bit tiring. And her garden associations are worse by far. She's all into flower shows and that sort of things. I suppose I should be grateful she's not a cat or poodle fancier, too." He laughed merrily. "Are you enjoying yourself, Alexandria?"

"Parties such as this usually bore me," Alexandria replied. "But then, people bore me if they're not particularly interesting. I prefer quiet little gatherings with few people."

"I'm terribly sorry this isn't more to your liking, Alexandria," Tim returned, trying not to look annoyed as his brothers came to join them.

"I say," Charlie exclaimed, "what are you three doing off in the corner here?"

"Breathing—at last," Alexandria said. "It is much too late for me. I should have retired an hour ago."

"Not to bed so early?" Augustus commented. "The party has just begun."

173

"Training to be a dancer is as rigorous as preparing to be an athlete," Alexandria explained. "One does not burn the candles at both ends if one hopes to maintain physical stamina."

"Perhaps that's what's become of Oliver," Augustus suggested. "He may have simply toddled off up to bed."

"I saw him with Xan not long ago," Tim inserted. "They were in the library."

"Your Cousin Oliver?" Alexandria questioned.

"I suspect Alexandria finds Oliver provocatively handsome," Letty commented. "She's asked about him, haven't you, Alexandria?"

"I find all the Phenwick men I've met particularly handsome," Alexandria replied.

"I say, Oliver was off speaking with that Prussian whatever he is," Charlie announced as if it was important.

Ursala Phenwick joined the young people. "Why isn't anyone dancing?"

"I hadn't planned to dance," Letty said. "We do enough of that every day."

"Not ballroom dancing, I trust," Ursala added. "Well, my husband is busy gadding about and I would like to dance."

"I would be honored if you would dance with me, Cousin Ursala," Augustus said after Tim had nudged him.

Ursala allowed Augustus to lead her to the floor.

"Would you like to go for a stroll, Cousin Letitia?" Tim asked. "The moon is bright, and strolling isn't near as strenuous as dancing is."

Letty thought for a moment, curiously eying Alexandria and Charlie. "Yes, that would be pleasant."

Alexandria asked Charlie to get her a glass of water. While she waited for him to return, she observed Oliver go back upstairs and Xan step to where Peggy Phenwick was standing in a small group of people.

"I feel as if more is going on here tonight than meets the eye," Peggy commented when she and Xan had moved away from the others. "And what ever has happened to Oliver? I thought he would be the life of the party here."

Xan guided Peggy to an isolated spot not far from where Alexandria was waiting for Charlie to return. "There are any number of things going on here tonight, dearest Peggy. As to Oliver, well, he's preoccupied and about to venture into a highly dangerous and secret mission."

"How's that?" Peggy questioned.

"Not so loud, Cousin, or the secret is liable to be out."

"You didn't tell me any of this."

Xan smiled toward Alexandria. "Let us go where no one is present. Be warned, I can tell you very little."

Chapter Eighteen

THE PHENWICK HOUSE was extraordinarily quiet all of Sunday morning. The party had lasted late and even the servants were permitted to rest after their late-hour cleaning and straightening after the gala occasion. The only person to rise early was Letty, who was so accustomed to doing so that she found it impossible to sleep after the sun shone behind the blinds in her room. Not wanting to disturb Alexandria, she tiptoed from bed, freshened herself and dressed before she quietly left the room.

The garden, while not enormously large, was far more spacious than most gardens in that section of London. Manicured to garden show perfection, the landscaping was most impressive, with rows of hedges and brightly colored flowers, a lily pond and statuary. Sun glistened off the surface of the water where the fountain had not been turned on. Sparrows chattered and splashed, quibbled and seemed to be playing bird games. Letty watched with curious interest, and tried not to think of Moss Grove and the interminable mornings she had gathered eggs.

Standing by the trellised rose arbor was what appeared to be a blurred figure of a man. Letty's eyesight was usually quite good, but for a moment she thought her vision was playing tricks on her. Rationalizing that it was probably the gardener, she turned away and went toward the lily pond, where she sat on a wrought-iron bench and watched the large carp swimming beneath the surface.

Several minutes later, Letty glanced again at the rose arbor to observe that the figure of the man seemed to be as it had been. Now she could see that the man was well dressed and not in the uniform of a gardener. A moment later he appeared to be coming toward her. Still she could not make out his features as a feeling of apprehension came over her.

"Do you not recognize me in an English garden setting?"

"It's you! But what are you doing here in London?" Letty asked when she was able to contain her surprise.

"You'll discover that I appear and disappear in the most unusual places and at the most singular times. Time and space, as you know it, have little to do with me, and quite the other way around."

"What brings you here?" Letty asked.

"Simply keeping a watch over my latest choices."

"Choices? Plural?" Letty asked. "I declare, Adam, you are certainly puzzling."

"That's part of my nature. A little intrigue helps fend off boredom. And, being enigmatic, I won't explain 'plural.'"

"In that case, I won't ask." Letty laughed. "Since time and space have little to do with you and the other way around, can you see into the future?"

"I can in a sense, but I certainly wouldn't want to spoil your enjoyment of playing out the course of events by telling you about it. Dear heart, that's what makes life interesting, seeing it unfold one day at a time."

"Do you know what's become of Jeremiah? I can't help but think about him," Letty said.

"Jeremiah will surprise you one day."

"You're being evasive, aren't you?"

"I do hope so."

"Then why have you come?"

"Simply to let you know I'm near by. I won't be far."

"Adam?" Letty questioned as the image seemed to dissolve before her eyes.

As Letty ruminated on what had just transpired, she wondered if it hadn't occurred simply through her imagination. Yet she would like to believe that there was more substance to Adam than that. The thought amused her. In a way it was comforting to know that, imagination or not, Adam Truff was still around her.

A breeze came up and with it several leaves blew across the lawn. Among the leaves was a white object which caught her attention. Going to it, Letty discovered it was a piece of partly burned paper upon which was Oliver Phenwick's name. As she studied it, she presumed it was some sort of identification document.

"What's got your curiosity?" Alexandria asked as she walked up behind Letty.

"Merely a piece of paper I found blowing with the leaves." She handed it to Alexandria.

"What a silly thing to capture your interest!" Alexandria commented and handed it back to Letty.

"Perhaps. But why do you imagine it had been discarded and burned this way?" Letty persisted.

"I can't begin to guess the motivation behind certain happenings." Alexandria adjusted her lavender morning dress and curled her legs beneath her on the grass beside the lily pond. "I'm surprised to see you up so early today. This is supposed to be a holiday."

"I can never sleep late in the day," Letty replied as she folded the piece of paper and tucked it into her bodice. "At the risk of letting the household think I was a bit on the balmy side, I was contemplating doing a few of my dance exercises right here in the garden."

"I limbered up in the room. However, I've come to believe that one needs a certain holiday from dancing, too." Alexandria plucked a blade of grass and ran it over her exotically-shaped lips. "I hope we will return early to Somerset. It's pleasant enough here, but I don't like to spend excessive time socializing."

"All work and no play is liable to make Alexandria a dull dancer," Letty teased.

"Or a great *artiste*," Alexandria returned. "I feel that I am already technically skilled as a dancer, now I must examine the spirit of what I am doing. Skill is acquired, learned, if you will, while the matter of interpretation comes from the very soul. Pavlova dances with her soul, as does Nijinsky. It is that quality of the soul showing through which sets them apart from other dancers. I've seen a depth of spirit in your interpretations, Letitia, as I have been told about myself."

"I never really thought about it like that," Letty replied. "Fact is, I don't even know what my soul is."

Alexandria rose and went to throw her arms about Letty. "You don't need a definition, Letitia, you simply have it—and there's no way that you can keep it from shining through. I predict that you will become a great artist—that we *both* will."

Many of the guests remained at the home of Daniel Charles Phenwick and family, and some were destined for extended stays. Tim and Charles drove Letty and Alexandria back to Somerset in the mid-afternoon. The Phenwick men offered to treat the young ladies to an early repast, but both declined, saying that they had eaten far more than usual during their brief stay in London.

"When shall we see you again?" Tim asked when it came time to separate from Letty and Alexandria.

"You'll be starting your new teaching position soon, won't you?" Letty asked.

"Shortly, yes. But I'll have weekends," Tim replied. "The four of us could go to the country for a picnic and boating. I know some marvelous places. And we wouldn't even have to go into London. It would be jolly fun, rather."

"We shall see." Letty smiled sweetly, but she had difficulty disguising the fact that she was anxious to say good-bye.

"I'll drop you a line when I get situated at school," Tim assured her. "And perhaps I'll motor out here from time to time. I promise not to make a nuisance of myself. I say, Charlie, old man, shouldn't we be getting on our way?"

"Rather." Charlie gazed deeply into Alexandria's eyes. "I've immensely enjoyed this weekend with you, Miss Muzakova."

"It has been most interesting," Alexandria said in a husky voice that seemed to have an invitation underlining it.

The young ladies went to the room they shared without speaking. Once within it, Alexandria removed as much of her clothing as she could to be comfortable. Letty changed into a dressing gown and sat in the window seat with her knees up. She stared dreamily out the window.

"What are you thinking about, Letitia?" Alexandria questioned. "You seem a million miles away."

"I may be."

"Contemplating the genteel handsomeness of Timothy Phenwick?"

"Doing what?" Letty blushed. Then she smiled. "He is remarkably handsome, isn't he? So are his brothers."

"Yes, I noticed." Alexandria stretched and did a few limbering exercises. "Charles has an amazing sensuality about him."

"They call him Charlie."

"Yes, I know. But I prefer to call him Charles. It sounds far more dignified. It strikes me as being singular that you have such a soft, slow American accent and your cousins sound so British."

"Naturally so. I was born and raised in the Southern part of the United States and my cousins were raised in

180

London," Letty returned, still somewhat absently gazing from the window. "We're not closely related, you know."

"Your family is in the shipping industry, isn't it?" Alexandria questioned after she had made several other movements and was presently standing on point.

"Part of the Phenwick family is in shipping," Letty said. "Not my side of it. Why do you ask?"

"Merely curiosity." Alexandria twirled and used the back of a chair to support herself as she stood on the toes of one foot and lifted the other leg to form a perfect right angle to her body. "Did you see these letters here on the table?"

"Letters?" Letty turned her attention back into the room. "What letters?"

Alexandria scooped up the two envelopes. "Only one is for you. The other is for me." She danced toward Letty and handed her the one. "Mine is from my mother. It's addressed from Paris. And yours?"

Letty opened it. "From Jeremiah in Moscow."

"Jeremiah?"

"Jeremiah James."

"Oh, the black person."

"My best friend."

Alexandria continued her exercises as she danced away from Letty and she read her letter.

Jeremiah's penmanship was familiar to Letty, since it was very much like her own. She had taught him and he had copied her every pen-stroke. She smiled.

Dear Miss Letty:

I have been in Moscow nearly two weeks and I have done nothing but dance the whole time. Every day that I dance, the stronger I become and the more endurance I have. Worth says I am progressing well.

Worth has become a very good friend and companion, as well as my patron. He sits in at many of my classes and often when I practice by myself.

Last week Worth invited Sergei Diaghilev to our apartment for supper—Diaghilev and his young protégé, Leonide Massine. Worth insisted that I dance for them, and they were honestly impressed with my performance. The following night we were invited to a performance by Massine and a few other dancers. Mr. Diaghilev whispered to me that I had as much promise as Leonide.

Worth believes that I have far greater potential than what Mr. Diaghilev suggested. But I do believe Worth is prejudiced about me and my talent.

If you are wondering about this letter and my vocabulary, I am learning many things. However, Worth has helped me with this and I have simply recopied after he made corrections.

I am deeply devoted to Worth for all that he is doing for me. I believe you will be amazed when you see me again and how well I have improved.

I have seen little of Moscow, but that is unimportant. Worth says that I am a natural talent and that I have the soul of a dancer and that dancing must be first and foremost in my life. I agree with him.

I must close for now, but I promise I will write to you again, once you write to me.

Sincerely,
Jeremiah.

Letty reread the letter twice. Initially, she was thrilled by the progress Jeremiah was making. Secondarily, she began reading something into the written words, and wondered how many of them were Jeremiah's and how many were actually those of Worth Bassett. The man was greatly influencing Jeremiah, she could well understand that, and she wanted to believe that it was solely for his own good. Still there was a question of doubt.

"What is it, Letitia?" Alexandria asked as she reclined on the bed practically unclad. "Is anything wrong?"

"No, everything is fine. Jeremiah is progressing beautifully, and he seems to be quite content," Letty replied as she folded the letter. "The contents don't sound like Jeremiah's words, but he assured me that Worth Bassett had helped him with it. He is devoted to Mr. Bassett."

Alexandria remained in a reclining position. "Your friend is well off in the company of men. Male dancers are a breed unto themselves. Men can best teach men dancers because a woman does not know how to instruct them to increase their strength. Your Jeremiah is most fortunate to have a patron such as Worth Bassett."

"I wonder."

"How's that?"

"Nothing." Letty rose and went to run a cold wet cloth over her face and arms. She turned her thoughts from Jeremiah and considered Tim Phenwick. What feelings did she have about him? And were they honest feelings? He was certainly most attentive and patronizing. Furthermore, he had taken every opportunity he could to make physical contact with her, touching here and there, letting his hand gently brush over her shoulder, pressing his thigh softly against hers as they sat in the automobile while driving back from London. She was impressed with him in a favorable way. When her thoughts began to explore fantasy projections about him, she forced herself to put such images from her mind. That sort of speculation was unfamiliar to her and she questioned why that had appeared.

"My mother is considering marrying a wealthy French count," Alexandria announced. "But she is only *considering* it. Knowing Mama, she won't take any drastic steps until she is certain of the man and what she can get out of him. Mama is quite young looking—we resemble each other—and she has a way of attracting the most unusual men. Are you listening to me, Letitia?" She sat up. "Letitia?"

"What is it? Oh, I'm sorry. I was deep in thought."

"So I see." Alexandria laughed, which was something she rarely did. "Who is it you're thinking about? Jeremiah? Or is it Timothy Phenwick?"

Letty excused herself to go bathe.

Chapter Nineteen

DURING THE REMAINDER OF SUMMER Letty and Alexandria accelerated their long hours of balletic study, dancing until, exhausted, they collapsed early at night. Both displayed tremendous promise and progress. The remarkable thing that was absent between them was a sense of competition with each other, whereas there constantly appeared to be that among the other dancers at the Academy. The instructors commented about their attitudes and agreed that it was most unusual to see two young lady students who had become such good friends.

"We simply have such a close rapport with each other," Alexandria explained, "because we love each other as sisters—more than just sisters, rather as if we were identical twins."

Letty wasn't sure her definition of their relationship was quite that, but she agreed that Alexandria's appraisal was not far from wrong.

Sundays were the one day of the week when the young ladies would permit Charlie and Tim Phenwick to call on them; and, if they felt up to it, the four would go for short outings. The Phenwick brothers were both conservative in their attitudes and manners, properly polite and considerate. Far from being stuffy, they were nevertheless reserved and considerate. However, it progressively became apparent that Tim was developing a romantic attitude and an emotional response to Letty; this became far more apparent to Alexandria than it did to the principal involved.

"Timothy is most attentive to you," Alexandria remarked one Sunday in mid-September. They had returned from a motor trip to Bath where they had wandered about the ancient Roman ruins of that extraordinary city.

"Charlie is attentive to you, too," Letty countered.

"Charles is sweet in his way," Alexandria returned. "And, I must admit that he is a perfect escort for me at this time because he is so basically passive. I enjoy his company. But I cannot say that Timothy appears to be as passive as his brother."

"Tim is indulgent and patronizing," Letty admitted, "but he never oversteps the bounds of propriety."

"Sometimes I come to the conclusion that women are not so much seduced by men as men are seduced, inadvertently, of course, by women. I've no doubt that if either of us was so inclined, we could force an intimate situation with the Phenwick men."

"What a thing to say!"

"I'm perfectly serious. Certainly men are eager, but I believe we cause them to be stimulated to action," Alexandria observed. "That, of course, is not true of all men. There are certain of them who are constitutionally different. They are self-centered egotists, who really have no feelings or consideration for the feelings of others. They are brute animals. Fortunately, neither Charles nor Timothy fall in that category. We are most fortunate, considering our objectives and our goals."

"You sometimes amaze me, Alexandria. You are so worldly-wise and far more analytically aware of what is going on. I admit I react with my emotions; and were

I to do so to an extreme, I could well not have control over the situation."

"Letitia, do you actually know what your priorities are?" Alexandria asked as she began her exercises, stretching forward one leg supported on the back of a straight chair and reaching for her toes.

"My priorities?"

"Yes, your priorities in life." Hands wrapped about her foot, Alexandria held that position as she spoke. "To me, first things must always come first, and the first consideration in my life is dancing, my career. I do not criticize my mother for her life as a courtesan, as it were, but I never wish to have myself put into such a position. I could never condescend to pleasing a man or any number of men as a means of making my way. I have to first and foremost be true to my ideals, my own sense of moral values, and that which I like to think as my appointment with destiny."

"Appointment with destiny?" Letitia had begun her exercises, but she stopped to gaze curiously at her friend. "You contradict yourself. One minute you say you believe you are largely responsible for your own destiny, that you create it, and now you speak as if your destiny was some preordained matter."

"Not so." Alexandria stretched back, moved her body from side to side and returned to gripping her foot. "I believe I set forth my own goals, make the plans and strive toward them, and therefore my destiny is given a direction. But I do believe there is a spiritual force, call it God, if you like, that guides me toward that destiny. It is to that end with which I have an appointment. I have confused you, haven't I?"

"Quite a bit."

"I believe you will come to understand in time," Alexandria replied after again pulling back and moving from side to side. She put the other leg up and repeated the exercise.

"What about outside influences like—well, say like someone like Charlie and any romantic interest he might have in you?" Letty asked. "Couldn't that change the course of your destiny?"

"It could, if I allowed it," Alexandria returned. She bobbed her head forward until it went to her knee. "But I like to think that I am in control and, therefore, attract as much attention and interest from Charles—or any other man—as I care to allow."

Letty shook her head. "I declare, I simply can't understand all of that. You are a mystery, Alexandria."

"I *do* hope so," Alexandria said, her face still at her knee. "And I trust that I will always remain so . . . at least to the outside world."

After their exercises the girls bathed, then each massaged the other where their muscles were extremely taut. The closeness that had developed between them was beautiful, pure and loving in a kind of spiritual affection. The greatest thing between them was the fact that they truly cared for the well-being of each other, and for the progress they were each making with their dancing.

In mid-October Georges LeVeque returned from Paris with Madame Ivanovich and Vladimir Popkin. Both Roselle and Popkin appeared miraculously rejuvenated, working and living in an artistic environment that agreed with them. Popkin still continued to drink, but not to the excess he had done while in Savannah.

Roselle greeted Letty with open arms and explained that she had accomplished much while in Paris. "It was so good to be back among my own kind again. I was such a fool to isolate myself in Savannah. Still, I have been thinking about that, and I wonder if the reason I had gone there in the first place—I mean the real reason—was to discover your talent, Letitia."

"You make me blush, Madame Ivanovich."

"You mustn't. I am sincere. And once I've caught my breath, you will dance for me. I want to see the progress you've made," Roselle stated. She didn't seem to lean as heavily on her cane as she had done in the past. "It is most important to me."

Alexandria and I have learned a sort of *pas de deux*," Letty said. "Would you care to see that?"

"Alexandria Muzakova?" Roselle questioned. She frowned before she smiled. "Very well, you will let me see it."

Later that day Letty arranged to use a rehearsal hall at the Academy and delivered a copy of the piano score for Popkin to look over.

In tights and well-worn tutus, Alexandria and Letty performed for Madame Ivanovich. Their movement and timing was perfect as they danced in remarkable unison. In the midst of the number, each girl did a solo turn before they came together, hands joined to complete the work.

"I am most impressed," Roselle commented at the conclusion of the piece. "Most impressed, indeed. You show important improvement. I can make no further comment about it. However, I wish for you each to relax briefly and repeat it for me in half an hour."

"Repeat it?" Alexandria questioned.

"Not only for me," Roselle assured her. "I am impressed enough that you two can audition with what you have shown me."

"Audition?"

"I will say no more. Prepare yourselves."

Letty and Alexandria went to a small room to wait, continuously doing stretching exercises to keep their muscles in limber condition. Although they speculated about what the situation might be, Alexandria convinced her friend that they should not think about anything but doing a perfect job of dancing. It was unimportant who would be watching their performance; the essential thing was to put forth their best effort and concentrate only on that.

"But what if—"

"Don't even mention what you are thinking, Letitia," Alexandria warned. "Think only of perfection."

"What is perfection?"

"It is not only technical accuracy," Alexandria explained, "but it is also projecting into your dance that which is in your soul. Let the gods of dance create through you."

"Sometimes I don't understand you at all, Alexandria. I declare, you do confuse me."

"Don't be confused by anything. Stop a moment and think of what perfection means to you." Alexandria stood arms akimbo. "What is the first thing that comes into your mind when I say the word 'perfection'?" She snapped her fingers. "Quickly, what is it?"

"A rose."

"A rose?"

"A red rose with the most pungent, sweet spicy fragrance I've ever known." Letty recalled a morning in a park in Savannah when she was taking eggs to be sold.

"Then continue to think of that rose and that you and your dancing are as perfect as it is," Alexandria said.

When the young ladies returned to the rehearsal hall, their attention briefly went to Madame Ivanovich, Georges LeVeque, Laura Donnally and Tiziano Spolini, who were all seated.

"My legs are trembling," Letty whispered as Popkin stepped to the piano and flexed his fingers before he put them to the keys.

"Don't let them," Alexandria returned. "Think only of that scarlet rose of perfection."

Vladimir Popkin began to play and moments later the girls were dancing. As they did, they both seemed to be surrounded by the overpowering fragrance of roses. If possible, their interpretation was even better than it had been when they first danced for Madame Ivanovich.

At the conclusion the room was held in stark silence with the exception of the aspirant breathing of the dancers. It was Laura who broke the perfect stillness with gloved applause, but her clapping ceased with a reprimanding look from Tiziano.

Madame Ivanovich nodded to Letty in an indication that they were excused.

"Were we as bad as all that?" Letty asked as she and Alexandria went back to the small room, the door closed behind them.

"One thing I've learned about people in the arts is that they are not to be judged from their immediate apparent reactions to situations. There is a tendency to be dramatic—if that indeed is what it is." She hugged Letty. "Rest assured, we each did our best. It's done. Simply forget about it."

"Forget about it?" Letty all but shrieked. "How can I possibly?"

"But you must. Good or bad, whatever has been done has been done, and it can't in any way be changed," Alexandria said. She watched Letty's confused expression. "Now would be an excellent time to go for a motor ride with the Phenwick brothers."

"Alexandria! How can you be so calm?"

"It takes practice, Letitia, much practice." She breathed deeply and sighed. "We had better change into our dresses."

When Letty and Alexandria emerged from the dressing room nearly twenty minutes later, where they had not been interrupted, they were met by Georges LeVeque and Tiziano Spolini.

"Vladimir Popkin has accompanied the ladies to a small café nearby," Tiziano said. "We will join them there."

"Our dancing—?" Letty questioned impetuously.

"Your dancing?" Tiziano raised an eyebrow.

Georges LeVeque smiled for the first time. "Being cold is one thing, Tiziano, being icy is quite another. Rest assured we found your dancing most interesting and accomplished."

"Extremely accomplished," Tiziano added as he seemed to thaw. "But there is a problem."

"What is it?" Letty asked.

Alexandria nudged her in hopes of keeping her from continuing with the interruptions.

Georges LeVeque cleared his throat. "The fact is, we are seeking one replacement for the company—only *one*."

"Then you must choose Alexandria," Letty quickly said. "So much of what I have learned, not about technique, but about performing, she has taught me."

"Letitia is being modest," Alexandria inserted.

"I will be perfectly frank with you," Georges continued. "We were deeply impressed by each of you, but we are faced with a financial situation, which simply will not permit us to hire both of you. And since Thomas Phenwick has been so generous in his support, naturally we feel that we must select Letitia."

"No! That is all wrong!" Letitia exclaimed.

"But facts must be faced, Letitia," Alexandria said.

"I won't dance if you are not to be included," Letty returned. "Since I am getting financial assistance from the Phenwicks, couldn't I simply continue to do that and work without additional remuneration?"

"We will be traveling about," Georges stated. "The expense of an additional person must be considered. To please Madame Ivanovich as well as your family, mam'selle, we must select you."

Alexandria forced a smile. "He is right, Letitia."

Letty moved away from where the others were standing. "No!" She turned around. "Let me beg of you not to make a choice at this time. I don't know what I can do, but I will do something. If only Tommy and Evelyn were here in London now. Please, Monsieur LeVeque, postpone making a decision until later."

"Later? But time is of the essence."

"Two days. Please give me two days," Letty pleaded.

Georges LeVeque drew Tiziano aside. Alexandria went to where Letty was standing.

"What can you do in two days?" Alexandria asked.

"I don't know. I simply don't know, but I will do something," Letty assured her.

"Very well, mam'selle, two days," Georges said. "Now we must join the others."

Chapter Twenty

AFTER SEEING THE REACTION of Tiziano Spolini and Georges LeVeque over the audition of both Letty and Alexandria, Laura Donnally decided to take matters in hand. She went directly to Daniel Charles and Louise Phenwick and through them and their friends, she was able to practically double the backing money for Geroges LeVeque's ballet company. She had never before undertaken a project in which she had obtained such rapid results. It pleased her, too, because she didn't have to go directly to her husband to put up financial backing, which gave her a sense of independence she had never previously had.

Within a week arrangements were made for Letty and Alexandria to go to Paris with LeVeque, Spolini, Madame Ivanovich and Vladimir Popkin. Laura would travel there once she had completed her money-raising mission in London.

"I don't mean to criticize you, Cousin Laura," Louise Phenwick said on the afternoon Letty crossed the Channel to Calais, France, "but it has been brought to my attention several times that you appear to be having a rather close relationship with Tiziano Spolini."

"It has been brought to your attention? By whom?" Laura shot, unable to disguise rising anger.

"By your very actions, dear," Louise returned. She tried to be as tactful as possible, but she had heard chatter about her American cousin and she wished to draw it to her attention before word somehow got back to Pruman Donnally about his wife's behavior.

"I find Signor Spolini to be an extremely interesting and artistic person," Laura returned, her annoyance still bubbling. "I am rapidly becoming a patroness of the arts, and have every right to associate with whomever I please."

"I do not dispute that in the least, Laura," Louise replied. "Discretion, however, is sometimes a most valuable ally."

Laura attempted to cover her tracks, but she was aware that she had shown her hand. She decided to take another approach. "Louise, my husband and I have been married fourteen years. They have basically been good years—but not the best. Perhaps it would have been different if we had had children as you and Daniel Charles have. I love Pruman in my own way, as I'm certain he loves me. Still, I fear we have grown too used to each other. There has been love these past few years, but little romance, if you know what I mean. And Pruman spends a great deal of time traveling. I don't dare speculate about what sort of adventures or misadventures he encounters while away. I try to put that from my mind."

"Do you mean to imply that this affair with Signor Spolini is *not* the first such liaison that you have had?" Louise questioned.

"I don't care to answer that question. It isn't really important."

"And what are your feeling for Signor Spolini?"

"My feelings?"

"Is he nothing more than a physical encounter?" Louise asked.

Laura clenched her fist as if she were seeking something to hit. Then she sighed, shook her head and formed an almost pathetic expression on her pretty face. "No, Louise. At first that is all I anticipated that it would be. But I fear I've foolishly let my emotions get out of hand."

"Are you in love with him?"

"I—I don't honestly know," Laura replied, now trying to control embarrassment. "Tiziano is so many things that Pruman isn't. He represents excitement, the arts, the magic of adventure and I love his dear eccentric friends and associates."

"Has it occurred to you that love may have blinded you?" Louise seemingly gave her attention to a bouquet of chrysanthemums that needed rearranging, allowing Laura time to express her reaction. "Artists and people in an artistic ambience are notorious for their peculiarities, *sub rosa* plots and counterplots. I wonder if you have only seen one small side of Signor Spolini —the only aspect of him that he has wanted you to know."

"Meaning?"

"I really can say no more than that," Louise said. "But it strikes me peculiarly that you have dived into raising so much backing money for Signor Spolini and Monsieur LeVeque. Is it possible that you have been manipulated by your unbridled emotions?"

"Are you suggesting that Tiziano has used me?" Laura fired.

"You wouldn't be the first lady of wealth and society who has been so used. History repeats itself." Louise turned from the chrysanthemums. "Believe me, dearest cousin, I am not being in the least bit unsympathetic. I merely tell you this—and without grounds of justification—because I have known others who have found themselves in uncomfortable positions with people of the art world."

"How well have you know of such incidences?" Laura asked.

Louise moved away from her and went to a large, ornate, gilt-framed mirror and stared curiously at her own reflection. "Quite well, I reluctantly admit."

"Louise? *You?*"

Louise stared at Laura's reflection through the mirror. Her smile was dim. "And Daniel Charles and I *do* have children."

"Oh, dear."

"You needn't say 'oh, dear' like that." Louise turned back. "I fortunately have a most understanding husband. He's a bit Victorian at times in certain conservative attitudes. We sensibly discussed the situation and Daniel Charles ultimately admitted that he is not without an untarnished past—and for that matter, I do have some questions about his present. Still, we have come to an agreement, an arrangement of sorts, and have got on remarkable terms with each other and our life together. The fact is, our feelings of love for each other are far greater now than they've ever been in the past. The novelty of romance has a way of wearing thin after a few years."

"I had no idea."

"Nor should you have had. I would not have revealed this to you, Laura, were I not concerned for your present situation," Louise said. "My father, Dr. Augustus Ornby of Vienna, has dealt with human emotions and mental conditions most of his professional life. To some he is an authority. He very sensibly advised me to relinquish any feelings of guilt about myself. Life is, in reality, a very short span, and one should do one's best to be happy while living it. I want you to be happy, not unhappy or hurt. That is all, Laura. Please know that you have me to come to should problems arise."

Laura stood as if in a trance, unable to move. She didn't want to think about the possibility that she might be setting herself up for disaster; still she had been around long enough that she knew that such could be likely. Suddenly she ran to Louise and threw her arms around her, remaining in that position for several minutes without speaking.

During the next three months while Laura was in Paris, Tiziano Spolini's time was largely occupied with preparations for the coming ballet season, wherein he worked closely with Georges LeVeque. Tiziano handled much of the business aspect of the company and fancied himself another Sergei Diaghilev. As a result, he spent little time with Laura and more and more time with his artistic friends. She tried to understand. It was difficult.

1914

Letty displayed extraordinary promise as did Alexandria Muzakova and they were both given prominent roles in the fledgling company of dancers. In some instances they were given the same parts so that they could dance alternating performances. It was a big risk putting such basically inexperienced young ladies in essential roles, but Laura Donnally had been responsible for insisting that they be given every opportunity. Georges LeVeque complied with her wishes, at Tiziano's urging, but protected himself by having each of the ballerinas covered by other dancers. The opening performance was scheduled in Amsterdam the first week of March.

By the last week of January, word came that Worth Bassett would be in Paris, where he had scheduled a recital performance for his protégé, and he insisted that both LeVeque and Spolini be present for the grand event, with the suggestion that the entire company be in the audience to lend moral support. The enticement was the fact that Diaghilev was also to be in attendance.

Over the months Letty had received several letters

from Jeremiah James, all of which had been edited and embellished by Worth Bassett. More and more they sounded less and less like the young black boy with whom she had been raised in Savannah, and increasingly like Worth Bassett. Alexandria twice made the comment that it seemed as if Jeremiah had become possessed by his patron and had been infused with the older man's personality. There was no doubt that Jeremiah was intelligent and a fast learner, able to grasp ideas and mimic mannerisms. If Worth was clever, and indeed he was, the young man could quite conceivably become that which Worth designed.

The concert hall was relatively small and intimate. Since it was not meant to be a money-raising situation, every seat would be occupied by members of the dance world as well as patrons, artists, and students. Such an audience could be extremely difficult to play before, but, by the same token, if the performer was good, they could be highly supportive and far more enthusiastic than a paying crowd.

Laura purchased a new gown for Letty to wear to the recital, one which was designed especially for her. She was radiant in soft blue satin and Laura's chinchilla fur-lined cape. Alexandria was not as elaborately decked out, but she made a striking appearance in a pink brocade creation which Laura had worn several times before and had had altered for the occasion.

Jeremiah was accompanied only by the piano artistry of Worth Bassett, who played everything from memory. The Russian school of ballet was apparent in Jeremiah's style and technique. His artistry was close to perfection, dramatic, moving, totally impressive and won the standing acclaim of all who had been privileged to witness him.

"He is perfectly marvelous," Diaghilev was heard to exclaim during the intermission. "I have never before seen a young dancer progress as rapidly as he has. I must have him!"

"We may be too late," Tiziano said to Georges

LeVeque. "Diaghilev is spouting superlatives in all directions. Unfortunately, he has more to offer than we do."

"Ah, but Worth is our friend," Georges countered.

"He's also become very thick with Diaghilev."

"We have one trump, Tiziano."

"And that is?"

"Jeremiah's deep friendship for Letitia Phenwick."

"I fear it will take more than that," Tiziano replied. "We shall see."

The second half of the program was even more impressive than the first part. Jeremiah's leaps and suspensions were enough to surpass Nijinsky who was then in his prime. The audience applauded until their hands were raw and aching as time after time he topped his previous exhibitions.

Collapsing with utter exhaustion, Jeremiah retreated to the dressing room and asked not to be disturbed until he had rested from the intense exertion. Worth Bassett stood outside the room and accepted the cacophony of praise and adulation of the throng that had come backstage to give congratulations.

"Amazing, absolutely amazing," Roselle Ivanovich uttered as she stood away from the crowd. "And to think how foolish I was not to accept him as a student in Savannah because of his race. Yet it would have been madness of me to have taken the boy into my studio as Letitia had begged me to do."

"You must not chastise yourself, Roselle," Vladimir Popkin said. "First, you could not have known of his tremendous talent. Second, my little one, you know as well as I the climate in Savannah, and I am not referring to the weather."

Worth announced that there was to be a reception party later that night in the backroom of a large restaurant near the theater, which everyone was invited to attend. Displeased that they could not immediately congratulate Jeremiah in person, but contenting themselves with the eventuality of meeting him, the enthusiastic throng finally disembarked from the stage. Still their enthusiasm would not be quelled.

Letty waited alone, standing in the shadows. Alexandria wanted to remain with her, but Letty begged her friend to go with Madame Ivanovich and Vladimir.

"Ah, Mam'selle Phenwick," Worth said, acknowledging her presence, "you have waited after the others have gone."

"Jeremiah is a very special friend of mine, as you well know," Letty said.

"Jeremiah is *now* an extremely special friend of mine," Worth replied in a haughty, arrogant tone that he was known to use. "It would be best if you were to go to the restaurant and see him there with the others."

"No. You don't understand," Letty protested.

"No, dear child, I fear it is you who does not understand," Worth stated. "Jeremiah has made a metamorphic transition. And after tonight, I am certain the metamorphosis will be even more profound. Diaghilev himself wants Jeremiah. He can quite possibly become a greater celebrity than Nijinsky in his greatest hour. The color of his skin makes him absolutely unique and without peer."

"I believed in Jeremiah before he ever knew what a pair of ballet shoes were," Letty said softly. "Something inside of me told me to teach him to dance. Jeremiah may be your extremely special friend, Mr. Bassett, but we were raised together. Please permit me to see him."

Worth braced himself. "Not until he arrives at the party."

The dressing room door opened. Perspiration was still oozing down Jeremiah's face. He stood in a partially gaping Japanese kimono, which clung to his still liquid body. "Miss Letty." He held his arms open and she went to him.

"You were wonderful tonight, Jeremiah, just wonderful."

"I done did it, didn't I?" Jeremiah said. "Don't correct

201

me, I know what I said." He stepped back to appraise her. "I've never seen you look so much like a queen Miss Letty, never."

"*Miss* Letty?" Worth questioned sarcastically. "This isn't Savannah, Jeremiah, and you don't have to be subservient to any white person."

"Pay no mind to him, Miss Letty, he's jus' 'cited 'bout all dis fuss dey's a-makin'," Jeremiah commented. "I'se still de same ol' me deep down inside. Ain't dat de truth!"

"Stop it! Stop it, Jeremiah!" Worth shrieked. "I'll not have you put yourself down this way. Don't ever let me hear you talk like that again."

Letty kissed Jeremiah on the cheek. "We'll see each other at the party."

Worth pushed Jeremiah gently back into the dressing room after Letty walked across the stage and out of sight.

Chapter Twenty-one

AS IF A NEW STAR HAD BEEN DISCOVERED in the early evening sky, Jeremiah James's successful première recital received the positive acclaim of critics and audience alike. By the following day, those who had not been in attendance at the spectacular performance began asking about when he would next appear. Worth Bassett was besieged with inquiries about Jeremiah; writers and reporters begged to do special stories on the phenomenal sensation of the dance world. Artists and photographers wanted to create his likeness—from caricatures to formal poses—of the young man who surely must have descended from Negro royalty. Those who had reviewed his performance were so ecstatic with their praise that no less a conclusion could be reached.

Every offer that Georges LeVeque made, Sergei Diaghilev topped, the famed impresario who had discovered the likes of Vaslav Nijinsky. LeVeque bargained on the grounds of long-term friendship with Worth Bassett, Diaghilev bartered with his very reputation at stake. When the three men finally came together in the same room, Worth managed to finagle an unheard of arrangement whereby Jeremiah would be exclusively handled by Diaghilev with the exception of a twelve-week annual period when the young artist would dance with the LeVeque Ballet. But Diaghilev managed to hold certain options and stipulations that might be difficult for LeVeque to comply with. Still the agreement seemed to resolve a sticky situation, and all but guaranteed the certain fame and success of the young man in question.

The same day following the recital, despite Worth's protests to the contrary, Jeremiah kept the luncheon date he had made the day before with Letty. They dined in a remote, out-of-the-way café.

"I can't believe it, Jeremiah, I simply can't believe it," Letty exclaimed as she greeted her old friend. "Every newspaper in Paris is proclaiming your fame."

"I find it all so very difficult to believe," Jeremiah replied, his handsome bronze face aglow, his eyes bright and wide with incredulous amazement. "Worth told me how it would happen, but I didn't really take him seriously."

"How very much you've changed!" Letty said a short while later. "I hear Worth Bassett in every word you say. Is it possible that such a transformation can have taken place in such a short span of time?"

"You, too, have changed, Miss Letty," Jeremiah observed.

"Me? Well, I've worked hard at it," she admitted.

"And you don't think that I haven't?" Jeremiah laughed.

"I always knew you were intelligent, far more so than anyone in Savannah realized. I knew that you could learn rapidly, but I never dreamed—"

"Worth Bassett is a remarkable man, quite extraordinary," Jeremiah explained. "He's a hard taskmaster, as he has told me countless times over these past months. My life became completely dominated by him. I've been his private student practically twenty-four hours a day, every day. But the secret is that I wanted to learn, I wanted to excel, and I was determined to do so. When I wasn't dancing or doing my exercises, I was forced to read and spend hours in intellectual conversation with him. Then, from time to time, when he thought I had made noticeable progress, he would arrange for me to be in the company of other learned people wherein I was expected to hold my own in rhetoric. It was often commented upon that I sounded like a carbon copy of Worth himself—and is it any wonder?"

"How do you actually feel about Mr. Bassett?" Letty asked.

"How do I feel about him?" Again he laughed. "He refers to himself as my Pygmalion." He smiled again before the flicker of a frown crossed his face. "I greatly admire Worth for all he had done and is certain to do for me in time to come. He has filled me with ideals and dreams I could have never dreamed myself. I allowed myself to be clay in his hands and he has molded me."

"I, too, have lived among dancers and people of the ballet world," Letty said as she watched Jeremiah's expression. "I have heard many stories about the eccentricities and singularities of men like Worth Bassett, certainly tales of Diaghilev and his relationship with Nijinsky as well as the speculations about why the impresario and Nijinsky are no longer associated."

Jeremiah put his large hand atop Letty's much smaller hand as it rested on the table. Long artistic fingers wrapped around hers. "Had I been born a white man in a white man's world, perhaps my life would have been completely different. I cannot say that for a fact. But I was born a black man in a white man's world. I've tasted of the gross injustices of the echoes of slavery, injustices brought about simply because of the color of my skin. Had we not escaped Savannah when we did, I would have been lynched simply for being your friend and because of ungrounded suspicions about my relationship with you. Miss Letty, in all honesty, I must tell you that such a relationship as was suspected between us never could have been. It simply couldn't have. I know that now. I've often wondered if it would have been different if I had been born white. I don't believe it could have been."

"Jeremiah—?"

"If you don't understand now, I believe you will someday. I can say no more about it," Jeremiah stated. He squeezed her hand again and shot her a large, heartfelt smile. "You haven't told me how your dancing is progressing."

"I'm doing well." Letitia explained about the LeVeque company and told him about Alexandria, who had become her best friend and about the planned ballet season beginning in Amsterdam.

"I'll return to Moscow for at least three months," Jeremiah later related. "I was not entirely pleased with my recital performance. No matter what arrangements Worth makes for me, I made him promise that I could return to Moscow. It is a rigorous routine I must endure there, but I believe that is what is required to perfect my techinal skill as a dancer. The Russians know so very much about it. I am the only black person where I study; but there I am treated as if I were unique, someone spectacularly special."

"You've always been special to me, Jeremiah, even spectacularly so, now that I think of it."

"As you will always be someone spectacularly special with me, too, Miss Letty."

During the course of the luncheon, the old friends chatted on and on, catching up with news about themselves and reminiscing over past happenings. Shortly before it was time to leave, Letty excused herself to go freshen her face. While she was gone, an old woman came scuffing up to the table and begged Jeremiah to purchase a flower from her. He selected a red rose and placed it on the table where Letty had been seated.

"A rose? Wherever did it come from?" Letty asked when she returned.

"I remember the story about the rose you found in the egg basket," Jeremiah said, "so when the old lady came along, I purchased it from her. Every time I see red roses I think of you."

"Do you often see them?"

"Surprisingly; quite often." Again Jeremiah took her delicate hand. "Miss Letty, I believe we are both destined for remarkable careers in ballet, as we are destined to remain the best of friends for years to come—all of our lives."

"But only friends?" she stated as if it were a question.

" 'Lovers come and lovers go, but the best of friends go on forever,' " Jeremiah quoted. "Worth often says that to me."

"Lovers?"

Jeremiah laughed. "What do either of us know about lovers, except that we love to dance? Shouldn't we go now?"

Jeremiah dropped Letty at the inexpensive hotel where LeVeque housed his ballet company. They parted with a promise to meet again soon.

When Jeremiah was gone a veil of depression fell over Letty that she found difficult to shake herself from. Stopping at the hotel desk, she was given a letter that was postmarked from Savannah. She merely tucked it in her bag and moved listlessly toward the ancient lift. Staring down at the rose in her hand, she was pensive as the elevator rumbled up the three flights, which seemed to take an eternity.

"Nothing happens without a reason."

Thinking she was alone, Letty turned back with a startled look to see a familiar face. "I didn't see you there."

"Naturally you didn't, because I didn't allow myself to be visible until this moment."

"Oh. And what did you mean by what you said?"

"Simply what I said. Nothing happens without a reason. Accidents aren't really accidents. People don't

*merely meet by coincidence. Both fortune and fame are
not brought about by happenstance. There is a reason
for everything whether you or I, or the world in general,
accepts it or not. Jeremiah is as he is because it was
meant to be, just as you are as you are—and for that
matter, just as I am as I am, at this moment. Only in
retrospect, if one is truly perceptive, can one discover the
reason behind anything that transpires. But be happy,
Letitia, for yourself and for Jeremiah. Each in your own
way has been chosen. And what a transformation I've
seen in each of you."*

The elevator came to an abrupt halt.

"This is your floor, I believe."

When Letty turned back after looking forward to
examine where the lift had stopped, the image of Adam
Truff was gone. Stunned in the confused daze that
usually immediately followed her encounter with the
apparition, she drifted from the cubicle in a foggy state.

"Letitia!" Alexandria called from down the hallway.
She had climbed the stairs as she always did because
she believed it helped to strengthen her legs. "Letitia,
is there something wrong?"

"I beg your pardon." Letty shook herself out of her
trancelike state. "Oh, Alexandria! I was daydreaming."

"How was your meeting with Jeremiah?"

"Confusing," Letty replied.

"That isn't the answer I expected to hear."

"It was enjoyable. We had a very nice time."

"But you said it was confusing," Alexandria commented.

"Perhaps I'm naïve or just plain unknowledgeable
about certain things," Letty said as they arrived at the
room they shared. "Jeremiah has so greatly changed
that I hardly knew him. I saw that last night, but there
at the party he was the center of attention. Today I
could see the tremendous transformation that has taken
place in him. I wonder if I have changed nearly as
much as he has. Do you believe that nothing happens
without a reason?"

"I haven't really considered it," Alexandria replied as she made herself comfortable. "I believe everything and everyone has certain potentials which are often slow in unfolding. For instance I believe every dancer is born with the potential to dance, as every singer is born with the potential to sing. If the potential happens, it does so because there is a reason for it happening. But certainly not every potential is fulfilled."

"I don't believe that is what I was thinking about," Letty commented. "However, now that you mention it, perhaps the same logic applies to what I was thinking. I suppose it isn't important."

A short while later, after she had prepared herself to go to the rehearsal hall, Letty remembered the letter she had picked up at the hotel desk. Alexandria was still getting ready as Letty read it.

> *Dear Miss Phenwick:*
>
> *My name is Parker and I'm writing this for your granddaddy who is desperately sick here in Savannah. In his delirium he keeps asking for you. The doctor says his days are briefly numbered and believes that he will not die in peace unless he sees you again.*
>
> *Jim Phenwick begged to return to Moss Grove for his last hours. Enclosed is my check for your passage to return to Savannah as soon as possible.*
>
> *Yours sincerely,*
> *Ambrose Parker.*

"Ambrose Parker?" Letty questioned aloud, since the name was unfamiliar to her. Tears had come to her eyes at the thought of her grandfather dying. She was weeping when Alexandria appeared from the dressing room.

"What is it, Letitia?"

Letty held the letter for Alexandria to take and read.

"Let me see the check," Alexandria stated as she reached for it. "It looks perfectly good to me. What will you do?"

"There is only one thing I can do," Letty replied. "I must go to him."

"But your grandfather may be dead by now."

"That is the chance I must take."

"But what of the ballet tour?" Alexandria questioned, doing her best to console the grieving girl.

"It doesn't matter. I owe so very much to my granddaddy. I have to go to him." Letty burst into uncontrolled crying. "It will solve Monsieur LeVeque's problem with me gone."

"The problem has already been solved," Alexandria assured her. "You must think about your career. Leaving now could greatly jeopardize it."

"I would never be able to forgive myself if I did not go to Granddaddy. Such neglect would haunt me the rest of my life," Letty said. "I've only one choice to make."

"No, no! Think! What can you possibly do for your grandfather at a time like this? Nothing."

"I can give him comfort. He will be able to see the change that has come over me. I can tell him about Jeremiah."

Alexandria threw her arms around Letty. "You must consider this matter, objectively consider it."

"I must see what arrangements I can make to get back to Savannah as quickly as possible. I've made up my mind. Will you explain this to Monsieur LeVeque?"

"And what of your Cousin Laura? Shouldn't you confer with her in this?"

"She has gone to Amsterdam with Signor Spolini. They left early this morning."

"Then contact the Phenwicks in London," Alexandria suggested.

"I will do what I can, but I know I must go to my granddaddy."

Alexandria pleaded with Letty to reconsider and to think of the consequences of what such an action might bring about, but the distraught girl would not hear reason.

When Alexandria went to inform Georges LeVeque

about the turn of events, Letty went to a travel agency and learned that a ship was leaving in two days from Cherbourg, France for the United States. The check proved to be perfectly valid and she purchased a ticket to travel. Then she returned to the hotel to pack her belongings.

Chapter Twenty-two

EMOTIONS HAVE AN INSIDIOUS WAY of disfiguring logic; the distraught mind confuses rationalization and incubates disillusionment. With her concern for her grandfather, Letty could think only of going to him in a desperate attempt to comfort his last hours. Even aboard the French oceanliner, she was unable to sort rational thoughts about her career and the irreversible harm she may have done to it by leaving Paris so abruptly.

Georges LeVeque had attempted to reason with her; yet he had been understanding and not unsympathetic. He, however, had wished that Tiziano Spolini and Laura Donnally had been there to attempt to persuade Letty to reconsider what she was doing. Still the impresario had assured the young dancer that there would be a place for her in the LeVeque Ballet when she returned from her mission of sorrow.

Late in the day that Letty left from Cherbourg, Alexandria Muzakova encountered Madame Ivanovich, a person to whom she had never truly warmed, yet one for whom she had tremendous respect.

"I am saddened, to be sure, that Letitia left in such haste," Roselle remarked as she sat having tea with Alexandria. "Yet I know how deeply devoted the child has been to her grandfather over the years. And it has been a relationship of mutual admiration that goes without question. For years Mr. Phenwick had been parent, grandparent, confidant and friend to her."

"I never knew my grandparents, any of them," Alexandria confessed. "I suspect it is for that reason that I cannot quite comprehend how Letitia could drop everything and go to him."

"It is to your advantage that she has gone," Roselle observed, trying to avoid sarcastic overtones.

"My advantage?"

"Don't tell me you've never thought you were competing with Letitia," Roselle said. "It would be unnatural if you were not."

"I suppose there has always been a slight sense of competition, but it has been on a friendly basis," Alexandria assured her. "We both have learned many of the same roles, but we each have our own interpretations. I foresee that there will be a time when we are compared with each other; yet we are blessed with our individual personalities and, therefore, our own unique abilities. I could not love Letitia more if she were my own sister. In fact, I think of her as the sister I never had."

Roselle reserved her further comments. She fell into a few moments of meditation. "It strikes me peculiarly that Mr. Phenwick returned to Savannah after having been liberated from that place. I have heard of those who wish to go to the place they have known best to die. Still something disturbs me about all of that."

"Disturbs you? In what way?" Alexandria sat forward. She had had queer perceptive notions concerning the same thing. "Does it occur to you, Madame Ivanovich, that something is wrong?"

"Explain yourself."

"I can attempt to understand Letitia's feelings and the sadness she must be experiencing," Alexandria said, "but I have an inner sensation—call it a perception, if you like—that something is simply very wrong. I can't explain beyond that. Still I've come to trust my instincts and I just don't like the reaction I get."

"Are you psychic, Alexandria Muzakova?" Roselle questioned. "That was strange of me to say; when I believe that everyone is basically psychic in one way or another. The irony is that my psychic sense tells me that there must be substance to your instincts. I, too, cannot put my finger on what it is."

"Since we have the weekend off," Alexandria said a while later, "I believe I will travel to London."

"That will be a tiring trip and you need to conserve your strength."

"I have sufficient strength and more, Madame Ivanovich," Alexandria returned. "But you said something a few moments ago that has triggered a question within me. You mentioned about people going to a place they have known to die. Has Letitia's grandfather been away from Savannah?"

"Of course. He and Jeremiah James's family were moved to Boston some time ago."

"Was Letitia aware of this?"

"I presumed that she was. Still I received the information indirectly through Popkin," Roselle explained. "Vladimir has long been a friend of Thomas Phenwick, from whom he received the information."

"During your stay in Savannah, Madame Ivanovich, did you ever hear the name of Ambrose Parker mentioned?"

"It is not familiar to me, but I did not know many people in that dismal place," Roselle said with a sigh. "You are bristling with excitement, Alexandria Muzakova."

"If I am bristling with anything, it is my concern for Letitia," Alexandria replied, "which makes it all the more urgent that I get to London as quickly as possible."

At the conclusion of the rehearsal that day, Alexandria departed for Calais where she would cross the Channel to Dover.

"I wish to see Timothy Phenwick," Alexandria stated when she arrived at the home of Daniel Charles Phenwick. "He is not expecting me, but it is most important that I see him at once."

Alexandria was ushered into the sitting room where she was soon joined by Louise Phenwick.

"I regret that my son isn't in at the moment," Louise explained. "I thought it was Charlie who had captured your fancy, my dear."

"Neither of your sons has truly captured my fancy, Mrs. Phenwick," Alexandria replied. "But I do know that Timothy has strong feelings for Letitia, as she has for him."

"Ah, then you've come on a liaison mission."

"Not precisely that, Mrs. Phenwick. I come on an errand that may mean life and death to my dearest friend." Alexandria wanted to pace as she sorted her thoughts. "Do you expect Timothy?"

"He was to motor down from his school."

"Perhaps I should go there."

"You're liable to cross each others' paths en route."

Alexandria thought a moment. "Mrs. Phenwick, do you know the present whereabouts of Mr. Thomas Phenwick?"

"He's in Edinburgh for a concert. Curious that you should mention Tommy, his wife is our house guest. If you like, I'll ask Evelyn to join us."

"Yes, that might help." Alexandria moved restlessly around the room. The longer she waited, the more apprehensive she became.

Evelyn Phenwick always gave the impression of being the diva that she was. Despite her elegant appearance, and she was always dressed as if she were making a public performance, there was a simple honesty about her that made strangers feel at ease.

"Miss Muzakova," Evelyn said grandly as she extended her hand to Alexandria, "I don't believe we have had the honor of meeting in the past. I have a touch of arthritis, and Edinburgh is far too damp for me this time of the year."

"I am concerned about the location of Mr. Jim Phenwick," Alexandria stated after the formalities were concluded.

"Cousin Jim Phenwick? Why, he was in Boston when Tommy and I were there not a month ago," Evelyn replied. "He's a sweet old dear, and quite lively."

"Lively?"

"The North agrees with Jim," Evelyn went on to explain. "He's taken to working a short time each week at Medallion with Albert and the others. It's really given him a new lease on life to become active again."

"He was in good health when you last saw him?"

"Excellent health," Evelyn replied. "As a matter of fact, I had a brief session with Dr. Joseph Phenwick about my arthritis—Joseph is Louise's father's brother—and he mentioned at the time that he had examined Jim recently and that he couldn't be in better health. Why do you ask?"

Alexandria explained the situation to both Evelyn and Louise.

"But there would be absolutely no reason for Jim to return to Moss Grove," Evelyn stated. "The old plantation now belongs to Tommy and me. The money has been put in a trust fund and will ultimately go to Letty—a fact which Jim didn't want disclosed to her."

"I wish I had gone with Letitia when she made travel plans," Alexandria said. "Furthermore, I wish I had got a better look at that check she received from Ambrose Parker."

"Whoever is Ambrose Parker?"

"That, at the moment, is the prime question in my mind," Alexandria stated. "I only know Letitia was traveling on a French liner, I don't even know the name of it."

Augustus Phenwick arrived and informed his mother

that he had seen Tim at the club. Augustus was immediately dispatched to fetch his brother.

"I don't know if Letitia was headed directly for Savannah," Alexandria explained to Tim a short while later, "or whether the ship was to disembark in New York or Boston."

"Whatever the case," Tim said, "I must get a ship to the United States as quickly as possible. Will you come with me, Augustus?"

"Certainly. But I will have to make certain arrangements," his brother replied.

"Then make them. Time is of the essence," Tim stated.

Alexandria remained at the Phenwick house while the brothers scurried about to handle details.

"I suppose every mother thinks her sons are a bit unusual, above other young men of their peers," Louise said later in the day. "But I've never known of three boys who have such a close relationship with each other. My husband only had three half-brothers, and there was a distance between them. Perhaps that is why he encouraged such a closeness between his own sons. Do you have strong feelings for my son Charles?"

Alexandria looked away from Louise's intense stare. "I admire Charles. He is every bit a gentleman and I find his company most congenial."

"That is being a bit evasive, isn't it?" Louise countered. "Buy why shouldn't it be? After all, I asked an uncomfortable question, didn't I?"

"My love is for my career as a ballerina, Mrs. Phenwick," Alexandria stated. "An artist must have only one love, just one."

"But you are an exotically attractive young woman," Louise commented. "Surely you don't intend to deny yourself romantic attachments."

"In time, perhaps I will deviate from my single-visioned course," Alexandria returned. "I don't permit myself to think such things at this time. I am completely devoted to my dancing."

"Evelyn and I were discussing how very much you have the qualities of a Phenwick woman," Louise said. "Letitia has similar qualities, but then she was born a Phenwick. Since you are such good friends—Oh, dear, I suppose I shouldn't be speculating like this, should I?"

"I have heard reference to Phenwick women," Alexandria acknowledged, "but I put little importance on the title. I can understand your position, Mrs. Phenwick. You are a mother with three grown sons, and you must have concern that they are all unmarried at this time of their lives. Yet, as obvious as I see Timothy's feelings are for Letitia, I could never encourage her to marry him—not if she wishes to continue as a professional ballerina."

"Why is that?"

"I know you've immersed yourself in the arts, Mrs. Phenwick, and I admire you for that," Alexandria went on. "The fact is, I wonder if you are cognizant of the real soul of the creative person. I believe the true artist marries his art. Yet I try not to close my mind to the possibility that I may be mistaken."

"I hear wisdom in your words," Louise commented, "and I have admiration for you and your convictions. Still I wonder if the artist doesn't require a balance in his or her life—a balance between reality and fantasy. One can espouse an ideal—but ideals are often intangible. That I have seen only too often among my artistic friends. Still I know how peculiar it must sound for me, a person on the periphery of the art world, to even speculate about such things. Whatever transpires in your life, Miss Muzakova, I trust that we will come to be good friends. I have great admiration for your talent as well as for your beliefs."

"Thank you." Alexandria decided it was time to change the subject. "While I attended a party here a while back, a cousin of yours from Denver—"

"Oliver? Ah, yes, Oliver. A most unusual young man," Louise remarked, then she intently studied the mysterious expression that had come to Alexandria's face. "Oliver? Oh, yes, I see."

"What is it you see, Mrs. Phenwick?"

"It is Oliver who has attracted your fancy, is it?"

"Not necessarily. I merely inquired about him as a means of changing the course of our conversation."

Louise smiled dimly. "Oliver is presently in Munich, as I understand. I doubt that we will see much of him around here for some time to come. My husband could tell me very little about him and his escapades in Germany. Do you like opera?"

"I know little about it."

"I have an extra ticket at Covent Garden tonight. Speaking of Germany reminded me of it. If you would like, I would enjoy having you as my guest," Louise said graciously.

"May I consider it before I give you an answer?"

"By all means."

Alexandria thought that perhaps Louise's mention of the opera was her means of altering the course of their conversation.

Tim and Augustus returned with information that they could leave the following day from Southampton on one of the fastest oceanliners available.

Assured that the Phenwick brothers would do all they could to divert Letitia from disaster, Alexandria agreed to accompany Louise and Evelyn to the opera that night and return to Paris the next day.

Chapter Twenty-three

WITH THE PHENWICK FAMILY'S INTERESTS in the shipping industry, Augustus was able to make arrangements for the South America-bound ship to put into port at Charleston, South Carolina, long enough for him and his brother to disembark. That might help them catch up with Letty's ultimate arrival in Savannah.

The ship carrying Letty reached New York City. The winter crossing had been uncomfortable and tedious. She spent much time in her stateroom and only rarely ventured to the recreational areas aboard the ship.

After the initial few days at sea and her constant concern about her grandfather, Letty managed to control her extreme emotional reaction and began to become somewhat objective about her mission. How often she had heard Jim Phenwick say that he was just waiting around to die. She had never really taken him seriously. Now she reprimanded herself for not returning sooner to Moss Grove.

As rationality returned, Letty began to realize that it was wrong for her to chastise herself for seeking a life of her own and devoting her time to that which she loved most: ballet. She concluded that she had every right to pursue that which meant most to her.

To take her mind from the reason behind her trek to Savannah, Letty fell into her old practice of dreaming, building sand-castles about what the future might hold. She remembered the words she had heard in the hotel lift that day. *Nothing happens without a reason.* Then surely there was a reason for her to return to Savannah at that time. Was it to say farewell to a dying grandfather, or to bury him? Or was there something far more significant in the entire adventure?

She dreamed of the day when she would become successful as a ballerina. How often such dreams had sent her into mystical fantasies. Even in the days when she was regularly taking ballet lessons with Madame Ivanovich in Savannah, she had projected her day-dreams into the future. Yet, already she had discovered that reality was quite different from her dream images.

When she had exhausted speculations about dancing, Letty found her thoughts centered around Tim Phenwick. How strange? Memories of Tim and the happy times they had spent together in London, often returned to her while she was in Paris. She had to admit that she liked Tim. And occasionally, after he had made romantic advances toward her in a gentlemanly way, she had had other thoughts about her handsome cousin.

During the last day of the sea voyage, Letty found that Tim occupied many of her daydreams. Was it because for the first time since she had met him that she had time to entertain such ideas, and not be overwhelmed with her concern about her dancing? That was a possibility. She had listened to Alexandria's thoughts about romance in opposition to dancing, and found that she couldn't completely agree with her friend's persuasions. Now, alone with her dreams, Letty found romantic speculations kept her mind from the sadness behind her reason for traveling to Savannah.

Finally, when considerations of Tim became too intense and she realized she had to detach herself, Letty thought of Jeremiah and his triumphant recital in Paris. Jeremiah. She often dreamed in her sleep about him, and on several occasions the dreams involved erotic situations.

Most of all Letty was absolutely amazed by the progress Jeremiah had made with his dancing, and she realized beyond a doubt that Worth Bassett had been responsible for such accelerated improvement and maturity. Yet she feared that Worth was also leading her friend in another direction that might not be in Jeremiah's best interest. Who was she to say what was right or wrong for anyone else? *Nothing happens without a reason.* Even such thoughts about Jeremiah, even the erotic dreams? If only she had Alexandria to converse with at that time.

Upon arriving in New York, Letty attempted to contact the office of Simon Phenwick, Laura Donnally's brother. He was not available. She even went to the theater where his wife, Phyllis, had been starring in a play. The show had closed. Anxious about getting to Savannah as quickly as possible, she made no further attempt to contact any members of the Phenwick family.

As the train neared Savannah, Letty's thoughts again were held on the sorrow of her mission and she couldn't get her grandfather off her mind.

The train chugged into the state of Georgia with interminable slowness. For the first time since she left Europe, Letty remembered her Aunt Mattie and her pathetic, demented condition. Because she didn't like to think of the old woman being kept in an insane asylum, she did her best to consciously push thoughts of Mattie from her mind. What terrible horror the woman must have had to endure! Still, tragedy began in Mattie's life when she was just a small girl and was savagely attacked by Yankee soldiers during the Civil War. What scars of torment must have been indelibly cut into her mind. She wondered if the old woman ever had periods of rationality when she sometimes rose above her demented state and tried to fit together the pieces of her life. In a way, she hoped Mattie never did have to experience moments of temporary sanity. And, as she thought about her great-aunt, Letty prayed that she had died and had been released from her misery—poor soul.

There was little that had changed in Savannah during the time that Letty had been away. It was just as she remembered it. Never brittlely cold as the Northern climate, the February weather was comfortable. The great sprawling magnolia trees had already begun to form buds.

People moved about at a faster pace through the streets, but the tempo had never been exceptionally fast in Savannah. The significant thing was that more people were out and about that time of the year. Motorized transportation was an infrequent sight since most vehicles were still horse-drawn. There was something quaintly old-fashioned about that, but it all underlined the fact that time moved slowly in the picturesque Southern sea town.

"Ambrose Parker?" the short stout gentleman questioned when Letty had inquired about him. "Never did hear a' that name. Reckon I don't rightly know ever'one in Savannah, but I ain't heared a' no Ambrose Parker."

None of the three different people Letty asked had even heard the name.

A lank, long-legged man in his thirties ran through the back alley, bobbed around trash barrels and went to a familiar back entrance. Furtively he glanced about before he pushed open the back door and squeezed into the narrow hallway. A quick knock on a door and he went in. "She's come. She's a-askin' fo' Ambrose Parker."

"Good," was the reply through teeth that held a stump of a cigar in place. "Ya-all know what t' do now. An' I don't want nothin' t' go wrong, ya hear?"

"Yes, suh."

Letty wondered why people looked at her with curious interest. She had to conclude that it was because she was dressed more stylishly than she had ever appeared in the Savannah streets in the past. Even if they recognized her, her dress set her apart and seemed to label her as an alien in their midst. In a way it made her feel important; yet, on the other hand, it seemed she was ostracized because of the way she was dressed. Going to the blacksmith's shop, she made arrangements to hire a horse and buggy, assuring the smithy that she was quite able to drive it alone. She was advised that there would be an hour's wait before a vehicle was available.

Those eyes which had been curiously watching her, now seemed to stare with suspicion. As she moved down the main street, she increasingly became aware of the interest she was arousing; interest she had seen directed at perfect strangers who had come into town for one reason or another in the past.

Letty entered a small restaurant where she ordered a small amount to eat and a lemonade. Eyes turned to her.

"Ya-all from th' North?" a paunchy man in his forties asked, wiping his hands on a soiled apron that covered his belly.

"No, I'm from Savannah," Letty replied. "I've merely been away."

"Ya-all don't talk right fo' a Southerner."

Letty smiled and went about her business. Still she was becoming annoyed by the singular attention she was attracting. "I was raised at Moss Grove Plantation," she finally said when the paunchy proprietor passed, giving her the fish-eye.

"Ya-all ain't Letty Phenwick, is ya?"

"I am."

"I d'clare! Reckon ya-all up an' changed. No wonder ya don't seem natural-like. Ya-all up an' sold Moss Grove t' them Yankees an' got all high an' mighty on us, didn't ya?"

"Sold Moss Grove?" Letty questioned.

"White folk Yankees is one thin'," the man belched, "but a-sellin' t' mulatto Yankees is some'un else. Ain't ya-all got no Confederate pride?"

"I didn't sell Moss Grove."

"Ain't th' way we heared it." He made a contemptuous snorting sound. "Th' way I sees it, Yankee mulattos is worse than black niggahs from down here. Niggahs knows their place—er at least they'd better."

"Tommy?" Letty questioned aloud.

"M'name's Caleb, not Tommy."

"I'm sorry. I was thinking of someone else." Letty hurriedly paid for what she had had and went back toward the blacksmith shop. En route she passed the building wherein Jaspar Calhoun's office was situated. She started to enter, but she couldn't bring herself to face her overbearing, self-important cousin.

The smithy helped Letty into the buggy and gave her last-minute instructions. The horse was slow and plodding and she wanted to turn back, accuse the smithy of giving her a workhorse and ask that it be exchanged for a much faster one. Still she had had to wait for it, and chances are she would have a much longer wait for a substitute. She would make do.

The afternoon sky was a bit overcast and clouds appeared to be rolling in from the east. It almost reminded her of hurricane weather, but she knew it was the wrong time of the year for that. Still there was a distant smell of rain in the air and she had known sudden storms to arise even when skies were clearer than they were.

As the buggy rattled over the furrowed dirt road, the way so familiar to her from years of trudging over it, her memory was rekindled. How often she had walked to her dancing lessons, and how weary she had been on the homeward journey. Yet all of those tedious hours had gotten her to where she was. Despite the familiar surroundings, she was beginning to feel herself a stranger there. Alexandria had once mentioned how places she had known and lived in took on a foreign look when she no longer lived there. Her friend believed that meant some mysterious door had been closed to her in a particular given area and she had outgrown her purpose for being there. But it also meant that other doors had been opened to her. Even particular hotel rooms had a warmth about them as long as they were meant to be a current living space; later, when revisited, they were coldly unreceptive to her. That was the general feeling she had about Savannah now. It was no longer her place, she had gone forward, moved on, and things of the past were only memories that could never be again.

The days of February were short. Night came early. But that afternoon the sky grew increasingly dark an hour or so before nightfall. Wind had come up, blowing at the peak of the straw bonnet Letty had secured on her head. It ruffled her dress until she had to tuck her skirts under her. As the wind increased in velocity, the buggy swayed and the horse began to balk. "Get along, now!" she called.

Gritty dust blew into Letty's face and the peak of her bonnet was folded back as she clung to the reins with all the strength she could muster.

A flash of lightning streaked the eastern sky and the animal reacted.

"Hurry on, now, or we'll be caught in an awful downpour!"

The horse seemed to sense the urgency in her words and began to trot faster, which seemed to go against his usual constitution.

Raindrops had begun to fall by the time the buggy rounded the bend and trees surrounding Moss Grove came into view. Another flash of lightning splashed behind the old plantation house, forebodingly dark and mysterious-looking, silhouetting it. The two leaning gateposts had the appearance of weary sentries, who had perhaps died at their station.

Thunder rolled with a deafening crash and the old horse bolted forward as if his own safety depended on it. Clinging to the reins, Letty was nearly knocked from the buggy as it went between the gateposts. Yet she was able to navigate the horse toward the old carriage entrance where the animal would be sheltered from the certain downpour.

One hand at her bonnet and the other holding her skirts to keep them from billowing out, Letty went toward the front of the house when she found the carriage entrance locked. Many of the windows had been boarded over.

Dirt and debris covered the wooden boards of the front porch. The Corinthian columns appeared to be as weary as the gateposts. Letty stood back for a minute, observing the old house, before she climbed the steps. Only then her movement was motivated by an increasing amount of rain. She didn't really want to enter that place. Never before had it seemed so sinister-looking.

The front screendoor was hanging by one hinge, and the wind pushing against it caused it to make an eerie sound that was like a wounded animal whining. As Letty approached the front door, the screendoor came out at her and she just missed being hit by it. The old porch swing groaned back and forth as if some phantom spectre was rocking it.

No more did she turn the handle to the front door, than the wind pushed it and her into the building. It took all the effort she could force to get the door closed against the angry wind. Once it was accomplished, Letty pushed the bolt to hold it tightly shut.

The entrance room was in virtual blackness. Wind creaked the wallboards inside and out. A musty aroma permeated the place. Feeling her way to the parlor, Letty found that it too was nearly in pitch darkness. All of the windows had been shuttered and boarded over. She tried to open one, but found it impossible. A feeling of panic came over her. Why?

She went for the oil lamps, but found they were empty. Furthermore, she could find no matches.

As her panic increased, Letty went toward the stairway leading to the second floor. But she held her position at the balustrade before she could muster the courage to take the steps.

Chapter Twenty-four

A FAT RAT CAME BOUNDING down the stairs, made a sudden stop when he sensed Letty's presence, stood up on his hind legs, sniffed and quickly retreated in the direction of the second floor. Letty's eyes had grown accustomed enough to the darkness that she saw the creature and squealed more from surprise than fear. Still, rats caused her to have a feeling of repulsion, squeamishness and disgust. Dare she proceed up the stairs?

It occurred to her that she had not seen any of the cats or dogs who were usually in residence. What had become of them? Chances were the storm had frightened them and they were off hiding somewhere. She calculated that she had been away from Moss Grove for about seven months.

Before climbing the stairs, Letty groped her way to the kitchen where she knew a supply of coal oil was kept. She found the container empty, but she did manage to locate a single candle. Matches were near the wood-burning stove. The first two she tried to strike were soggy, but she managed to get a spark from the third.

As she held the lit candle high, she shrieked in terror. On the floor were three large snakes and a fourth was stretched out on the table. She must have inadvertently stepped over them when she went for the matches. The dogs and Horace James had kept the snakes under control in the past. Trembling with fear, her thoughts became irrational and she did her best to control the panic that had overtaken her.

The candlelight was not bright enough that she could determine the species of reptile that had invaded the kitchen, but even nonpoisonous snakes were repugnant to her. She didn't dare move for several minutes, staring hypnotically at them. One wiggled and slithered toward her, raising its dark head as if to get a better look at her. The predominant thought that occurred to her was that the snakes would not be in the house if any humans were occupying it. Could her grandfather be in the infirmary in town? And where were the Jameses? Perhaps the old man was out in their living quarters where Cissy James could keep a close watch over him. Still, that didn't seem logical. The other possibility was that the snakes had been purposely put in the kitchen. If that was the case, they well could be poisonous. Such reasoning didn't make much sense to her.

Recalling what Horace James once told her, Letty glanced around her, only making the slightest movement, for an object to throw. Snakes were attracted to motion and sound. Her one hope was to distract them long enough for her to retreat from the kitchen. Three large spoons were on the counter just within her reach. Grasping them all at once, she took aim and pitched them toward the stove. They banged against it and clattered to the floor. The snakes slithered in the direction of the sound.

The swiftness of her dancing feet propelled Letty from the kitchen and she violently slammed the door behind her, not once looking back to see if the snakes were in pursuit.

Breathless with hot terror burning in her throat, Letty braced herself against the door. The candleflame flickered, but it had miraculously remained lit during her escape. Overhead thunder exploded with a deafening blast as heavy rain was hurled with the wind against the house.

As Letty again reached the balustrade, she wondered if she shouldn't try to make her way out to the Jameses' living quarters. There was little doubt that the storm was close to its most intense force. The wind and rain would drench her, and chances were that she might not even make it to her destination until the downpour subsided. Still, if she penetrated to the second floor, might she not encounter some other horror, if indeed the snakes had purposely been allowed into the house?

The unknown was the most terrifying ingredient with which she had to cope. Yet she had to see for herself that her grandfather was not upstairs. Stealthily taking the steps one at a time, she climbed toward the second floor.

More thunder cracked directly above the old house. Letty stopped dead in her tracks. Did she hear movement in the house? Human footsteps? Or was it the scampering of rats? She wanted to retreat, but she took a desperate resolution to go forward. She had once overheard Peggy Phenwick state that the Phenwick women were chosen through an initiation of terror. No one knew the explanation for that, but it had without exception been the case. Was this the initiation of terror that would make her eligible to assume the title of a Phenwick woman? If so, she would just as soon forego that honor.

Bolstering her courage, she knew not how, Letty went toward her grandfather's room. Jim always kept the door open. It was closed. The heat and humidity in the old house was unbearable. With so many windows boarded over, there was no circulation whatsoever, which made it seem even more strange that Jim's door was closed.

Coinciding with the moment Letty jerked the bedroom door open, a bolt of lightning struck, seemingly just outside the open window to Jim's room. The room was lit with silver-white light. She saw the bed upon which was a multitude of horrid rats. The storm had panicked them and they came charging toward the open door. With all her strength, Letty pulled the door closed and held tightly to the knob as if she thought the rodents could somehow open it.

If her grandfather's body had been in that bed, it had been devoured by the ravenous rats. The thought turned Letty's stomach and she thought she was going to be sick. She had to escape that house before any more terror beset her.

By the time she reached the top of the stairs and paused briefly to catch her breath before descending them, Letty was so inundated with terrifying fear that her thoughts had become confused. She had to breathe deeply and gain her bearings.

"Le-titia!" a feeble voice called from somewhere on the second floor. But it was quickly drowned in another ominous blast of thunder.

Had she heard her name being called? Or was it only her distraught imagination?

"Le-titia!" the sound came again after the rumble subsided.

Dare she go investigate it?

"Help me, Le-titia!"

The voice was coming from the opposite part of the house from Jim's room.

"Aunt Mattie?" Letty questioned aloud.

"Th' Yankees! Th' Yankees!"

There was no doubt in Letty's mind that the voice was that of Martha Phenwick. How often she had called to her like that over the years when Letty was the only one who could manage the demented old lady.

Throwing caution aside, Letty went toward Mattie's room.

The door was ajar and the terrible offensive odors seeped out from it. Now they seemed infinitely worse than they had ever been in the past. Letty raised the hem of her skirt to cover her nose as a means of keeping away the dreadful stench.

The window was open in the room, but bars covered it. The place was a shambles, in such disarray that it appeared as if someone had attempted to demolish it in a fit of insanity.

"Aunt Mattie? Are you in here?"

The answer was an angry growl of thunder.

"Aunt Mattie? It's me, Letty," she said over the rumble.

A sharp, piercing, absolutely terrifying scream penetrated the room. Starting as a squeal it crescendoed into the hysteria of a mad banshee.

Letty twirled around and backed toward the bed. "Aunt Mattie?"

When she turned forward to the bed, the scream came again and Letty was suddenly attacked from behind. The candle was knocked from her hand and fell to the bed. The stunning blow momentarily dazed Letty as she felt clawlike fingers dig into her neck.

"Damn Yankee! Damn Yankee!" Mattie screeched as she lashed out with every ounce of strength in her frail body. "They tol' me ya-all was a-comin', but this time I'm a-gonna kill ya, ya hear! Kill ya-all dead onc't an' fer all, then maybe I'll be free, ya hear?"

Letty managed to push Mattie aside long enough to turn to face her. "Aunt Mattie, it's me, Letty—Letitia! Now you just stop this right now."

Mattie cowered back for a moment before she lunged at her great-niece with all the fury of an enraged tigress. Never had Letty known her to have such ferocious strength before and she suddenly realized that she was fighting for her life.

Ultimately able to wrestle Mattie to the floor, Letty

slowly began to get the advantage, her anxiety heightened by the continuing storm raging outside. It all seemed a dreadful nightmare from which she prayed to awaken at any moment. Gusts of violent wind blew savagely through the open barred windows.

The candle that had fallen to the bed had not gone out. The flame had ignited the ticking, which smoldered in the feathers beneath. The wind fanned the fire until flames began to leap up. Letty became aware of the all too familiar smell of burning cloth and goosedown. It hadn't occurred to her that the candle flame didn't go out when she dropped it.

"Aunt Mattie! I smell smoke. Don't you understand? There may be a fire!"

Mattie only knew that she was fighting some imaginary enemy, though very real to her demented mind. She was taking her last revenge for all the hurt, sorrow and agony she had endured over the many years.

When Letty was able to glance toward the bed, she could see flames dancing above it, bobbing with the wind, and reaching fingers of flame to touch and ignite whatever else it could.

"Aunt Mattie, we'll both be burned alive if we don't get out of here!" Letty yelled as she managed to catch Mattie in a hammerlock hold and apply enough pressure to cause her excruciating pain. She had had to use that tactic in the past when the old woman had become completely unmanageable. "Now get to your feet!"

Letty jerked at Mattie until she stood. By then the flames had crawled up the wall. Frantically the old woman was pushed from the room with Letty directly behind her. The fire had spread to the floorboards and appeared to be following them out the room.

As the two began navigating down the stairs, Mattie began to struggle and three steps from the bottom she forced Letty to lose her balance and trip to the floor below. Immediately Mattie headed back up the stairs, but Letty scampered after her and tackled her before she reached the top step.

"Aunt Mattie, if you've never listened to reason before, you must do it now," Letty pleaded. "That's an inferno up there. The entire house will go up in flames any minute now." Even as she watched, the fire, encouraged by the wind, went to the other side of the hallway toward Jim's room. "God help us if the fire burns down the door to Granddaddy's room and those rats escape!"

Mattie kicked and tried to free herself from Letty's hold.

"No, you don't, Aunt Mattie! If you go back up there you'll be cremated alive."

Mattie grunted and groaned. "Let me die, Letitia, jus' let me die!"

Tim and Augustus Phenwick had arrived in Savannah about the same time that Letty did. However, unfamiliar with the city and not knowing where to go for information, they had difficulty finding anyone who could give them directions to Moss Grove. Later, they had even more trouble arranging for transportation to drive out to the old plantation. For one thing they only had British money, and the other problem was that they were strangers who spoke with odd accents and the man at the livery stable wouldn't trust them. Finally the brothers put up their combined assortment of jewelry, two rings that were diamonds and set in gold, as well as two gold watches, and made the urgency of their mission plain to the dimwitted stable owner.

The storm began before the brothers had got halfway to Moss Grove, which made it almost impossible for them to make certain that they were going the right way. Several times they feared they had made the wrong turns and twice the flimsy buggy got stuck.

Sopping wet and covered with mud from lifting the buggy wheel out of ruts, both Augustus and Tim were about to give up and head back for the city when a charge of lightning lit up the sky and the old plantation house could be seen in the distance.

"I can't tell for certain with all this rain, Tim," Augustus commented as his brother drove, "but, I say, it looks to me as if smoke is coming from that old place. Rather."

"Maybe it's a fire in the fireplace," Tim suggested.

"In hot weather like this? And that's black smoke. I can see it now. It appears as if the house is bloody well on fire!"

"I can't make this damn nag go any faster. It's liable to up and die on us as it is," Tim yelled, but he did his best to force the horse to increase its speed.

Although the wind was still blowing at gale force, the heavy rain had moved west along with the lightning and thunder as the Phenwick brothers approached Moss Grove and drove through the opening between the sagging gateposts. Flames were shooting up from the rear of the house.

"We'd better leave the buggy as far away from the house as we dare," Tim commented as he pulled up beside a tree near the gateposts. "We'll tie it there."

Augustus went to move the horse and buggy that Letty had driven since the animal had already begun to panic.

Tim checked one side of the house while Augustus scouted about the other side. They met near the Corinthian columns in front.

"The doors are all stoutly locked," Tim announced.

"Yes, I say, and the windows are all boarded over," Augustus reported. "There's a couple of unboarded windows on the second floor, but flames are coming out of each of them."

"With the other horse and buggy still here," Tim said, "we can only assume that Letitia is still here and that she's trapped inside."

"What do you suggest we do?"

"I'm open to any idea you might have."

Chapter Twenty-five

TRACKING THROUGH MUD and puddles of water, Augustus went out in the direction of several small buildings in hopes of finding some sort of tools to use to pry open the boards over the window. The brothers had attempted to batter in the front door, but the stout oak was impenetrable.

As Augustus reached the toolshed, a bullet cracked the wooden siding next to the door, missing him only by a few inches. He fell forward in reaction, then crawled to his feet and hid out of sight as he saw two horsemen riding away toward the house.

Fortunately Tim had heard the report from the gun and managed to shield himself behind one of the Corinthian columns as he watched the masked horsemen ride past. Since they seemed to be circling the old mansion, he remained as well hidden as he possibly could.

When the riders came around again, one of them pitched a flaming torch onto the porch before they both rode through the gateposts and down the road. Tim scampered to get the torch and heave it away before it could ignite anything. His first concern was for Augustus's safety. He started in the direction his brother had gone before he saw Augustus come running toward the house, a metal bar in his hand.

"I say, there were two of the ruddy bullies!" Augustus shouted. "They damn near hit me with a bloody bullet, they did!" He reached the place Tim was standing. "They've set fire to other parts of the house."

Tim took the metal bar from Augustus and went to the porch with it.

Mattie kicked at Letty when the latter tried to force her to her feet. The old woman, cadaverously thin, lurched away and went in the direction of Jim's room.

"Brothah'll help me!" Mattie called. "Brothah'll save me!"

"No, Aunt Mattie, no! There's nothing but rats in there!" Letty called.

Smoke had filled the hallway and Letty again used her skirt tail to hold over her face. The door to Jim's room was a curtain of flames. Without hesitation, Mattie charged through it. The old woman's screams were mixed with the frantic squeals of the rats.

Letty got as near to the door as she dared, but she knew that to enter would mean her own death. Confused and turned around, she went in the opposite direction from the stairs. By the time she realized her error, she saw that flames were eating at the hem of her skirt. Desperately, she ripped the garment away and let it fall as she reversed her direction and headed for the staircase.

Flame laced along the wooden bannister as she carefully inched her way down. Smoke was coming from the area of the kitchen as well as from the parlor. Letty tried to put thoughts of Mattie from her mind, but the urgency of the situation seemed to magnify all of her terror. Reaching the main floor, and seeing the smoke come from the kitchen, she thought of the snakes and feared that they might at any moment come slithering toward her.

Finding the front door impossible to open, Letty hit her fists against it.

Flames were red hot in the parlor where the furniture was ablaze. Fire surrounded her and the smoke came at her in noxious clouds. She had begun coughing, her fingers bleeding as she scratched at the front door. Fitfully coughing, gasping for breath, her body fell against the door as she slid to the floor. Her mind swirled with a collage of strange images and colors before she had the sensation of brightness and an invasion of fresh air.

Moments later, Letty felt strong arms reach around her, urgently lift and carry her from the house. A light rain was still falling and the refreshing touch of it against her face had a reviving effect. As strength came to her body, she wrapped her arms about the shoulders of the man who was carrying her.

"Tim?"

The sensation of his lips against hers, despite the water pouring over their faces, was the stimulation she needed to bring her back to consciousness.

"Is it really you, Tim?" Letty questioned.

"It's me, old girl, in person."

"Then it all must have been a horrid dream," she sighed. "I'm not in Savannah after all. I'm still in England."

"You are very much in Savannah, dearest Letitia," Tim said gently. "I wish I could tell you it was only a nightmare."

Letty lifted her head from his shoulder and looked back at the old house, flames and smoke pouring out of the windows. "Oh, God . . . Aunt Mattie!"

"If there's anyone in that house, they're not alive to know what is happening," Augustus said as he joined them. "We daren't go back to town, and we can't stay here."

"There's a small village down the road in the opposite direction from town," Letty said, feeling weak and exhausted, yet strangely comfortable in Tim's arms.

239

Augustus drove one buggy, while Tim maneuvered the other with Letty beside him. The rain drenched them. Letty only looked back once. She sighed and leaned her face against Tim's shoulder.

Augustus tried several farmhouses before he found a family who was sympathetic to their plight and opened their hospitality to the three weary people. They were older people, a farmer and his wife and their thirty-two-year-old retarded son.

"Jeb an' me'll take them horses an' buggies into Savannah in th' mornin' first thin'," the farmer said. "Ain't no need a' ya-all a-riskin' more trouble. Best ya-all go t' Atlanta er some'eres else if'n ya-all wanta git t' th' bottom a' this." He shook his head. "Chances are, ya-all'ud better leave well 'nough alone, ya bein' foreigners an' all."

"But I've got to find out about my granddaddy," Letty persisted.

Tim and Augustus took turns relating the story as they understood it about Tommy purchasing Moss Grove and moving Jim and the Jameses to Boston.

"Why wasn't I told about all of this?" Letty asked.

"It may have been an oversight," Augustus commented. "Or maybe most of the family thought you knew about it."

"I suspect you weren't told because Cousin Tommy was abiding by your grandfather's wishes," Tim suggested.

"If Granddaddy isn't in Savannah and he's healthy and well situated in Boston," Letty questioned, "why was I sent word that he was dying here in Savannah?"

Tim shrugged. "That is the mystery."

"Even if it were all part of a plot to kill me," Letty continued, "what would it have accomplished? I simply can't sort this out. Unless—"

"Unless?"

"It sounds like something my cousin Jaspar Calhoun

might be in back of," Letty said. "I can't help but think that he is involved in some way, but I see no reason for him to want to destroy me."

Neither of the Phenwick brothers had even a speculative guess about that.

Early the following morning, Ezra Ellis and his son Jeb took the buggies back to Savannah, pulling a third buggy behind them. It was a tedious trip, but they reached the city shortly after sunrise and had to wait around for the livery to open. Their business transacted as quickly as possible, they returned to the farm without raising suspicion about their mission.

The Phenwick brothers paid the farmer well for his effort. After lunch, Ellis drove the three to Hardeeville where they could catch a train for Charleston.

"I must go to Boston," Letty insisted when Tim suggested that they could get ship passage from New York. "I've got to see my granddaddy and make certain that he is all right. Perhaps he can shed some light on all of this."

Augustus decided to take the first passage back to England, leaving Tim to travel with Letty. The young couple thoroughly enjoyed the time they had together. Despite the closeness and the sense of sharing, many unanswered questions remained at the periphery of their consciousnesses pertaining to that dreadful experience in Savannah. Certainly Tim had no solution to the riddles and, frankly, he was relieved to be away from Moss Grove and whatever evil forces had perpetrated burning the old plantation.

Letty had ideas, but they were only conjectures. At the root of them all was the name of her cousin Jaspar Calhoun. She had to conclude that Mattie had purposely been taken from the asylum and left unbound at Moss Grove. The person or persons who took Mattie to the plantation house must have known that Letty was expected there and that the old demented woman would attack her. But why? What was the purpose behind it?

She thought of Adam's words: *nothing happens without a reason.* But what reason could anyone possibly have for contriving such a situation? If the property currently belonged to Tommy Phenwick, what would be proved or accomplished by harming Letty? Jaspar Calhoun might have been motivated by revenge, but what possible gratification could he possibly get by torturing his cousin?

"Put it out of your mind, old dear," Tim advised her as they neared Boston and passengers were beginning to gather their things in preparation for leaving the train. "No need in letting it worry you silly, you know. Who knows what strangeness goes on in the minds of individuals? For all we know, the incident at Moss Grove could have been part of a more complicated and convoluted plot—the sort mystery writers delight in. On the other hand, it may have been merely a bit of a prank. A bloody bad joke, if you ask me, but nonetheless only that."

"You're not helping me dismiss it from my mind with all of those complicated suggestions," Letty said lightly.

Tim took her hand in his. "Perhaps I can best distract you this way, dearest Letitia. I'm not the best at making mad, frantic love, but I'm certain with what I can do with my limited experience, I might be able to keep your mind off other matters."

Letty laughed. "I don't know about that." She squeezed his hand. "I'm not really ready for love, you know. My only love is dancing."

"You certainly know the proper way to deflate a chap's ego, old girl," Tim replied. "With an attitude like that, you could damn well force a bloke into taking vows of celibacy. What a ruddy waste that would be!"

"Oh, Tim." She caressed his hand with her free hand. "It's not that I don't love you, because I do. But loving and being in love are two different matters. I'm in love with ballet."

"That's a bit of a bad blow! Playing second fiddle to a

242

ballet company is not an especially stimulating idea, you know."

"If you want to be in love and marry, dear Tim," Letty said, "then perhaps it would be best if you were to find another young lady to woo with your charms."

"You would drop me just like that?"

"I don't want to drop you period. But I can't encourage what you want, when my wants are entirely different. I appreciate you and I can love you—love you simply because you're my cousin."

"Jaspar Calhoun is your cousin, too. Do you love him?"

"Jaspar is quite another matter. All right, then, I can love you more than a person usually loves a cousin or any other close family member," Letty commented. "And maybe someday, just maybe, I will fall in love with you, Tim."

"At least you give me one ray of hope. Good show, old girl!" Tim lifted her hand to his face and kissed it. "I ask only this for now, that you let me be in love with you. We will remain close, and, in time, I'll do everything within my power to make you fall in love with me. How's that for being fair?"

Letty kissed his hand. "I do love you, Tim, I do. Please do your best to understand me. If I do not fulfill my dream of becoming a ballerina, I could never forgive whatever or whomever got in the way of my success. I don't want to hurt you, Tim. I never want to do that, but I can't allow you to hurt me or my aspirations, either."

Tim thought a moment before he again kissed the back of her hand. "I do understand, Letitia . . . I do."

Stately tall, silver-haired, craggily handsome Judge John Phenwick moved with the air of authority with which he presided over his federal courtbench. A man of distinction and honor, the patriarch of the Phenwick family had been offered important diplomatic positions, all of which he declined. He stayed clear of political affiliations, preferring to remain nonpartisan and chose

243

according to the dictates of his conscience rather than a platform set down by a political party. He was extremely well respected and praised.

When John entered the oak-paneled parlor of his spacious home on Beacon Hill, not far from Edward House, he did his best not to show the weariness that had come over him as a result of a hectic day in court. Smiling congenially, he went directly to Tim and shook his hand, then he put his other hand to the youth's shoulder and embraced him. "Welcome, Nephew, it's so very good to see you again."

"Thank you, Uncle John," Tim replied. "I don't believe I've seen you in eight years, still, you haven't changed a bit."

"Ah, but I have. There is far more silver on top and a greater hesitation in my step. It is kind of you to say that." John turned to Letty. "And this, I take it, is the famous Letitia Phenwick. My dear, you are an absolute beauty. Verbal descriptions do not do justice to that which is an actual fact. I am sincerely impressed."

"I am overwhelmed, Uncle—uh—Are you my uncle?" Letty asked.

"I suppose I must be, since your great-grandfather was my half-brother Prentise."

"Then you're only my half-uncle," Letty teased.

"At the distance we are related, it doesn't make much difference if I am half or whole." John embraced and kissed her. "Whatever the case, welcome to Boston and my home. Your grandfather has told me much about you, and my daughter has carried on via the post about both your beauty and your talent."

"Your daughter?" Letty questioned.

"Didn't you know that Laura Donnally is my daughter?"

"Oh. I suppose I did, but somehow I didn't quite make the connection. Well, then, since Laura is practically my adopted mother, we must be more closely related than we thought." She laughed.

"I like you, Letitia Phenwick. And I decree that you

are very much a Phenwick woman," John stated emphatically.

"A Phenwick woman?"

"Aren't you?"

"I was born a Phenwick."

"Rest assured you will take your place among the best of those ladies who are known as Phenwick women," John said.

Letty became flushed as a shiver of excitement trembled through her. "Uncle John, in your time did you ever know Adam Truff?"

"Know Adam? Did I know Adam?" He laughed loudly. "That is like asking me if I knew my left hand. And the very fact that you mention his name as if you are acquainted with him, merely proves I was right in labeling you a Phenwick woman. I can tell you tales about Adam Truff that would go on for days. Have you seen your grandfather yet?"

"Yes, we've had a wonderful visit," Letty replied. "And I must state that I've never seen him looking so radiantly healthy in years."

"My half-brother Prentise was grown and away from home before I was born," John explained, "but from what I knew of him, I can see a remarkable physical resemblance between Prentise and Jim. I only regret that Jim lost touch with the family so long ago and didn't come to us for assistance when he most needed it."

When she got the opportunity, Letty explained the circumstances surrounding events that had happened at Moss Grove. John listened intently, jotting notes as he did.

"I will have the federal authorities investigate the incident in Savannah," John said after hearing the complex details. "Furthermore, because of things Jim has told me, I'm going to have my nephew Jaspar Calhoun's affairs looked into, and if need be, I'll pay him a visit myself. Reconstruction and carpetbag governments in the South have made certain people ruthless. I'll say no more about it until an investigation is made."

"I will rest easier knowing that you are handling the matter," Letty said. "It's the name of Ambrose Parker that stands out in my mind and worries me."

"If there is indeed a person named Ambrose Parker," John returned as he drummed the tips of his fingers together, "we will get behind that, too. I'll even put Xan on the case once he has time. In fact, when next you see him, if I don't encounter him first, you might tell him that I suggested he look into the situation concerning Ambrose Parker while he's in Europe."

"In Europe?" Letty questioned. "But the letter I received from him came from Savannah."

"Quite so. I don't dispute that; my dear," John said, his eyes narrowing as several thoughts came to him at once. "Yet it strikes me peculiarly that the travel agency you booked ocean passage with so readily took the check from Ambrose Parker. Well, perhaps that isn't of great importance, but it's a curious situation. You might mention that to Xan, too."

Letty and Tim spent three happy days with Jim Phenwick. The old man was overjoyed to have their company. When it came time for parting, Jim presented his granddaughter with a bouquet of red roses.

"They won't hold up none like that'un ya had," Jim said lightly, "but they'll remind ya that ya're a Phenwick woman. Ya-all don't know how proud that makes me. An' I reckon, wherever she is, ol' Millijoy is right proud a' ya, too, Letty . . . right proud."

"Oh, Granddaddy, I have missed you very much."

"How in th' hell could ya-all miss me when ya've got all a' Londan an' Paris t' keep ya company?" Jim chuckled. "Now go on with ya, girl. An' ya-all be good t' that Timmy. I like that bo'. He's one cousin I approve of."

Letty hugged and kissed her grandfather until Jim

peeled her hands from around his neck. "Now-now, no tears an' stuff like that, Letty. They're a-liable t' rust that pretty face a' yourn. Ya-all give Jeremiah a good pat on th' back for me. Land, was I ever surprised t' read 'bout him a-dancin' in th' newspaper clippin's Laura sent from Paris. Who'ud a' thought that nigra bo' would be as famous as all that? Cissy an' Horace was tickled pink, all right. Maybe one day we'll pack up th' young'uns, Horace an' Cissy an' me, and traipse off t' Paris an' see Jeremiah dance for ourse'fs. Now go on with ya, Letty, ya Timmy is a-waitin'.'"

Letty kissed Jim one last time, held tightly and ran, without turning back, to where Tim was waiting.

During the return ocean voyage, Letty and Tim spent much of the time together. That feeling of love they had for each other magnified.

"Letitia," Tim said as they stood on the deck the last moonlit night of the trip, "I want you to marry me."

Letty stared out at the vastness of the sparkling black sea and swayed with the motion of the ship. The wind lightly brushed through her hair and, although it was cold, she found it refreshing.

"You know I'm ruddy crazy in love with you, Letitia."

Letty's lovely face was glistening with moonlight as a mistiness came to her eyes. She gripped her hands tightly to the railing and bit her lower lip. "We couldn't ask for a more romantic setting than this, could we?"

"I arranged it especially for us."

Letty continued to stare forward as Tim put his arm about her shoulder and kissed her cheek. She made no effort to resist. But, as he continued with his display of affection, Letty slowly lifted one leg, pointed her toes and did a stretching exercise.

"I am not in love with you, Tim. I'm sorry. I love you, I do truly love you, but—must I repeat that over and over again?"

"I don't give up easily, old girl. I say, I've got that

question about marrying you memorized, so you're liable to hear it often until you answer in the positive," Tim said as he nibbled a kiss at her ear. "You feel, you respond, I know you do love me in your way. That is enough for me. I'll be in love for the two of us."

"It wouldn't be fair to you, Tim," Letty replied. "Let me establish myself as a ballerina. Or, if the critics do not accept me and I get nothing but discouragement, then I will reconsider your question. Don't think badly of me for being this way. I have debated the situation within myself, and I must be true to my overwhelming desire to dance." she kissed him and responded fully to the dynamics of his masculine aura, his strength and the depth of his emotional feeling.

"You are such a lovely dreamer, Letitia."

"Letitia, the dreamer," she echoed and danced away from him as he was about to again take her in his arms. She twirled and spun over the deck.

Again Tim caught up with her and held her tightly. She accepted his affection, but she could not promise him that which he most wanted: the fullness of her love in marriage.

Alexandria, Charlie and Augustus Phenwick were at the dock in Southampton, England to meet the ship when it arrived. It was a festive occasion that continued as they motored back to London.

"How is it you were able to get away from Paris?" Letty asked Alexandria when they were alone at the Daniel Charles Phenwick house in London. "I should think rehearsals would be accelerated at this time."

"The opening in Amsterdam has been postponed for two weeks," Alexandria replied. "There have been problems."

"Problems?"

"Personal problems. Georges LeVeque will be in London tomorrow. He wants to speak privately with you," Alexandria sounded sullen and concerned.

"Can't you tell me what the problems are?"

"It has to do, directly or indirectly, with the relationship between Laura Donnally and Tiziano Spolini," Alexandria said. "They have had a heated dispute. It seems Laura encountered Spolini indulging in an indiscreet situation. Her feathers got all ruffled."

"Where is Laura now?" Letty asked.

"She has taken a suite at the Savoy. And, from what I understand, she is making plans to return to Boston within two weeks," Alexandria related.

Upon freshening herself from travel, Letty made arrangements to go directly to the Savoy. Alexandria accompanied her and waited in the lobby while Letty went up to Laura's room.

"Letty! Oh, Letty!" Laura ran to the girl's arms and began sobbing. "You can't know the torment I've endured these past few days. I've never had such an emotional upheaval."

"I can see you are distraught. What is this all about?"

Laura wept for several minutes before she managed to gain control of her emotions. "I was mysteriously tipped off about a rendezvous Tiziano was having. At first I couldn't believe that it was happening, so I went to investigate to see for myself that it wasn't true. But it was. I've been horribly deceived. Naturally, when I learned the truth about the man, I made arrangements to pull my financial backing from the LeVeque Ballet. I just can't believe this has happened."

"So to spite Tiziano Spolini you are going to hurt Monsieur LeVeque and all of the company of dancers, including Madame Ivanovich and Vladimir Popkin? Is that the case?" Letty asked, trying not to sound unsympathetic, yet at the same time being practical.

"I want to hurt Tiziano as he has hurt me," Laura wailed.

"I met your father while I was in Boston," Letty said, purposely changing the current of the conversation.

"My father?" Laura became wide-eyed. "You didn't

249

tell him—I mean—there was no mention of—well, of—"

"*Your indiscretions?*" Letty filled in. "Rest assured I respect your friendship too much to have done such a thing."

Laura sighed. "I wish you hadn't said my indiscretions as you did. Mine are hardly what Tiziano's are. He purposefully used me, tampered with my passions and emotions to get backing for the ballet company. And I fell for his line."

"Did you think you were buying Mr. Spolini for a lifetime, Laura?" Letty questioned. "How could that be when you have a husband back in Boston?"

"I've told you about Pruman and his ways."

"Did you first feel deceived when you learned of your husband's amorous adventures with other women?"

"At first, yes. But we worked that out."

"Then why can't you do the same with Mr. Spolini?"

"It's not the same thing. Tiziano has gotten money from me."

"And didn't you get money from Mr. Donnally?"

"That's different. I'm married to him."

"It just seems to me to be a case of the shoe being on the other foot," Letty observed. "Is it possible that the woman you discovered with Tiziano was either younger than you, perhaps beneath your social status, or even more affluent? In any case, if you truly analyze it, aren't you actually reacting to jealousy?"

Laura braced herself, stared at Letty, then abruptly turned away. She raised her head high and held it back as tears misted in her eyes. "It wasn't another woman. I could be more tolerant if it were, because I could compete with that. Letty, I gambled and I lost."

Letty stepped behind Laura and put her hands to the woman's shoulders. "Laura, you once told me that you wanted to prove yourself by investing and being involved with the ballet company. Is that true?"

"Yes, of course."

"Actually, you were fascinated by Tiziano Spolini,

and you invested in him. But you must have known of the predilections of some men associated with the arts, especially with ballet. Didn't you have an inkling about Signor Spolini?"

"I did, but I didn't want to believe it true."

"Or you thought you might change him. Isn't that the case?"

Laura moved away from Letty.

"Your father is a very wise man," Letty commented.

"I wish I had his wisdom."

"Don't do this to Monsieur LeVeque, to the company —and to me, Laura. Don't spite us because of your lack of wisdom in dealing with Signor Spolini. Find it in your heart to turn the other cheek and prove to him, to the world and to yourself that you can be successful. Put your wager on the ballet company now, not on Signor Spolini. Now that you know the truth, you can be your own person and not be influenced by the manipulation of your emotions. Please, Laura, do this for yourself, not for me, or for anyone else, but for yourself."

Laura stood silently for a moment in impassioned contemplation. Then she rushed to Letty and childlike embraced her. "Perhaps now I know why you were chosen to be a Phenwick woman and I was not. Help me, Letty. Let us do this together." She wept and Letty wept with her.

As Alexandria waited in the lobby, she became restless, got up and moved about. Periodically she went to the front desk to check the time. She hadn't dreamed Letty would be so long; still she prayed that her friend would be successful in her mission.

A well dressed woman, wearing black with a heavy veil covering her face, stepped to the desk as Alexandria was close by.

"I've come to pick up a letter for Mr. Ambrose Parker," she said confidentially.

"Ambrose Parker, was it?" the clerk repeated in normal tones. "Is he a guest, ma'am?"

"No. The letter was simply sent to him here."

Alexandria tried to get a closer look at the woman's face, but it was well concealed. A few moments later the clerk handed her an envelope. She glanced over at Alexandria, put the envelope in her purse and quickly left the hotel lobby.

Alexandria was still standing by the desk when Letty appeared.

"It's taken care of," Letty said proudly. "Laura will not withdraw her financial support, nor will she return to Boston until after the Amsterdam opening. Come, we must celebrate over a cup of tea."

While they had tea, Alexandria told Letty about the woman in black and the letter for Ambrose Parker.

"Ambrose Parker?" Letty thought. "Then Judge Phenwick may not have been mistaken in his theory. I'll think about that later. Oh, Alexandria, aren't you happy that Laura has changed her mind?"

"I am overjoyed," Alexandria said, but she didn't sound it.

AUTHOR'S NOTE:

Due to the complexity and interweaving of Letitia, Alexandria and the yet to be introduced Romula, this volume (#35) along with the next two (#s 36 and 37) will constitute a trilogy to round out the stories of the abovementioned ladies, the three Phenwick brothers, and their enigmatic cousin, Oliver Phenwick.

The year, as was mentioned earlier, was 1914. By August 4th of that year, the world was thrown into turmoil when Germany declared war.

This has been a prelude to that war. What evolves in the rest of this trilogy is the effect that war has on Letitia, Alexandria and the entire Phenwick family.

**A Home Subscription! It's the easiest and most convenient way to get every one of the exciting Coventry Romance Novels!
...And you get 4 of them FREE!**

You pay nothing extra for this convenience: there are no additional charges...you don't even pay for postage! Fill out and send us the handy coupon now, and we'll send you 4 exciting Coventry Romance novels absolutely FREE!

SEND NO MONEY, GET THESE
FOUR BOOKS FREE!

P0281

**MAIL THIS COUPON TODAY TO:
COVENTRY HOME
SUBSCRIPTION SERVICE
6 COMMERCIAL STREET
HICKSVILLE, NEW YORK 11801**

YES, please start a Coventry Romance Home Subscription in my name, and send me FREE and without obligation to buy, my 4 Coventry Romances. If you do not hear from me after I have examined my 4 FREE books, please send me the 6 new Coventry Romances each month as soon as they come off the presses. I understand that I will be billed only $10.50 for all 6 books. There are no shipping and handling nor any other hidden charges. There is no minimum number of monthly purchases that I have to make. In fact, I can cancel my subscription at any time. The first 4 FREE books are mine to keep as a gift, even if I do not buy any additional books.

For added convenience, your monthly subscription may be charged automatically to your credit card.

☐ Master Charge ☐ Visa

Credit Card #_____

Expiration Date_____

Name_____
(Please Print)

Address_____

City_____State_____Zip_____

Signature_____

☐ Bill Me Direct Each Month

This offer expires March 31, 1981. Prices subject to change without notice. Publisher reserves the right to substitute alternate FREE books. Sales tax collected where required by law. Offer valid for new members only.

GREAT ADVENTURES IN READING